Praise for Maggie McConnon's Bel McGrath mystery series

BEL OF THE BRAWL

"Don't wait until St. Patrick's Day to read this delicious mystery!"
—Nancy Martin

"*Top Chef* meets Sherlock Holmes to cook up a delightful menu of mystery, humor, and romance . . . Maggie McConnon knows the secret of concocting the perfect soufflé of fun. Bon Appetit!"
—Evelyn David, author of *Mind Over Murder*

WEDDING BEL BLUES

"A hilarious entry into a new series starring protagonist Belfast McGrath . . . This mystery is fun, light-hearted, and definitely surprising, making it a great summer read."
—*RT Book Reviews* (4 stars)

"Dorothy Cannell readers will savor this tasty starter to a culinary series."
—*Library Journal*

"McConnon has a surefire winner in Bel: a saucy, funny, flawed protagonist that readers are guaranteed to fall in love with."
—Susan McBride, *USA Today* bestselling author of *Say Yes to the Death*

Praise for Margaret McLemore's Hot McLemore
DRIVE'S SONS

ICE OF THE DEVIL

"Don't read until St. Patrick's Day... read with caution."
—Henry Hazel

"The characters show a tenderness... Delightful,
a mix of compassion, humor, and romance... Margaret Mc-
Clemon knows... to serial... Radiopsaint, the perfect recipe
out... New suspense."
—Lenni Doyle, author of
Nice to the Murder

WEDDING DESIRES

"A million-dollar mix of new verses... turning pages, just...
better McLeish... This mystery is truly unpredictable,
exquisitely surprising... and the... it... with... surprise..."
—McClennon's *Romance Times*

"Don't play Cupid... reason... this tale... to read to a...
Cupid's arrow."

"Take some luck... hidden... what... in her... who's found...
Read her mysteries... the results... are guaranteed to fall in
love with."
—Rhea Matilda Koss... best-selling
author of *Forever in the Dead*

"McConnon creates fetching characters drawn with warm humor and an authentic Irish voice. Bel McGrath will leave you smiling."
> —Nancy Martin, *New York Times* bestselling
> author of the Blackbird Sisters mysteries

"McConnon blends humor and intrigue like no other."
> —Laura Bradford, author of
> *A Churn for the Worse*

"Spirited, fun, and as Irish as a shamrock, *Wedding Bel Blues* sparkles. A rollicking read."
> —Carolyn Hart, *New York Times* bestselling
> author of the Death on Demand mysteries
> and the Bailey Ruth Ghost mysteries

"With dark family secrets, old flames, mysterious strangers and the odd dead body or two, McConnon has delivered a perfect blend of villainy and intrigue with laugh-out-loud witty one-liners and lashings of Irish bonhomie. A jolly good summer read."
> —Hannah Dennison

St. Martin's Paperbacks titles
by Maggie McConnon

Wedding Bel Blues

Bel of the Brawl

Bel, Book and Scandal

Titles by Maggie Barbieri

Murder 101

Extracurricular Activities

Quick Study

Final Exam

Third Degree

Physical Education

Extra Credit

Once upon a Lie

Bel, BOOK, AND SCANDAL

Maggie McConnon

St. Martin's Paperbacks

NOTE: If you purchased this book without a cover you should be aware that this book is stolen property. It was reported as "unsold and destroyed" to the publisher, and neither the author nor the publisher has received any payment for this "stripped book."

This is a work of fiction. All of the characters, organizations, and events portrayed in this novel are either products of the author's imagination or are used fictitiously.

BEL, BOOK, AND SCANDAL

Copyright © 2017 by Maggie McConnon.

All rights reserved.

For information address St. Martin's Press, 175 Fifth Avenue, New York, NY 10010.

ISBN: 978-1-250-07730-1

Our books may be purchased in bulk for promotional, educational, or business use. Please contact your local bookseller or the Macmillan Corporate and Premium Sales Department at 1-800-221-7945, ext. 5442, or by e-mail at MacmillanSpecialMarkets@macmillan.com.

Printed in the United States of America

St. Martin's Paperbacks edition / December 2017

St. Martin's Paperbacks are published by St. Martin's Press, 175 Fifth Avenue, New York, NY 10010.

10 9 8 7 6 5 4 3 2

To my dear friend, mentor, advisor, and sister-from-another-mother, Susan McBride, who has encouraged, cajoled, and championed me for thirteen books.

ACKNOWLEDGMENTS

I have had the good fortune of working with the same editor for the last twelve years, so a big thank you goes to Kelley Ragland of St. Martins Press/Minotaur Books for her continued support and encouragement of my various—and sometimes outlandish—ideas. Thanks, too, to Maggie Callan at SMP/Minotaur for her help and guidance during the writing process and beyond.

To Deborah Schneider, Cathy Gleason, and Penelope Burns go my gratitude for their help these last dozen years, as I have undertaken three series and the creation of multiple characters. I appreciate all you do.

CHAPTER *One*

I was wet, cold, and tired, but despite the fact that she was ready to kill me with her bare hands for staying out all night, my mother addressed all three of my immediate needs before saying anything else.

A towel to dry my hair.

Clean clothes in the form of a pair of jeans, a T-shirt, and a pair of socks. An Irish sweater, the most uncomfortable item of clothing ever made—a hair shirt, really—but welcomed, and probably deserved, at that moment.

A bologna sandwich. It would be the last time I would eat bologna, for many reasons, the most significant being that the smell would forever after remind me of Amy. And how she had disappeared the night before and would always be gone.

Mom was worrying a rosary in one hand, the other securely placed in one of my father's meaty ones. She turned and looked at me, asking me a question she had already asked and would continue to ask, along with everyone else even vaguely connected to Foster's Landing. "Where is she?"

I didn't know. I didn't think I would never know.

My brother Cargan, the closest to me in age and the one who had found me beside the Foster's Landing River, was across the room, looking out the window, his violin strapped to his back; he had a lesson later that morning and wouldn't miss it for anything, even if Amy Mitchell was missing and never to be seen again. No, he was gearing up for a big competition in Ireland and nothing stopped him from his lessons or his practicing. Although the mood was somber in the police station, I wouldn't have been surprised if he had whipped the instrument out right then and there and started playing a tune, a sad one, the type I had grown up listening to.

My other brothers were out and about in town now. They, too, had come running when Cargan first discovered me but were less concerned about me now that they had joined the hunt for Amy. It was another night for Bel, one said. She was going to be in a lot of trouble, said another. They were both right: It had been another typical night and now I *was* in a lot of trouble, the last to have seen Amy alive with nothing to tell that might lead to her whereabouts. They were a self-protective bunch, caring little as to why I would be hauled into the police station, happy that, for once, they were not the ones in trouble. Feeney, especially. He was always in trouble. Derry and Arney, not as much, but both had a way of finding their way into situations that were beyond their control. Feeney was a much more calculated and deliberate hooligan.

Next to Mom, Dad let out a barely audible sob, the kind that told me that he was, first and foremost, a father and one who felt the pain of a missing child. He looked over at me, almost as if he wanted to confirm that I was still there, and reached out the hand that didn't hold Mom's, patting me awkwardly on the thigh.

"Ah, Belfast," he said. "Ah, girl."

"It's okay, Dad," I said. "They'll find her. They'll bring her back." I thought about those words a lot over the years, wondering where that confidence came from. Youth, I eventually decided. When you're young and nothing bad has ever happened, you think everything will always be better, every wrong will be righted. It's only with age that you realized that that wouldn't always be the case and that disappointments would stack up, like the layers of my famous mille-feuille cake, the one with seemingly a thousand layers of goodness that cracked upon the first dip of the fork. But even then, in my heart, I had a feeling it wasn't going to turn out the way we all wanted, something I couldn't give voice to at that moment.

Lieutenant D'Amato came out of the conference room at the Foster's Landing police station and looked at me, frowning. Behind me the door opened, and his expression suddenly lightened, the sight of his only child, his daughter, coming through the doors with a cup of coffee in one hand and a bag of something delicious in the other, the greasy stain at the bottom indicating that it was probably a Danish from the local bagel store. It smelled better than my bologna sandwich, which I wrapped up in the wax paper that Mom had put it in and which I stuffed under my thigh.

Mary Ann handed her father the food and then turned to me, tears in her eyes. "Oh, Bel," she said, and ran toward me, enveloping me in a hug. She smelled good, not like river water and stale beer like I did, but more like the soft grass that I felt beneath my feet when I ran from my house down the steep hill toward the river. Beside me, my mother's silent reproach hung over me like a fetid cloud.

Why can't you be more like Mary Ann D'Amato?

I had heard it more than once in my seventeen years and hoped eventually it would die a natural death as I got older and more accomplished, setting off to take the culinary world by storm, another thing that left a distinct distaste in my mother's mouth. I was supposed to be a nurse. A teacher. A wife, mother. Not a chef.

It was your idea to open a catering hall, I wanted to say. Your idea to have me in the kitchen every moment I wasn't studying or swimming on the varsity team. Your idea to ask me how the potatoes tasted, if the carrots needed another minute. Your idea to let my brothers learn the traditional Irish tunes and put me in an invisible, yet highly important, role—that of sous chef to you and a myriad of other cooks who had come through the doors of Shamrock Manor, only to discover that yes, our family was crazy, and no, they didn't really care all that much about haute cuisine.

Mary Ann was going to nursing school; of course she was. She was the daughter that my parents never had and she would make everyone in this town proud.

Years later, in what could only be from the "you can't make this stuff up" files, Mary Ann would marry Kevin Hanson—my Kevin Hanson—and I would cook the food for their wedding. We would all be friends and we would laugh together and eat together and have a generally good time in one another's company. Before, I felt the lesser, but in the future, the now, I would be the

equal, the one who had gone away and come back, realizing that my heart was in this little village, at least for
a time. But back then, Amy was still missing and everyone thought I held the key to her whereabouts.

"Where is she?" Mary Ann whispered into my curly
hair.

"I don't know," I said. And I didn't. Amy Mitchell
was my best friend, my confidante, my sister from another mother, and she hadn't said a word about where
she would go after a night on Eden Island. My last words
to her, an angry sentence (*You'll be sorry. . . .*), burned
in my gray matter. I don't know where she is, I wanted to
scream. It had been just fun and games until I had seen
her kissing my boyfriend, Kevin Hanson. We had been
celebrating our waning days at FLHS, and it was the
best night we had ever had up until that point.

I don't know why she wouldn't tell me where she was
going, but maybe I did.

Maybe of everyone here in the police station, she
wanted me to be the last to know.

I broke the embrace with Mary Ann and sat down
again; I would never smell a certain floral-scented sham-
poo again without thinking of that morning. I would
never feel the grass beneath my feet without thinking
of the smell and where it brought me in my mind. Mary
Ann's face, tear streaked and pale, made me feel bad
about my own: dry as a bone, not a tear in sight, stunned,
resigned. Amy was gone, and deep down I knew that she
was never coming back. How I knew it so well in the
early morning hours I had no idea. Why I had told Dad
things would be fine was a mystery. But I knew it as well
as I knew my own name that it was over and wondered
how everyone else was still clueless to that fact.

"Belfast McGrath?"

I looked up at a cop who clearly didn't know who I was but whose face told me he knew why I was there.

"That's me," I said, and walked into the room where I would tell them everything and nothing.

CHAPTER Two

"Belfast!" my father cried from the foyer. "Belfast McGrath!" he said again, as if I, as an adult, had forgotten my full name and that would bring me running. It had to have something to do with the Christmas tree that he put up in the foyer every year. My brothers, who were supposed to help with the massive tree, had scattered into the wind like fallen leaves at first sight of the tree, making me Dad's choice as the de facto trunk holder as Dad balanced precariously on the banister, trying to get the tree straight without the benefit of a level or a tall able-bodied man (ahem, Derry).

I was in the kitchen at Shamrock Manor preparing for an upcoming wedding. I had taken over the reins as chef a few months earlier, and while it never got easier to be in the midst of my family, I had found a certain rhythm—a certain peace—in the kitchen. It was now my own and everyone treated it as such, leaving me to do what I did best: cook. Dad poked his head in the door. "Been calling you, girl. What's going on?"

I waved a hand around the kitchen. "This," I said, bringing his attention to a plate of macaroons. "And that," I said, brandishing a tray of raw cylinders of piecrust dough. "I hope you're not implying that I'm slacking off, mister."

May Sanchez, a sous chef I had hired a few months earlier, backed me up. "She's working, Mr. McGrath. Like always." Her job done, she went back to fileting a large piece of beef with a razor-sharp knife, her hands working quickly. Although her formal training in the kitchen was less than mine, she was a natural, her knife skills as good as anyone's with whom I had worked.

For some reason, Dad took May's word over mine. "All right then," he said. "We've got a couple in the foyer, tall drinks of water, both of them, who just happened to be passing by on the Taconic and they think this might be the perfect place for his daughter's wedding."

The couple was standing by the bust of Bobby Sands, Irish martyr, that Dad had sculpted, reading the plaque that he had put there. Dad is nothing if not sympathetic to "the Troubles," a Northern-Irish boy himself, someone violence had touched, if only tangentially, but leaving its emotional mark. When I emerged from the kitchen, they both looked at me, a smile breaking out on the woman's face and a worried one breaking out on the man's. The woman, a tall brunette wearing clogs not unlike the ones I wore in the kitchen, pointed at me.

"Hey!" she said. "I know you."

She didn't look familiar to me, but that didn't mean anything. As I had worked in a New York City restaurant for years, faces had come and faces had gone, and if you wanted to be remembered you had to be a "special order," someone whose favorite dish, their "usual," resonated with me. A face meant nothing, but a fan of my lamb shank? That was the person I remembered.

She started for me, her rubber-soled clogs squeaking on the glossy marble. "You're Belfast McGrath, right?"

"I am," I said. The woman was very excited to see me and I didn't know why, two things that left me a bit wary.

"No, *the* Belfast McGrath. The chef. From The Monkey's Paw?" she said. She held out her hand. "Alison Bergeron."

Didn't ring a bell, and I still didn't know who she was. Her husband shoved his hands deep into his pockets and looked up at the ceiling; something told me that he had never gotten used to his wife's enthusiastic, if misguided, outbursts.

"Nice to meet you," I said. "You were at The Monkey's Paw for dinner?"

"At the Monkey's Paw *for dinner*," she said, dropping her voice an octave, giving the words import. "That dinner."

And there it was. Now I did remember her. There had been a few couples in the restaurant the night I had lost my cool and my job, and she and her husband had been one of them. Max Rayfield, a reality-TV executive who desperately wanted to follow my every move, and her husband were seated with them. At the other table were the former president of the United States and his First Lady and, unfortunately, an unexpected guest, a fish bone in his snapper that had nearly killed him. Not my fish bone exactly, but the fish bone of my sous chef and ex-fiancé who had let me take the fall with a gratefulness that left me stunned.

Alison grimaced. "I'm sorry," she said, looking from me to my horrified father. "I shouldn't have brought it up."

"Nope. You shouldn't have," her husband said, his

eyes still trained on the ceiling. Although he seemed to be practiced in the art of not reacting to his wife, he had not perfected it.

"But I have to say that it was one of the best meals I ever ate," she said. "Later events notwithstanding."

Did she mean the broken bottle that I brandished at the celebrity restaurant owner, the famous award-winning actor? Or how I was "escorted" from the premises by some muscle the owner had called in? Either way, it had been the stuff of my nightmares, come to life, and certainly was an event I was hoping to forget.

"No offense," she said.

"None taken," I said. I held my hand out to her chagrined husband. "Hi, I'm Belfast. But you already knew that."

"I did," he said, and I started to wonder if he ever said more than three or four words at a time. Alison was chatty; he probably couldn't get a word in edgewise. "Bobby Crawford."

The introductions made, Dad led the couple into the dining room, which wasn't set up for a client visit but which was impressive nonetheless. The bank of windows facing the river offered a view that would never get old, even now in winter when the trees were bare, and a thin layer of ice coated what was left of the river, mostly dirt now, a drought the previous summer having brought the water down to a dangerously low level. It was because of that drought that weeks earlier the police had discovered Amy's things, buried underneath the water for years, but not Amy. That was something else I was trying, and failing, to forget. We took seats at a round table next to the largest window, the couple facing the river, and Dad's and my backs to it and the great lawn that rolled down to the water's edge, the perfect view if you were trying to sell someone on what we had to offer.

"So, your daughter is getting married?" I said.

"His daughter," she said, not unkindly. She set the folded newspaper that she had carried into the Manor on the table; an advertisement for the Manor was visible on one of the pages. So that's what had brought them here. "She has a mother. A nice one. A great one, in fact. She's just not me."

"Yes, my daughter. Erin." Bobby Crawford looked at my father, beseeching him with his eyes, trying to telegraph something. He finally blurted it out, my father blissfully unaware of what he might be trying to convey. "She's young. Twenty-four. Too young."

It didn't seem too young, but I didn't have children so couldn't fathom why the father of the bride looked so bereft at the thought of his adult daughter getting married. "And her fiancé?" I asked. "Young, too?" I had learned along the way that in addition to booking parties, Dad, Mom, and I also acted as therapists when the couple, or their family, had an issue. She was too young; he was too old. (Or, in the rare case, vice versa.) She was Catholic; he was a Protestant or, worse yet for the devout parents, an atheist. She had a big family; he had only a few cousins on his father's side and most of them didn't speak to one another. It was a constant juggling act, making the couple happy while keeping their parents—who usually paid for the grand event—from having nervous breakdowns.

"You were barely out of your teens when you got married the first time," Alison said to her husband. "We've had this conversation."

He crossed his arms over his chest. "Too young."

Alison turned to me. "We were driving around and happened to see this place. It looks perfect for what we have planned and in terms of location. We'll have to bring the happy couple here, of course." She looked out at the river. "Can't beat that view even if it's a little bare right now."

She didn't know that the view for me had changed since the discovery of Amy's belongings.

"Hopefully we'll get some rain and it will fill up nicely by the time you have your event," Dad said, ever the optimist.

"When's the wedding?" I asked.

Bobby rolled his eyes. "Memorial Day."

As handsome as he was, he was crabby, too. He was my people, fitting the mold of almost every Irishman I knew and/or was related to. One minute sort of happy, the next in a black mood. "Oh, that's soon. In the wedding-planning business, that is," I said, making a note on the pad that I kept in my coat pocket. "So, I don't know if you know anything about the Manor, but we do traditional Irish service, right down to my brothers as the house band, if you'd like." I watched as Alison's face lit up and Bobby's face fell. Right, she was clearly not Irish if she got that excited about Irish music. Only someone who hadn't been exposed to years of traditional fiddle and accordion playing got that excited about jigs and reels. For the rest of us, it was commonplace, the soundtrack to our lives. "Dad can give you a sampler CD. They play music besides Irish tunes," I said. "My brother Feeney does an amazing Elvis impersonation."

"Even better," Bobby said dryly.

Dad straightened a bit. "You don't like Elvis, son?" he asked, his face contorting, suggesting that he couldn't fathom this, someone not bowing at the feet of "The King."

Alison looked at her husband and then back at me and Dad. "Would you excuse us for a second?" she asked, taking her husband by the arm and leading him to the back of the dining hall by the bathroom where I had discovered a dead groom a few months earlier. It had been an exciting year, to say the least, and not in the best possible way. Dad and I tried to amuse ourselves with talk of the weather, the number of days until pitchers and catchers reported to spring training, anything so we didn't overhear a rather spirited discussion between the potential clients for a Memorial Day wedding.

When they were done, they returned to the table, Bobby's mood considerably lighter, if not a little resigned. "Thanks for the information. Yes, we'll take the sampler CD and a menu, if you don't mind. I'd like to bring my daughter and her . . ."

When words failed him, his mouth hanging open in silence, Alison jumped in. "Fiancé?"

"Yes, fiancé. I'd like to bring them here to see the place, get a sense of what it's like." He smiled for the first time since walking into the Manor, but it was still a little strained. "It's very nice here."

Dad clapped him on the back, the larger man lurching forward in his chair with the force of it. "Excellent!" Dad stood, gestured toward the window. "You won't be sorry if you choose Shamrock Manor. Belfast here is one of the best cooks in America, if not the world!"

"Thanks, Dad," I said, looking at the couple. "I can do whatever it is you'd like. As a matter of fact, we had a wedding here in October at which we served duck to the guests." Bobby looked at his wife, stricken at the thought of something besides a big hunk of meat being served at the event. "Not that I'm suggesting that," I said. If I never had to poach another duck in my life, it would be too soon. "We have a large array of options for you. Bring your daughter and her fiancé and we'll do a tasting."

"That sounds great," Alison said. She poked her unresponsive husband in the ribs. "Right? Sounds great?"

He made a little grunt in agreement.

"Why don't I give you a call when we can get Erin and Fez up here?" she asked.

"Fez?" Dad said. "Is that a Christian name?"

"It's short for something," Bobby said, his eyes wandering around the dining room. "We're still not sure what."

Dad put his hand on Bobby's back. "Come, lad. Let me show you around."

After they left, Alison turned to me. "Sorry about all of that. Great guy, Crawford. But wildly protective."

"He wouldn't be the first and he won't be the last," I said.

She studied my face, searching for something. "You're back home now. How is that going?"

"I love it here. I love cooking at the Manor." Even to my own ears, the words rang hollow, but it was closer to being true than it had been when I first arrived. "It's where I need to be. Should be."

She cocked her head, confused. I hadn't convinced her. "You're an amazing chef. If I have my say, the wedding is here. But we're contending with in-laws, the girl's mother, Bobby's intractability." She rubbed her fingers together. "He's a little tight."

When she saw my confusion, she elaborated. "With

the dough. The bank. Moo-lah-di. Thinks we can do this whole thing with a hundred people and about two grand."

"Ah," I said. "Probably not."

She shrugged. "To me, it's a no-brainer. With you, the Manor is the place to have this wedding. I could be wrong, though. We've got a lot of opinions to consider." She gave me a hug, catching me by surprise. "I don't know if it's because of that night at The Monkey's Paw, but I feel like I've known you a long time."

I let myself be hugged and stopped myself from telling her how long it had been since I had had that kind of human contact. A bad breakup, followed by another bad breakup, had left me a little hollowed out and craving companionship outside of my brothers and parents. Moving back to the Landing had been the right thing to do at the time, but I'd be lying if I didn't admit that it was kind of lonely. One could only get so much comfort from talking to parsnips all day or even one of my brothers, one more eccentric than the next. "Me, too," I said. "And please, don't judge me or the Manor based on what you saw that night in the city. That was a really bad time in my life."

"I'll say," she said, laughing. "But the broken wine bottle was a nice touch. And P.S., the former president blew me a kiss on the way to the bathroom when his wife wasn't looking, so I wasn't terribly upset to see him choke, if only for a little while." She put a hand to her mouth. "Jeez, did I say that out loud?"

"You did," I said. "But I can't say as I blame you."

Outside on the front porch, Dad, recovered from the Elvis slight, was extolling the virtues of a May wedding at Shamrock Manor, pointing out all of the evergreens that would be a backdrop to the photos of the wedding party, and the ones that would be flowering. "Planted them all myself about a hundred years ago!" he said, his voice booming in the morning air. Without hyperbole, Dad was an empty shell. "Do come back with the happy couple. We'll have lunch. Have a delightful case of Malbec in the basement that I've been saving for a special occasion."

He did? My next stop was the basement. He was holding out on me.

Alison gave me another hug. "We'll see you soon. Thanks for letting us drop in."

Dad and I watched them drive away. "I hope they come back," Dad said.

"Me, too," I said but for different reasons. Despite Mr. Crawford's unrelenting pessimism about the wedding, I liked them. I went back into the Manor and walked past the dining-room door. The newspaper that Alison had brought in still lay on the table, so I walked over and picked it up, ready to throw it into the recycling bin in Dad's office.

The paper fell open to a page of advertisements for various antique stores in the area, popular destinations for people from other parts of the Hudson Valley. At one of the places she had circled, I had found some antique cooking utensils that were in a box somewhere in my apartment over Dad's studio. At another, with Amy, I had unearthed a prom dress from the 1950s that I had worn proudly, a photo of me and Kevin still sitting on the mantle in my parents' living room despite my mother's heartbreak that we didn't go to Macy's like every other girl and her mother in Foster's Landing to buy a new dress. I smiled at the memory, sitting at the table in the dining room and flipping through the rest of the newspaper, mostly ads for Christmas trees to be hand cut and craft fairs in the area. Yes, the paper had to go. All Dad needed was another place to exhibit his "installations," sculptures made from anything he could forage in town. Some were good, but most were downright awful, but no one had the heart to tell him.

An article caught my eye, nothing more than a little blurb at the bottom of the third page, the photo blurry, the people in it barely recognizable. It was a story about a commune that had originated in the late sixties that was something of a legend in a town about an hour north of here before communes became a thing of the past and turned into "holistic healing centers" or, better yet, "spas." Living together and massaging one another—and the general public—was a convenient cover, not to mention a source of income, for people who had come together during the Summer of Love and had stayed on cheap land until development began to encroach.

Maybe I needed glasses. Maybe I was just tired. Maybe the weight of the last many years played tricks on my mind. But my blood turned to ice in my veins as I stared at the photo of the barns and large farmhouse on a big tract of Hudson Valley land and the image of one young woman, long blond hair, her head turned slightly so you could only see her in profile. I traced a finger over the photo, trying to divine the symmetry of her face, the curve of her nose.

The girl in the photo—Amy, wearing what I thought was a necklace she had had when we were kids, a dolphin on a chain—smiled up at me, as if to say, See, you were wrong, Bel. I didn't die. I lived.

CHAPTER *Three*

"Dad! May!" I shouted across the foyer. "I'm going out for a while!"

I made haste out of the Manor, wanting to get out of there before anyone in my family could ask what I was up to and I also wanted daylight on my side. The trip to Wooded Lake was going to take an hour and it was December, the shortest day of the year just a few weeks away.

The article had been full of history but short on actual facts about the actual inhabitants of Love Canyon; it did include a map, with a little pin drawn to the upper right, detailing where it had been in the little burg. I didn't read the entire article, but skimmed it pretty well, preferring impulse over planning (one of my fatal flaws). I jumped in the car I had recently bought: a 2003 Volkswagen Beetle that Dad had procured on one of his junking trips around the county. It was a faded blue and a little long in the tooth as vehicles go, but it ran, if a little noisily due to a wonky muffler. I never had to go far to do what I wanted to do around Foster's Landing so it was the perfect car for me.

It was cold and I realized that as I got onto the highway, with the car blowing cold air, my chef's coat, which

I had forgotten to take off, would not provide the warmth necessary in thirty-degree weather. I blew on my hands, the car finally starting to heat up after ten minutes. In my pocket, my phone buzzed with a text, then another, and then with the ring tone that I had assigned my brother Cargan, a chirpy sound with a requisite tone of annoyance—his usual state with me—that let me know when he, and he alone, was calling. Mom, Dad, and the rest of the crew had the same, standard ring tone because when they called it was the rare instance I wanted to talk to any of them. There were so many of them—six in all, four brothers, two parents—that I wouldn't be able to remember their individual ring tones. Arney and his wife considered me their personal babysitter; Derry only called when he wanted to complain about Feeney; and Feeney only called . . . well, Feeney was another story entirely and that story had to do with bad decisions, bail, and "time served." But Cargan was a different story. Siblings and, more to the point, friends, since we were little, he had kept a lot of secrets from me over the years, but I didn't hold that against him. Rather, to me, it high-lighted his protective side, the side that wanted the best for me and for my life to be worry-free. Sure, it was a shortsighted and naïve approach, but after years of my sticking up for him against my other brothers he had wanted to give it a shot for me.

He would have killed me if I had taken out my phone while driving, so I let it ring in my pocket; it made a little sound after he left a voice mail message. I wondered what he wanted and then my mind started to wander. Maybe this was the year that Dad had taken a header off the balcony, the Christmas tree being the only thing to break his fall. Or Mom had tried to make a grilled cheese on the George Forman grill in the kitchen (the only appliance she used anymore) and burned the place down. After going through all of the things that had gone wrong and finally landing on "everyone's dead," like a true Irish lass, doom and gloom around every corner, I pulled off at an exit and parked the car in the lot of a strip mall.

He answered on the first ring. "Did Dad fall off the balcony?" I asked, holding my breath until he told me everyone was safe and sound. Even better, alive.

"Bel, you've got to settle down. I was just calling to tell you that I took a look in the walk-in and it looks pretty bare considering we have a wedding in five days. Did you place an order with Belhurst Farms for the poultry?"

I exhaled loudly. "Yes, I did."

Cargan was now a manager at the Manor, but he was also an almost-retired New York City Police Officer on leave after years of dangerous undercover assignments. The latter gave him a keen sixth sense, so I shouldn't have been surprised that he immediately picked up on the fact that I was in the midst of something that had nothing to do with weddings, my family, or my work. "Where are you?" he asked, suspicious.

"Nowhere," I said. Truth was, I didn't really know. Maybe Parkersville? Maybe farther north? "I don't know actually."

"What does that even mean?" he asked. "Dad said you ran out of the Manor like 'a house afire,' even though I really don't know what that means, either. It makes no sense, a house running anywhere, let alone one on fire."

" 'I left in a rush,' " I said, translating "dad speak" for my brother.

"Well, I got the meaning from context." I heard the

whirr of the printer in the background. "So where are you? And if you can't answer that, just tell me why you left so suddenly. Dad said you had a good meeting with potential clients right before you ran out."

"Yeah, it's not that, Car," I said. I debated how much to tell him. He had loved Amy once, probably as much as I had, maybe more, so tell him that I thought I had found her? Break his heart all over again if I was wrong? "There's a sale at a restaurant-supply store in Wooded Lake and I want a new knife."

He sighed. "Bel, you were always the worst liar."

"I'm not lying."

"Yeah, you are. First of all, there is no restaurant-supply store in Wooded Lake. Second, your voice just went up an octave, a sure sign that you're lying."

"How do you know there's no restaurant-supply store in Wooded Lake?" I asked. The inside of the car was becoming uncomfortably steamy, the heat now cranking. I turned it off, thinking that going home would be a good plan, but it was not an option. I was going up north to poke around, even if it meant that I sounded crazy.

"Bel, we've been over this," he said. "I know everything."

It sounded like an exaggeration, but he wasn't too far off. If he didn't know everything, he knew an awful lot.

I decided not to tell him. "Cargan, I had to get out of the Manor for a while. To clear my head. I'll be back in a little while."

He stayed silent for a few seconds before lowering the boom. "Is this about Brendan Joyce?"

He did know everything, at least when it came to me. He knew that after coming home, my life in shambles, I had gone right into another relationship, one that had seemed promising, the guy a "keeper," as Mom would say. Turns out I had been wrong. Small-town boys can break your heart into a million pieces just like guys in the big city. I still hadn't cried about it because I had learned not to cry over the years, with my brothers a tough bunch who smelled fear—and emotion—like dogs did. Cargan was different, but sometimes he was still "one of them," the pack who had a little sister whom they had toughened up to the point where she wouldn't shed a tear lest she seem weak. A baby. "It might be, Cargan," I said as breezily as I could, but he knew better.

"Did he ever give you a better explanation than 'I didn't know it was in there'? to account for Amy's high-school graduation photo being in his wallet?" he asked.

"Nope," I said. "That's his story and he's sticking to it, as they say."

"Stupid story."

"The worst," I said.

"It's almost so bad that it could be true."

"I doubt that," I said. "He looked pretty chagrined but not chagrined enough by the whole thing. Made me feel like he was lying."

Cargan's pregnant pause told me nothing. Outside, in the parking lot of the strip mall, people were scurrying about, holiday shopping, running errands, looking both stressed and chipper, happy and anxious. It was that time of year. The holidays had that effect on people.

"I don't know, Bel," Cargan said finally. "He seemed like a good egg."

"He did, Car." I looked out the window at a mother pushing twins in a stroller. My mother hadn't had such conveniences when we were small. Dad carried me and

Mom carried Cargan when we were too big for a baby carriage. I would look over Dad's shoulder and make funny faces at Cargan and he would smile back, laughing uproariously at the funniest face of all, crossed eyes, my tongue out. The other boys, a ragtag lot, would dart and weave on the sidewalk, the admonition of "don't go in the street!" heard again and again. "He did indeed."

"So, maybe he's telling the truth."

That was a possibility I had never considered, cutting the guy out of my life on Halloween, making our first dance together at Kevin and Mary Ann's wedding our last. "How are you always so sure about everything, Brother?"

"It's my gut, Sister. It's never been wrong."

There's always a first time, I thought, before bidding him good-bye and hanging up. He still didn't know where I was going and, if I were to be honest with myself, neither did I. I guess, like always, I'd figure it out as I went along.

CHAPTER Four

Wooded Lake boasted one high school, two middle schools, and as for an elementary school, I wouldn't know. I hadn't passed it during my hour-long drive around the small town, the only major building I hadn't identified. I went down the Main Street one more time, finally stopping in at a coffee place that looked like it had sprung up recently, cheap rents and a burgeoning hipster population putting this whole town on the map, making new businesses necessary. It was called The Coffee Pot, with a little leaf as its insignia, and I wondered at the double entendre. I went in, and while the place definitely smelled like coffee, there was also a musky undertone to that odor, one that spoke of an old building or something else, something more organic in nature. Being a chef for as long as I had gave me a great nose, one that could identify smells with accuracy.

I went up to the counter and ordered an espresso and being as it was snack time—who am I kidding? Every minute of my day is snack time—added a chocolate biscotti to my order. Before I walked away, I took another look at the guy behind the counter, who was around my age and sporting the longest, bushiest beard

I had ever seen. He asked me what I wanted. I sniffed the biscotti.

"Made fresh today," he said, and winked at me, giving me pause.

I held up the biscotti. "Will this make me feel better than I was hoping? A little lighthearted?" I asked without asking of its ingredients directly. "Light-headed, even?"

He gave me a quizzical look. "I hope so?" he said. "It's not like it's magic biscotti or anything like that."

" 'Magic biscotti'?" I asked. "Do you have other baked goods here with magic properties?" The last thing I needed was to disappear from the Manor, drive around a town I didn't know, and then get as high as a kite, so high that I would be forced to spend more time here than I originally anticipated. I hadn't seen any hotels and my car wasn't what you'd call comfortable for sleeping.

He leaned on the counter and I could see that behind that bushy beard was a very handsome guy. Not that I was noticing that kind of thing these days. I had sworn off men if not for good, then at least for a really long time. They all stunk, in my opinion, Cargan being the only standout. And my father, of course. And they were my relatives, so it was weird. Maybe I had set the bar too high, but in my heart I knew that I had set it too low. On-the-ground low. Maybe I would get high and think about that, an altered state being just what the doctor ordered.

He continued to look at me, my face giving away a mental tug-of-war going on behind my eyes. "Biscotti's not magic, Chef McGrath," he said, pointing at my chef's coat when I cocked my head, confused as to how he knew me.

"Oh, right, that," I said. "So, the name here, The Coffee Pot, the leaf insignia . . ."

"No double meaning," he said. "I forgot when I opened it where exactly I was setting up shop. I root for the Toronto Maple Leafs. That's where the leaf came from. The maple leaf." He lifted his chin toward what looked like an original Woodstock poster over the big grinder. "Summer of Love really cast a spell around here."

There were a couple of stools at the counter in addition to a bunch of mismatched tables and chairs. I sat on one of them and opened my biscotti; it wasn't magic, but it could have been. I held out a hand. "I'm Belfast. Belfast McGrath."

"Tweed Blazer," he said, holding out his hand. "And before you ask, yes, that's my real name, and no, my mother didn't smoke a lot of weed. She just liked the way it sounded."

I resisted the urge to laugh. I thought "Belfast" was a lot to carry around, but at least I wasn't named after an article of clothing. "You could pronounce it the French way," I said. He looked at me quizzically, so I explained further. "Blah-zay."

"I don't think that would make things better," he said, picking up a rag and wiping up a sticky spill on the scarred oak. "Call me crazy."

I took a sip of my espresso. "Crazy Blazer would be even worse," I said.

It took him a minute, but he smiled and pointed at me. "Ah, a jokester." He leaned on the counter. "So what brings an honest-to-goodness chef up to these parts? Please tell me you're looking to open a farm-to-table restaurant on Main Street. I can be your coffee vendor."

"Oh, sorry," I said. "Although that's not a bad idea. I bet you have some great farms up here."

"The best," he said. "My neighbor raises chickens, so we always have incredible eggs. And their chickens are all free-range and fed an organic diet."

I thought about the fresh ham and prime rib I served at 80 percent of the weddings I cooked for at the Manor and shuddered internally. I would have loved to do something with free-range chickens, but showing Dad the difference in price and having to listen to him scream about "organic this and holistic that!"—two mutually exclusive things—was not what I wanted to do. Yes, we had had duck at Mary Ann and Kevin's wedding, but that was only because Mom and Dad thought Mary Ann walked on water and would have given her the sun, moon, and stars if they could have.

"Real estate's really cheap," Tweed said. "Get in before all of the city people come up here and start snapping everything up."

"As tempting as that sounds," I said, "I have a job and a life in Foster's Landing and no funds to start a restaurant right now. Heck, I barely have enough money to go to a restaurant, never mind open one."

"So what brings you to Wooded Lake?" he asked. "I'd like to think it's my delicious coffee, known for miles around, but something tells me it's something else." He clapped his hands together and waved them in the air, the flour that had been on his hands creating a cloud between us. "Magic, perhaps?"

Maybe a little bit, I thought. "Actually, I was wondering how I could find Love Canyon? I've been driving around, but there's no sign of it."

He stopped smiling and stood up straight. "You're about twenty years too late on that one."

"As in it's gone?" I asked.

"Yep. Gone," he said. "Bought by a developer. It's condos now. Mostly."

That explained it. That's why I couldn't find any evidence that the place ever existed in this little town. But just bringing it up had erased any of the banter that Tweed and I had going and the subject of Love Canyon seemed to be one he was suddenly not interested in talking about. He turned and went back into the area behind the place where the baristas made coffee, and didn't come out again. I flagged down a girl behind the counter and had her ring me up, my espresso suddenly not so tasty, the biscotti tasting like paste in my mouth. This had been a mistake. The people of Wooded Lake had moved beyond Love Canyon and didn't want to talk about it; that much was clear. I pushed my little cup toward the barista and got up, heading for the door.

Outside, it was getting dark and it was colder than when I had entered; I hoped the Beetle hadn't gone back to arctic temperatures in the short time I had been in the coffee place, but I didn't have high hopes. The car was across the street and I waited for the light traffic to pass before stepping out into the road.

"That's not a happy subject around here," a voice behind me said. I turned and an older man, nattily dressed in a blue suit and a bow tie, a scarf around his neck, was standing close to the door of the barbershop a few feet north of the coffee place.

"What's not?" I asked, stepping onto the sidewalk.

"Love Canyon," he said. "Lots of bad memories in Wooded Lake." His hair, white like cotton, brushed his shoulders, lifting slightly in the breeze that seemed to seep into my bones.

"Why's that?" I asked.

"There's been a lot of interest in it lately, the anniversary of its closing coming up, but it wasn't all sweetness and light there," he said. "You can do a search. Look online. That will tell you everything you need to know." He turned away from me, looking over his shoulder. "And some things you probably don't."

"Like what?" I called after him. "What things?"

But he was gone, ducking into an alley next to the barbershop. When I followed him into the same alley, I found that it was empty, the only sound a cluster of dead leaves scuttling along the edge of the brick buildings on either side.

I don't know what I had hoped to find. That Amy would just appear and all would be explained? Forgiven? I felt stupid for having been so impulsive.

One thing was clear, though: I was coming back up here. And next time, I'd have a plan.

CHAPTER *Five*

Back home, the Manor was shuttered for the night, the only light cast by the big chandelier in the foyer, which was always blazing and could be seen through the large transom over the door. I pulled the Beetle into the spot next to the stairs that led to my apartment and let myself into my darkened home. The bulb had burned out over my door, and like everything else at Shamrock Manor, it would only be replaced after being out for far too long. My parents, brothers, and I were nothing if not practiced procrastinators and that trait would be our downfall eventually.

I threw my purse onto the counter, poured myself a glass of Merlot, and grabbed a plate of cheese from the refrigerator. A sleeve of crackers completed my meal and I went into my bedroom where my computer sat on my bed, right where I had left it that morning after I had checked the weather for the upcoming Saturday wedding. I didn't have a desk; heck, my nightstand was one of those particleboard rounds on a spindly tripod covered with a tablecloth. I positioned myself on the bed, carefully placing the wineglass on the nightstand, making sure that it wouldn't tip the table over, the wine filled to the brim. I opened my laptop and typed in "Wooded

Lake," something I should have done before I had driven there, a fool's errand if there had ever been one.

While I hoped that a photo of Amy would jump out at me and assure me of her existence past that one night on Eden Island, every photo of Love Canyon was blurry, faded, or both. It seemed the residents of the commune had been notoriously camera shy and the photos that did exist were taken by someone considered a "mole," the brother of a girl from Ohio who had disappeared years earlier and whom he had traveled east to find. The guy, one Gary Mertens, had been discovered as not really being into free love and communal living and banished from the place; the article I read said that he had eventually found his sister, Chelsea, living with a poet in Greenwich Village. She was already gone by the time he got there. She went on to fame as a painter and sculptor but never publicly spoke of her time on the commune.

A Svengali-like leader, the article said, had started Love Canyon in response to the "repressive, capitalist, patriarchal society" that existed in the United States at the time, and invited people to share "brotherhood, sisterhood, love and light" among the tall trees of the village of Wooded Lake. Sounded like a load of hooey to me, but I was a modern-day Monday-morning quarterback, looking at the whole endeavor through a historical looking glass that made the whole idea sound quaint, if not a little kooky. I couldn't imagine Amy getting caught up in something like that. A commune? Although all she had wanted was to get out of Foster's Landing, its tiny landscape and small borders hemming her in, a place an hour north and boasting free love didn't seem her style. She wanted to see the world, to spread her wings. That meant getting out of here and going somewhere else, somewhere bigger and better, not a town that was so much like Foster's Landing.

I couldn't imagine that Wooded Lake had been her idea of flying the coop.

The Svengali's name had been Archie Peterson before he changed it to Zephyr. The land had been family owned, deeded to him by his late father as sole owner upon the man's passing. It was fifty acres and had once been a working dairy farm until it had been turned into a place that promised "serenity and hope in a battered world," a contention for which the writer of the article, a man named Dave Southerland, could barely contain his disdain. The piece was tabloid journalism at its best and contained adjectives that portrayed the writer's bias: "Hokey." "Misguided." "Unrealistic." And finally, "Unsustainable."

No mention of the people who had been there, just that the population skewed more female than male, which didn't strike me as a huge surprise. I suspected that if someone changed his name to Zephyr and opened a place called Love Canyon, his idea was to get as many women up there as possible. I'm not sure his idea would work in today's world, but back then his promise of communing with nature, living off the land, and finding respite from what was a very turbulent time probably appealed to a lot of people, women in particular. Be a feminist or stay in your traditional lane? Protest Vietnam or hide in your suburban tract home? Vote for Nixon or probably the safer choice, Hubert Humphrey? When I thought about all of that, my decision to come back to Foster's Landing and live with my family seemed a simple one, even if it was setting up to come with its own challenges. Moving to a commune had never crossed my addled mind, thank God. It had crossed some people's, though, and that had kept the commune working in some capacity at least until fifteen years prior when it seemed Amy had arrived. It had disbanded not too long after.

What had taken her there exactly? And why hadn't she told me that this was her plan all along? Maybe it hadn't been. Maybe it had been a stop along the way to somewhere else, somewhere great. Maybe I'd never know. But I was definitely going to try to find out.

A knock at the door interrupted my mental gymnastics. Cargan was standing in the dark, looking up at the burned-out bulb. "Why didn't you tell me that the light needed replacing?" he asked when I opened the screen door to let him in.

"I could fix it myself, but why bother when I can wait a year and then only do it because I've fallen down the stairs in the dark?"

"Good point," he said, looking into my bedroom on the right. "Hey, got any more of that wine? I could use a drink after today."

I went into the bedroom and grabbed my glass. In the kitchen, I poured a healthy glass for him in a stemless wineglass that said "Queen of Everything" on the front. Before taking a sip, he looked at me. "Really? This is the only glass you have for me?"

"They didn't have 'Nosiest Brother Ever,' so this will have to do."

He took a seat on the couch and put his feet up on the stained and scratched coffee table. "Want to tell me the real reason you ran out of the Manor?"

I looked into my wineglass, hoping that I could find the answers there. I had tried that before and knew it

wasn't a surefire way to the truth. "I really don't, Cargan," I said. In my car, visible on the front seat, was the
article about Love Canyon and the photo of Amy. I wondered if he saw it and already knew where I had gone.
"Sometimes I get a little . . ." I looked for the right
words. ". . . hemmed in? And I need to get out of here
for a while."

"Never like this," he said. "Was it something about
the clients that came in? Did they upset you?"

"Not at all. They were lovely. The father of the bride
was beside himself at the thought of his daughter getting married, but the stepmother was really nice."

"Dad said that they were there that night. At The
Monkey's Paw." He took a sip of wine. "That it?"

I didn't realize I had such a convenient cover. "Yeah.
That's it," I said.

He studied me for a while, seeing if I would crack,
but I held his gaze. "What are the chances?"

"That they came here? Today?" I asked, shrugging.
"One in a million, I suppose. But the stepmom is friends
with the woman who wanted me to do that reality show,
so maybe Shamrock Manor was always on their radar."

"Maybe," he said. "Who's the friend?"

"Max Rayfield," I said. "If I recall, Max is married
to a cop and so is Alison, the stepmom."

"Names?" Cargan asked. It had been a while since
he had been "on the job" and when he was he was deep
undercover, but I still suspected that he knew everyone
and that his reputation, even just in name, preceded him.

"I don't remember Max's husband, but Alison's husband is Bobby Crawford," I said. "Ring a bell?"

He nodded. "Yeah. Good reputation."

"Well, that's good," I said. "I was hoping the wedding wouldn't be filled with a bunch of crooked cops."

He ignored that. "When's the wedding?"

"Memorial Day."

"And they didn't book?" he asked. "That's not a lot of time." To Cargan, six months out might as well have been two weeks from now. "That's a busy weekend."

"Do we have it booked?" I asked.

He also had a photographic memory, or something approaching one. "Booked on Saturday, free on Sunday."

Back-to-back weddings. Big fun. We barely had time to recover from Saturday before Sunday was upon us.

"Did you get contact info?" he asked.

"I'm sure Dad did," I said.

"Since you seem to have a relationship with the step-mom, why don't you give her a call and try to close the deal?" he asked. "We're in no position to lose a booking, and even though back-to-backs are the worst, it's money," he said, rubbing his thumb and index finger together.

"I wouldn't say we have a 'relationship,'" I said. Witnessing my complete and total meltdown at The Monkey's Paw should have ensured that Alison Bergeron and Bobby Crawford wouldn't want anything to do with Shamrock Manor, but there they were, looking at the place, leaning toward it, if Alison's enthusiasm for the place had been any indication. She liked good food and I made good food. That might be all the incentive she and her husband needed to pull the trigger, as it were.

"I'll call them tomorrow," I said. I yawned, signaling to my brother that it was time to hit the road. "I'm exhausted, Car."

"Me, too," he said.

I walked him to the door. "Did Dad get the tree secured?" I asked.

He shook his head. "Nah. Found him on top of it in the middle of the foyer. Thankfully the tree has soft needles and broke his fall. Gave him a nice black eye, though."

The scenario he described had been the one I had been most concerned about coming to fruition. After confirming that Dad's injuries were minor, I said, "I'm sure Mom has some old Irish remedy for that."

"I don't want to know," he said, his hand on the door handle. "She once made me a 'poultice' for a bruise I got playing soccer, I smelled like cabbage and Vicks Vapo-Rub for a week."

"But the bruise?" I asked.

"Gone in a day," he said, smiling. "She's still got a few tricks up her sleeve."

After he left, I returned to my computer, considering my next steps. My brother was on to me; he knew I was lying to him, but I wasn't ready to involve him just yet. His time would come; he would be valuable at some point. For right now, though, I was going it alone, setting out on a mysterious adventure that had room for only one traveler.

CHAPTER Six

While lying in bed that night, I realized I had overlooked one important detail in the story, that of the sculptor who had lived at Love Canyon, a woman who was easily found by googling her name: Chelsea Mertens. I knew a little about sculpture because my dad fancied himself a mixed-media artist, doing weird sculptures that bore no resemblance to their models, paintings that were strange in their conception and execution, and the aforementioned installations that looked as if they had dropped from the sky—and some alien planet—and that took a lot of brainpower to decipher their meaning. Dad was incredibly creative . . . just not terribly talented.

Chelsea Mertens was still alive and, while once the owner of a gallery in New York City, she had closed that and moved to Farringville, a bedroom community about an hour south of here right along the river, now plying her trade in an old barn behind what seemed to be a grand and spectacular Colonial. The photos on her Web site were the equivalent of real-estate porn and I wondered just how good her sculptures were—or how much she sold them for—for her to be able to live in such splendor. I wish Dad were more talented; maybe then I could get that professional stove that I craved. I was practically drooling onto my keyboard at the sight of her kitchen, a study in marble and stainless steel, fitting for an almost-hundred-year-old house yet functional in the contemporary world. I read through her site to find out if one needed an appointment to see her or her sculptures and found that she worked in her barn every day and that "walk-ins are welcome."

Walk in I would. Thank you very much, Chelsea Mertens.

The timing was off; she had left years before Amy had landed there, I was sure, but it was worth a try. I was looking for anything that could help and I had found exactly one person who had been there at all. Chelsea Mertens was a dead end, most likely, but since when did I let something like that stop me?

I drove along the river, taking the scenic route. Winter hadn't hit officially yet, but it was cold, the river on my right showing whitecaps that looked like they would be positively bone-chilling to the touch. It didn't take me long to get to Farringville; I had left after rush hour and it was a weekday, so the route I traveled was light on commuters. I still couldn't wrap my head around what I had seen in the paper and I knew I was tilting at windmills, as it were, but I felt the adrenaline coursing through my veins and thought that this was a reason for being, a reason to be alive. To see if my old friend had been at Love Canyon and, if so, if she was still on this planet at all, waiting to be found, hoping to see me and all of her old friends again.

It was a long shot but one that I was willing to follow.

A few months earlier, there had been a big-city reporter who said she was looking into the case, a woman with the improbable name Duffy Dreyer, a callback to the Amazin' Mets catcher of old. I wondered if she was any closer to finding Amy or had given up on the story, tired of chasing a cold lead that went nowhere. I wouldn't be sharing anything I had learned with her; I was on my own and didn't need any help here.

It took me several tries to find the street on which Chelsea Mertens lived. It wasn't a street exactly, but more like a lane, a long, paved stretch of road that was flanked on both sides by trees, some still green, even in late fall. The house appeared in the distance, but before that, a sign directed me to pull off to the right to the barn that housed "Mertens Art." Less a barn and more a rustic outpost to the main house, it sat on a big clearing, devoid of trees, with a little pad for a few cars to park next to the big wide doors that had the same name of the studio stenciled across the front.

Mertens Art was a business, plain and simple, with a receptionist at the front desk asking what I might be interested in viewing before letting me pass into a large room that held paintings, sculptures, and even some blown glass. I figured out after browsing by myself that it was an artist co-op, a detail that I had blown past on the Web site that I hadn't visited while looking for information. I was so intrigued by the artwork I figured I would get the lay of the land before asking for Chelsea, but I didn't have to wait long. Above me, on a lofted area that was accessed by a spiral staircase, a woman appeared, long, flowing gray hair billowing out behind her, skinny and fat silver bracelets adorning each arm. She swept down the staircase and landed next to me, her face open and smiling.

"I've been waiting for you!" she said.

"You have?" I asked, looking around to see if anyone

else was in the room or even if I was part of a weird reality show where unsuspecting art gallery patrons were pulled into some strange prank.

"I have!" she said. "Delilah, hold my calls."

The receptionist at the front of the room gave Chelsea a thumbs-up in response, an odd response for a subordinate to her boss.

At her request, I followed the woman into a back room that smelled just like Dad's studio, a combination of paint, thinner, wood, and, for some strange reason, burning rubber. There was a giant wooden slab that functioned as a desk; Chelsea took a seat behind it, motioning for me to sit across from her.

"I'm very excited to have this conversation," she said.

"You are?" I asked.

"I am!" she said. "It's like you've been dropped from heaven so I can tell my story. My true story. The story of my art."

"I think you may have me confused with someone else," I said. "My name is—"

"I know your name," she said. "*Everyone* knows your name."

I hoped that wasn't true, because if it was it meant that more than a few people knew about my stint at The Monkey's Paw and even more than I thought knew that I had a bad reputation. That I had been required to take anger-management classes in order for my former boss not to press charges against me for brandishing a broken bottle in his presence. "You do?"

"Why, you're a woman of few words, aren't you?" she said, placing one hand over the other atop her desk. "Now, shall we get started?" She leaned back in the chair and closed her eyes, putting her feet up on the desk. "It was in my mid-thirties that I decided that I needed to express myself in another medium, one that went beyond sculpture to bring—"

"I have to stop you, Ms. Mertens."

She opened one eye and looked at me. "Why?"

"Well, I don't think I'm who you think I am."

She repositioned herself into a sitting position, her feet on the floor, her eyes on a datebook in front of her. She riffled through a few pages. "It's Tuesday. It's ten o'clock. You're Francesca Dell'atoria."

I'm a plump redhead with the map of Ireland on my face. My father, an Irishman himself, probably looked more like a Francesca Dell'atoria than I did.

"*Rizzoli News*?" she asked. "Francesca?"

I held out my hand. "Belfast McGrath. Shamrock Manor."

"I don't even know what that means," she said. On her desk her phone buzzed, and she pushed a button.

The voice of the receptionist came through. "Chelsea? Francesca Dell'atoria is here."

"I'll be right out." She looked back at me. "So you're a customer?"

"Not exactly," I said, knowing I didn't have a lot of time. "My name is Belfast McGrath and I work at Shamrock Manor in Foster's Landing and I had a friend who disappeared . . . her name was Amy Mitchell . . . and she went to Love Canyon and we haven't seen her in fifteen years and I know you were there did you ever go back?" I asked, taking a deep breath when I was done. "I know you probably left before she even got there, but you're my only link to the place and I'm hoping . . ."

"No," she said, definitively and with finality. "I didn't see her."

"This girl?" I asked, pulling out a photo from my purse I had thought to bring with me, the same photo that Brendan Joyce had had in his wallet a few months earlier and that had caused our breakup, Amy's graduation photo. I put it on her desk. "Please. Have you been back to Wooded Lake? To see Archie Peterson? Zephyr? Did you ever see her?"

She looked at the photo nervously biting her lower lip, finally pushing it back toward me. "I didn't see your friend," she said, standing. "I left Wooded Lake a long time ago."

I got up, taking the photo and putting it back into my purse. "Are you sure? Can you tell me anything?"

"Ms. McGrath, is it?"

I nodded.

"I have an appointment." She ushered me to the door of the office and into the shop's space. She said nothing else to me before depositing me at the receptionist's desk again and whisking a gorgeous leggy Italian woman back to the office, the Chelsea I originally met returning, her fires stoked by the thought of telling her "story" to the arts reporter.

The receptionist, an Indian woman in her early twenties, watched her go. "I don't know what you said to her, but she looked pissed."

"I didn't really say anything," I said, trying another tack. "Hi, I'm Belfast."

"Delilah," she said, holding out a hand. "Chelsea's my mom. I can read her like a book."

"Your mom?" I asked.

"Adopted," she said, noticing my confusion at their disparate complexions. "Found me when she was in an ashram in Bangalore."

"Found you?" I asked.

"You know what I mean," she said, taking disaffection to a whole new level. "Anyway, are you a customer or what?"

I leaned on the desk, at shoulder level for me. "Well, not exactly," I said. "You mentioned your mother was in an ashram. Did she ever mention a place north of here called Love Canyon?"

"Oh, yeah," she said, her tone full of portent. "For sure. That's the commune-y place, right? The one her brother thought was a cult?"

"That's the one," I said.

"Yeah, she brings that up every now and again. Wasn't a good experience," Delilah said. "The guy that ran the place was a real lech. Broke her heart into a million pieces."

"Did she say anything else about it? Has she ever gone back?"

She shook her head, her black curls, some pink ones interspersed, shaking with the motion. "Nope. Just that he had lots of women and that was what led her to leave. Told me most men were scum and to stay away from them," she said. "Except for my father. She loves him. Says he's different."

"Well, that's a relief," I said. "Sorry I upset her. I'm looking for a friend." I started for the door.

"Aren't we all?" the girl asked, looking at her fingernails.

CHAPTER *Seven*

I ran into Dad first thing when I returned. He did have a shiner and it was a good one. I whistled appreciatively, glad to have something besides Amy to think about. "That's a good one, Dad," I said. "But you're lucky you didn't kill yourself."

He waved me off, walking into the dining room. The Christmas tree was on its side in the foyer, a beached conifer waiting to be upright once again. I followed him into the big hall.

"Maybe this is the year we hire someone to put it up for us? Secure it to the railing?" I asked.

"You know, Belfast," he said, bending to pick up an errant piece of paper that hadn't made its way into the garbage bin, "I thought there might be a reason I had four sons. Four strapping sons! I thought maybe, just maybe, that they would help me in my old age, make it so I didn't have to hang onto a Christmas tree like a surfer riding a wave." He pointed to his black eye. "They're useless. All of them."

Dad usually overlooked my brothers' shortcomings, but landing on his face in the foyer seemed to have put him in the darkest of moods, particularly where they were concerned. I went up to him and studied his face, the bruise that circled his usually bright, and twinkling eye. "I'll handle it, Dad. You're right: You're getting a little too long in the tooth to try to put up a twenty-foot Christmas tree."

"It's only eighteen," he said, "and I'm not long in the tooth. Just tired. Sick and tired," he said, storming toward the back of the dining room toward the bathrooms. "And would it kill anyone to restock the toilet paper?" he asked from the confines of the men's room. "For God's sake!"

My father was generally a congenial sort so his outburst was a little disturbing. Even if he was angry at my brothers, he never took it out on me or let me see just how annoyed he really was. He blustered a lot but that's all it was: bluster. I pulled my phone out of my pocket and started a group text among the five McGrath children and tapped out a message.

Family meeting. Ten o'clock. Manor kitchen.

Arney practiced law in town, so unless he had a meeting with a disgruntled divorcée he'd be free. Feeney's only source of employment at the moment was as lead singer in the McGrath Brothers band, so even though he didn't get up before noon most days, I was hoping he'd see the message and grace us with his presence. Cargan was in the Manor, so his attendance wasn't an issue. And Derry was now a stay-at-home father, probably just finishing up his viewing of the morning news programs; I didn't think I was interfering with anything very important that couldn't be handled at a later time, like laundry or the preparation of the evening's pot roast.

My brothers all sent questioning texts asking what this was about, but rather than explain, I let them twist in the wind. Giving them any explanation of why I wanted to meet would only justify their excuses and we needed this tree put up, trimmed, and full of lights before the weekend's wedding.

Dad passed me, a bag of garbage from the bathroom in one hand. "We'll handle it, Dad. Leave the tree to us," I said.

Muttering about ungrateful kids—the youngest of whom was me, making it that we really couldn't be defined as "kids"—he marched past me. Out back, I heard him throw the garbage into the Dumpster with gusto and then take off for parts unknown. We had a lot of land, so he could disappear pretty easily and be gone for hours.

I went into the kitchen, checked over my to-do list, and spent the morning working on a few of the items on there. I had just put the last of a tray of canapés into the freezer, popping an extra one in my mouth, when my brothers showed up in the kitchen, Cargan the only one not looking put out.

"I've got a meeting at eleven, so you've got exactly fifty-nine minutes," Arney said.

Feeney had some other kind of excuse and Derry just shrugged, knowing that we knew he had nothing to do ever and that his days were filled with car pool, volunteering at the school, and writing the great American novel, something he had been doing since he was twenty-two and had graduated from Sarah Lawrence with a degree in creative writing.

I had held back an assortment of canapés and proffered them on a plate. "Here. Try these," I said, hoping to mollify the angry crowd. While they ate, I pointed to the foyer, to the prone tree, something that none of them had commented on upon arrival. "We need to get that tree up. Dad fell off the balcony last night and has a black eye. It could have been much worse."

"I told Dad to hire someone," Arney said. "I even told him I would pay for it."

"Cheap bastard," Feeney said between mouthfuls of a miniature spinach quiche.

"Hey, now," Cargan said, a warning in his tone. "It will take all of twenty minutes with your help and I for one don't want to have the old guy laid up in the hospital with a broken neck."

"You generally die of a broken neck," Derry added. "Instantly."

"Not helpful," I said. "Now, who's in?"

Cargan had already gotten one of the groundskeepers to help bring up the extendable ladder. The Shamrock Manor grounds crew had long ago decided to strike against putting up the tree, their own safety of paramount importance; Dad had gone along with the decision because he is an old softie, first and foremost. He's also a great boss if you have a good excuse for why you don't want to do something. While I stood on the secondfloor balcony, which overlooked the entire foyer, Arney, Derry, and Feeney righted the tree while Cargan stood behind it. He scooted out from behind it when it was clear it was standing and assessed its levelness.

"A little to the right," he said. "Okay, left. Just a smidge." Below me, I heard cursing that, if Mom had heard, would have landed us all in time-out, sent to our rooms without supper like in the old days. There was also a lot of whispering, furtive, tense words between Feeney and Arney in particular that ceased when they saw my face peeking from around the tree, up on the second floor. I held the very top of the tree, leaning over the balcony, knowing exactly how Dad felt as he did moments before he rode the tree down to the ground below.

I tied a piece of rope from the top of the tree around one of the spindles on the balcony and pulled the knot tight. With five of us working on it as opposed to Dad's and my two-person show, it was bound to stay upright longer. I hoped I was right.

I came down the stairs and noticed Arney and Feeney deep in conversation by the dining-room doors and I didn't think my ears were deceiving me, but I definitely heard the one word—the one name—I didn't want spoken in my presence ever again.

Brendan.

"All right," I said, marching up to my two very guilty-looking brothers. "What gives?"

Feeney was a practiced liar and all-around charlatan. It wasn't hard for him to look me straight in the eye and say, "Nothing. Nothing gives."

But Arney, the oldest of our lot, and the one on whom Mom and Dad pinned all of their hopes and dreams, was still an altar boy at heart and, as a result, probably the worst divorce attorney one could hire, giving away the store to one aggrieved partner or another. I had gleaned from conversations between Mom and Dad that whoever was represented by Arney usually lost the battle and the war and I wondered how he stayed in business. It didn't take more than five seconds, and a harsh stare from me, for him to blurt out, "We saw him. We saw Brendan Joyce."

An old slogan went through my head—"Easy. Breezy. Cover Girl"—but I wasn't an easygoing type, couldn't do breezy, and definitely was not a cover girl. I attempted a combination shoulder shrug/hair flip to indicate that I didn't care, but something on my face told my brothers that I definitely did care. Too much.

Behind me, Cargan whispered, "I believe him," while in front of me, Feeney said, "It was all I could do not to punch him in the teeth."

"For what, Feeney?" I asked. "Carrying around a photo of a missing girl?"

"For breaking your heart, Bel," Feeney said. "For messing up probably the best thing that he had ever had in his miserable life."

And the look on my brother's handsome face, his black hair hanging on to his forehead and making him look as he had when we were little and our relationship wasn't quite as close, his protective nature not in full view, coupled with his hand on my shoulder, brought tears to my eyes. My brothers encircled me and muttered all the right things: He was a jerk. He didn't deserve me. He would pay. (That was from Feeney, totally alarming; his brand of justice was one that I didn't want meted out.)

They were wrong, though. He wasn't a jerk; rather, he had been a warm blanket on a cold night, with strong arms to hug me. He did deserve me and I him. That day, the day of the Kevin Hanson and Mary Ann D'Amato wedding, when I had found a photo of Amy Mitchell in his wallet, a heart drawn on it, my own heart had stopped. He claimed it wasn't his, that he didn't know how it had gotten there, and to me, that sounded like the protestations of a middle schooler, one who would think that his word was enough to make me believe the unbelievable. He did know and it was his and I told him that I never wanted to see him again, the look on his face unlike any I had ever seen.

He was shattered.

I knew the feeling.

He honored my wishes, though, and I hadn't seen him again. It was a small town, though; we were bound to run into each other and that was not a day I was looking forward to.

I wiped my eyes and extricated myself from my brothers. "Let's move on," I said. "That's over and we have a lot to do." I pulled the lid off a box of Christmas lights and handed the balled-up spool to Derry. "Here, this should take you a while," I said, noting that every year that I had been involved in this maneuver—and admittedly, I had been gone for many of them—we implored Dad to wrap the lights up in a neat fashion and every year we opened the box to find a knotted-up spool of lights, some of which didn't work. I bent over another box and pulled out more lights, my brothers now silent as we continued with our mission to decorate the tree.

When it was done, we stood back in a semi-circle admiring our handiwork. "Good job, boys," I said, and high-fived Cargan, standing next to me, as always. "Dad will be happy."

"Dad's never happy," Arney said before racing out of the Manor, late for his appointment.

We managed to decorate the tree in spite of the wonky lights, and when I flipped the switch the tree was ablaze, silver tinsel glinting in the morning sun streaming through the windows on the second floor and through the transom over the big front double doors.

"It looks beautiful," I said, giving them each a brief hug as they left. The whole project had taken no more than an hour. Cargan and I stood in the foyer, admiring our collective handiwork.

"They come through sometimes," I said.

"Rarely. But sometimes," he said. Before he walked away, he turned to me. "He was a nice guy. He made a mistake."

"Sometimes it sounds like you're on Brendan Joyce's side," I said.

He didn't say anything, going into the office next to the kitchen, leaving me to appraise the tree, alone.

CHAPTER Eight

This darned job was getting in the way of my social life (which was basically nonexistent anyway) and this new mystery (which was my new reason for being). That Saturday, I got up early and got to work preparing for the upcoming afternoon affair, a small wedding by Manor standards, sixty people, a former local girl and guy who were a few years older than me but who had met on an online dating site, not realizing until they met that they had both grown up in the same town.

The boys were tuning up their instruments in the dining room while Feeney sang some kind of love song into the microphone, his tenor on point as always. Cargan was playing around on the violin, his fiddling—musical doodling really—better than that of most people playing an actual tune.

The menu was simple: a sampling of our best canapés, a cheese station, tenderloin with roasted fingerling potatoes, and a cauliflower mousse. They were bringing in their own wedding cake. It was the simplest of meals and I could have done it in my sleep.

Dad came into the kitchen, looking spiffy in his tuxedo, which he wore when we hosted an event. Mom was behind him in a classic little black dress, a strand of pearls around her neck. "We ready, Belfast?" Dad asked as he did every time we began a wedding service and my answer was always the same.

"I was born ready, Dad."

He still didn't get the joke but appreciated my being on the job and ready for the action to come.

When the family arrived, entering the foyer, I could tell by the wrinkle of her nose that Mom was not a fan of the bride's gown, a fitted, off-the-shoulder number that showed every curve the voluptuous woman had, the low-cut neck highlighting her ample bosom. Dad glad-handed the men in the group and then led the family, sans bride and groom, into the dining room. The happy couple made a grand entrance to my brothers' practiced introductory music, the bride shimmying before going through the doors that led to the party.

I went back to cooking, loading up Colleen and Eileen, our two remaining longtime servers, with trays of canapés, my special mini-quiches always a hit, even if I found them a touch boring. Give the people what they want and all. That was Dad's motto, along with "the customer is always right" and, inexplicably, "it never rains in Southern California."

I was deep into meal prep when the doors to the kitchen swung open and a man came in, smiling. "Belfast!"

"Mr. Malloy," I said. "Long time, no see."

"Well, there was that quick hello a few months ago," he said, reminding me that we had seen each other since high school when I was a student and he was a teacher as well as my swim coach. "Still doing the hundred-meter free in your spare time?"

"Do I look like I get any exercise at all?" I said,

laughing. "I think it's pretty obvious that I don't. But you're very kind."

"Your food is amazing, Bel," he said. "You really knocked it out of the park today."

I put a large pot in the sink and filled it with water. "So the guests are happy?" I asked. "The bride and groom?"

"Everyone is beyond happy," he said. "You know, I've never been to an event at the Manor. Or it's been years if I have. Crazy, right?"

"You didn't chaperone our junior prom?" I asked.

"I don't think I did," he said. "Or maybe I did? That was a long time ago." He pointed to his head. "The memory isn't what it used to be."

"No one's is," I said. Colleen and Eileen came into the kitchen with trays of dirty dishes, loading them into the big industrial dishwasher while I chatted with my former coach.

"I should let you get back to work," he said.

"I think they are going to cut the cake," I said, peeking out from the kitchen into the dining room. "And you don't want to miss that. That's usually the most entertaining part of the wedding." I thought back to a few Mom had told me about from past events: The one where the groom got a chipped tooth from an overzealous bride; the one where the bride slipped and broke her leg on some icing that had fallen to the floor; the one where the bride's mother had left crying because the whole tradition had gotten so far out of hand, cake smeared on her daughter's lovely décolletage and ten-thousand-dollar dress.

Mr. Malloy stood there a minute longer, his hands in

his pant pockets. "Remember when I used to the 'cool teacher,' Bel?" he asked.

"You were never *that* cool, Mr. Malloy," I said, smiling. He had been, though, a young guy teaching kids not that much younger than he was, the teacher we went to with complaints and problems and issues related to teen-aged angst.

"Guess you're right, Bel," he said. "We men are an odd bunch. Always trying to hold on to our youth. Women age much more gracefully, go into middle age without a complaint."

An odd, serious sentiment given the jovial nature of our conversation, but I went with it. I thought about Mom in her Pilates studio, stretching and toning the older ladies of Foster's Landing; neither she, nor they, were going into middle age gracefully, without a complaint. "You're quite the philosopher, Mr. Malloy."

"Please. Dan. It's just that this wedding is making me feel old."

"Okay. Dan," I said, but it sounded weird coming out of my mouth. To me, he was still our teacher, our some-time confidant, not the almost contemporary standing in front of me, still handsome in that ruddy Irish way that I was familiar with, a little more heavyhearted, it would seem, than in our high-school days. I heard my brothers strike up the song that announced the cake cutting. "You'd better get out there. Cake cutting is getting under way."

"Just wanted to tell you what a great job you've done here, Bel," he said, walking toward the doors to the dining room. "You've come a long way from swim team."

I watched him go. Yes, I have, I thought, even though I was right back where I started.

CHAPTER Nine

The next morning, alone in my apartment, I studied the photo in the newspaper, finding a small magnifying glass in the desk that had been here when I moved in, making it hover over the girl, half-turned, on the side of the frame. It was Amy, plain and simple, and no one would ever convince me otherwise. It probably made sense to ask Cargan as he had known her almost as well as I had, but this was my mystery to solve and involving him meant relinquishing control, something that I had done enough of in the last few months. I had left my job, and it hadn't been my decision. I had moved back home, and while that had been my decision, the lack of control I had over my life—not to mention lack of privacy—was starting to concern me. Four brothers and two parents equaled meddling squared.

No, I would go it alone.

I found an e-mail address for the person who wrote the story, a guy named Dave Southerland, and e-mailed him, asking if we could talk further about the article and anything else he may have found out.

I got dressed, for the first time in a long time, in civilian clothes, not in chef's clothes. I put on jeans and a sweater, wrapping a scarf around my neck, letting my curls go free from the confines of the head wrap that I wore in the kitchen. I pulled on a pair of boots and grabbed my bag, heading down the stairs outside my apartment, hoping to get out of Foster's Landing before the inhabitants of the Manor and their attached residence were stirring.

I drove back to Wooded Lake, the drive less fraught for me almost a week after my last visit, thinking about that photo, the sun shining, the morning brisk but not terribly cold. I drove down the winding Main Street, finding a parking spot not far from The Coffee Pot, this time on the same side of the street. I didn't know if Tweed Blazer owned the place or just worked there, but I hoped he was behind the counter so I could apologize for whatever I had done to offend him and, more important, get more information about the village and Love Canyon itself.

The seat I had sat in that first day was unoccupied. Although he didn't appear at first and I had to place my order with another person who worked there, he did come out of the kitchen a few minutes later, smiling warmly at me as I took my first sip of espresso.

"Hi," he said, and by the way he said it, I could tell that he didn't recognize me out of my uniform. I didn't want to prolong the charade, so I held out my hand. "We met the other day. I'm Belfast McGrath."

He took a good look at me and realization dawned on his face. "You were asking about Love Canyon."

"Guilty as charged." I don't know why I said that, implicating myself in something more sinister than he needed to know. "Yes. Love Canyon. I'm doing a little research. Wanted to get a feel for Wooded Lake."

Today he wore glasses, thick, dark rimmed, and

square. Behind them, his eyes narrowed. "Why the interest?"

I came up with the lie on the spot. "In addition to being a chef, I'm kind of a part-time historian. I've been looking into stories of the Hudson Valley and am hoping to publish a book. I started with the history of my parents' catering hall, Shamrock Manor, and it just led me to think about other places in the area and their pasts."

"Sordid pasts?" he said.

"Well, maybe," I said. "I just think there are a lot of interesting stories to be told and I'd love to be the one to tell them."

"So full-time chef, part-time historian, and part-time writer?" he asked. "Sounds like you've got a lot on your plate." He grimaced. "No pun intended."

"I see what you did there," I said. I took another sip of espresso, the caffeine giving me clarity, enough to continue the lie in convincing fashion. "There are a lot of stories to be told."

"Some that shouldn't, too." He turned to the cashier and asked her to cover. He pulled up the hinged counter and stepped under it. "Let's grab a table so we can talk more about this."

I picked up my coffee and biscotti and followed him to an old Formica kitchen table in the corner of the store, two cane-seated chairs on opposite sides of it. We sat down, me facing the big picture window that looked out on to Main Street. I considered why I didn't just tell him the truth, ask him if anyone ever spoke of a teenager living there, if the name Amy Mitchell meant anything to him, but I wasn't ready for all of that. Slow and steady, I thought. Let it unfold naturally, I told myself.

Don't be impulsive, or more impulsive than you normally are.

After we sat down, he pointed to a spot on the table in front of me. "How come you don't have a notebook? Write things down?" he asked.

Because I'm not really a historian? I thought but didn't say. I put a finger to my temple. "Good memory. All up here."

"You must have done great on your SATs."

"Pretty good," I said. "Good enough to get me where I wanted to go."

He turned at the sound of the door opening, a little bell above it announcing a new customer. He leaned in, lowered his voice. "Love Canyon is something we're all trying to forget," he said.

"Why?" I asked. "It seemed like a commune for hippies? The 'free love' set? From my research anyway."

"Well, that's one way to look at it, I guess," he said. "It was a pretty interesting place, and not in a good way."

"How so?" I asked.

He looked around, rubbed a hand, a workman's hand, calloused and rough, over his face. "Listen, this was a nice little town. Off the grid. Under the radar. A place where you could play in the woods and be a kid and no one would bother you. That's what I've been told. When the sun rose, you went outside. When the sun set, you came back in. But after Love Canyon opened people started coming here, looking for something we didn't have."

"Like what?"

"I'm not sure," he admitted. "But whatever they were looking for, they weren't going to find it in Wooded Lake." He looked at a spot over my head, thinking.

"What's that they say? 'Wherever you go, there you are'? That's what it was like here. People running from something, looking for a way out, I guess." He shook his head sadly. "It was never here."

It was more of an existential conversation, one that focused less on facts and more on musings. "You have a lot of opinions about the commune."

"I guess I do," he said, sitting up straighter, a little defensive.

"Why's that?" I asked.

"Well, you're a part-time historian," he said, considering how much to tell me but deciding I was worth it, my fake profession giving me credence. "So, I guess it's okay to tell you."

"Tell me what?" I asked after a few seconds of weighted silence.

"Archie Peterson was—is—my father."

CHAPTER Ten

He told me that he and his father were estranged, Tweed never getting over the fact that his father had turned the family compound into a sketchy commune that collected lost souls. Lost female souls. His mother had legally changed his name to her maiden name—Blazer—and he had kept it that way.

"Love Canyon had been Merrill Farms, in Archie's mother's family since the 1700s. It was bucolic and beautiful and had so much history." He smiled at the memory. "It was reported to be a stop on the Underground Railroad. It housed some soldiers for a time. It was a place of history and American solitude. Not a place for 'free love' and all that came with that."

He was sharing, so I took the time to listen, but in the back of my mind, I thought about when I would ask about Amy, if I was ready for what he would say.

"The article didn't mention that," I said.

A look crossed his face. "What article?"

"The one in the *Hudson Courier*."

"Rag," he said. "Not really known for its in-depth investigative journalism."

I pondered that; I had had a negative reaction to the

journalism. Tweed continued. "Archie eventually ran the place into the ground and soon we had no money. I was about to leave for college . . ."

So we were about the same age.

". . . and I didn't realize that what I came back to would be a completely different place from the one I left."

"And your mother?"

"She was long gone," he said. "I think it started out as a good idea, but as time went by, it was clear that it was really just an excuse for him to be the philanderer that he had always been in his heart and nothing else; she took off." He took his glasses off and wiped his eyes, even though they were dry. "She hung in there a long time. I was a teenager when she left, but I decided to stay. We did stay in touch over the years until she died. Two years ago. Breast cancer."

"I'm sorry," I said. Suddenly, I felt a little dirty, my lie bringing back terrible memories for what seemed like a nice guy trying to tamp down the past.

"Thanks," he said. He looked up suddenly, directly at me. "Hey, do you want to see it?"

"See what?" I asked. "Isn't Love Canyon condos now?"

"Most of it, but not all of it," he said. "That's why you're here, right? To see what's left?"

I didn't think anything was left, but I played along. "Sure. Yes. I'd love to see it. But don't you have to work?" I asked.

"Hey, that's the best part of being the boss," he said, getting up and taking off the apron tied around his waist. He called over to a young girl behind the counter, "Hey, Julie. I'm going to be out for about an hour. Cover?"

"You got it, Tweed," she said while ringing up the customer in front of her.

The coffee shop was filling up, but I wasn't going to point that out to him, now that his reluctance in showing me the remaining part of the place where he had grown up had turned to enthusiasm. Outside, Main Street of the little village was bustling, Christmas lights adorning every door and window of the quaint shops, small decorated trees in pots that lined the sidewalk. He led me through the alley that I had seen the old man disappear into a week earlier. "We'll take my truck," he said, motioning toward an old pickup, cherry red, in pristine condition. The inside smelled of whatever oil he had used to clean the leather seats and the dashboard, not showing a hint of the lint that collected on mine. The truck started and idled smoothly, sounding better than the Beetle and riding more smoothly as well.

We drove through the streets of Wooded Lake, past one of the middle schools I had seen the other day and around a collection of new town houses and condos that had been built to blend in with the surrounding area, looking as if they had been there for far longer than they had. Someone had taken the time to make sure that the landscape remained unblemished by new construction, the complexes reflecting a rustic style and sensibility. He turned off on a dirt road, trees on either side of the narrow lane, the sun struggling to peek through the myriad branches that crisscrossed overhead. It must have been spectacular in the other seasons, spring's greens giving way to summer's lush, mossy overhangs and fall's beautiful metamorphosis from gold to red to amber. I looked out the window and saw a small lake on the right side of the property that we were approaching, a dilapidated barn standing at its edge. A small cabin was next to the barn, tended carefully, two rocking chairs on the porch. Why hadn't I run here when I was leaving New York? Why had I stopped at Foster's Landing? This was way more my speed, a place to heal. Home was probably where my heart was, but it was also where my family was, and that complicated things, to say the least.

"Nice place," I said. "Is this where you lived growing up?" I asked as he pulled the truck onto a slab of concrete that fit it perfectly.

"This is where I live now," he said. "It's all that's left over from Love Canyon. Want to look around?" he asked.

We got out of the truck, and walking across fallen spongy pine needles, the scent redolent in the brisk winter air, he led me to the barn, which still had an odor of horses and manure even though there were no signs of animals anywhere. I wound my scarf tighter around my neck, a little breeze coming in off the water turning my cheeks pink.

"Nice barn," I said, wondering why he had brought me here, what he wanted to show me. The interior was rustic but looked as if someone had recently been in here doing something; there was a large space heater in one corner and a long table against one of the side walls. "No more horses?"

He walked deeper into the barn, sunlight splintering through the gaps in the beams above us. "No more horses. Lots of work. And I don't have a lot of free time."

"So you kept some of the land for yourself?" I asked. "For your home?"

"Four acres," he said. "I sold the rest."

"Why?" I asked.

He shrugged. "Not sure. Exorcising old demons maybe?"

"What happened here?" I asked as he walked deeper into the barn, realizing at that moment that I'd gotten in a truck with a guy I didn't know, driving out to the woods for a tour that was sure to be unenlightening, given what I was seeing. I don't know what I was expecting—people running around naked? Old hippie men and women frolicking in the freezing lake? The smell of pot wafting in the stiff winter wind?

Or better yet, the sight of Amy, older now and still wise beyond her years, walking across a meadow, her long blond hair flowing behind her, her arms outstretched as if to say, Bel! I've been waiting for you!?

I stood in the middle of the barn, one shard of light spiking the ground in front of me, realizing that this was a mistake. All of it. If I was going to find Amy in Wooded Lake, I didn't have to lie.

I just had to ask.

Tweed had disappeared into the shadows of the barn, and when he reappeared seconds later his face wasn't the relaxed coffee-place owner's visage but the face of someone tense, concerned.

Before I had a chance to speak, he approached me, lifting a hand to expose his wrist, the one wearing a bracelet that was mostly wooden beads but on which something silver—a dolphin charm—glinted in the sunlight. I resisted the urge to grab his wrist to ask him the real question: Was she here and did you know her?

But before I could do that, he asked the question I had been dreading.

"So, do you want to tell me who you really are and what you really want?"

CHAPTER *Eleven*

I backed up a few steps.

"Really," he said, coming toward me. "Who are you? Why are you asking around about Love Canyon? Didn't you learn everything you needed to know on all the stuff on the Internet? There's nothing here that isn't there."

It was too late for lies. "I'm looking for someone. Her name was Amy. Her name *is* Amy. You knew her."

He stopped dead in his tracks, the space between us just a few feet. "Amy?"

"Yes," I said, sorry I didn't have a photo with me, or the newspaper where I thought I had seen her photo. I took his wrist in my hand. "This," I said, grabbing the charm, "this was hers."

He pulled his hand away. "This is my mother's," he said. "She was a swimmer."

He was lying. I don't know how I knew, but I knew.

"So was Amy. She got it when she broke a school record. From our swim coach."

He pulled out his phone and punched at the screen. He held the phone to my face, showing me a site that featured the exact same dolphin charms in all sizes and finishes. "You're grasping at straws," he said. "This was my mother's. And these charms are literally a dime a dozen."

I wasn't convinced, but I let it go. She had been here. I could feel it. "She's our age. She was barely eighteen when she disappeared. It was right after our high-school graduation."

"What did she look like?" he asked, his brow creasing, concerned.

"Blond. Thin. Athletic." I looked up at the rafters, willing back the tears that were pressing at the back of my eyes, my throat. All of a sudden, the seriousness of what I was doing became apparent to me and my reaction gave me pause. I knew I was invested in finding her but wondered if this was where I should let the road end.

"There were a lot of girls here. A lot of women in general," he said. "All through the years. Archie kept it going a long time."

"I'm talking fifteen years ago," I reminded him.

"That would have been around the time I was going to head out of here and go to college."

"Were you here then? When she got here?"

"How do you know she was here?" he asked.

"I saw the article. In the *Hudson Courier*." I turned, starting for the door. The room suddenly felt stifling, like the air was leaving it, floating up to the rafters and out of the patchy roof. "I need to get out of here," I said, suddenly feeling short of breath. I needed to get out of the barn, out of Wooded Lake, back to the safety and security of Foster's Landing. "This was a mistake," I said, suddenly as scared and unmoored as I had been years earlier when I had awoken on the shore, cold and wet, with no one to hear me ask where I was, what I was doing there by myself. It had been my family—my brothers—who had come for me and I needed to remember that, not push them away when I needed their help, a safe place to land.

I started for the truck, feeling Tweed's hand on my shoulder. "Wait," he said. "Wait."

I turned and looked up at him, the sun framing his thick hair.

"I'm sorry. It's just that it wasn't a good time here for a lot of different reasons. I can tell you about them sometime. I can think about your friend, if I knew her."

"How many people were here at that time?" I asked. "It was the beginning of the end by that time, right?"

"You'd be surprised," he said.

That didn't answer my question at all, but I didn't pursue it. There had been nothing on his face to indicate that the name Amy meant anything or sounded familiar at all. Nothing to say, Yes, I remember a young blond girl who arrived in June and left . . ." whenever she had left. "Is there anyone still here in town who was at Love Canyon?" I asked. "Anyone but you?"

"Honestly, they scattered like the wind once it was clear that Archie was a fraud, there was no money, the food had run out." He laughed ruefully. "Once the electricity was gone, around August the year I left for school, that sealed the deal." He smiled, any of the annoyance he had displayed earlier gone. "I can try to remember more, answer any questions you might have. How about on your home turf?"

"I don't know," I said. I looked around the place, the beautiful log cabin, the old barn, the lake in the backyard. Thoughts of Amy having been here maybe brought the tiniest bit of uneasiness to my consciousness. Here, out in the sunlight, the place seemed like a comfortable existence, a happy one for the right person. "I don't know."

"Think about it," he said. He pulled a card from his pocket and, picking up my right hand, placed it gently on the palm. "Here're are my numbers. But you can always find me at The Coffee Pot. That's where I spend most of my time."

I looked around, taking in the surroundings, trying to ground myself again. "A dog," I said, changing the subject, wanting to move away from what we had been discussing. If I was going to learn more, I was going to need to disarm him, to make him think that my intentions carried no bad intent.

"'Scuse me?" he said.

"A dog," I repeated. "This place is calling out for a dog."

"Had one," he said, walking toward the truck. "Lost him last year. Haven't had it in me to replace him."

"A big dog?" I asked. A guy this burly needed a Lab, a Bernese mountain dog. Something with heft.

"A Yorkie," he said, laughing. "He weighed eight pounds, soaking wet."

"Interesting choice," I said.

We got back into the truck and headed into town. When he parked in the lot behind the store, he turned off the truck and turned his head slightly, pointing to the card still in my hand. "Think about it. Bring a photo with you. I'll tell you whatever you want to know."

Would he? He seemed to be holding back, but maybe I was just paranoid. "Thanks," I said, before getting out of the truck, putting my feet on the grass next to the parking spot. Before I walked away, down the alley to Main Street on the other side, I called to him just before he went into the back door of the coffee shop, "Hey! Tweed!"

He turned and looked at me, his hand holding the door open. The scent of rich coffee floated out of the building and into the spaces around me, enveloping me, getting into the fibers of my clothes; I would smell it for hours. "I'm sorry. That I lied."

His reaction was a cross between a grimace and a smile. "You wouldn't be the first to say that. And you won't be the last."

CHAPTER Twelve

When I got home later that day, Mom called out to me from the office, "Belfast? Where have you been, girl?"

"Sorry, Mom," I said, not wanting to go into the whole thing about how I was adult, I could come and go as I pleased as long as my work was done, I didn't have anyone to answer to. "I was on an errand," I said, turning my face when she came out into the foyer so that she wouldn't see the lie written all over it.

"What kind of errand?" she asked.

The most important kind, but I'd never tell her. "Checking out a new egg farm."

She looked at me, studying me really, seeing when I would crack, *if* I would crack. "Hmmm," she said. "Taught my morning Pilates class and you were already gone."

Ah, Pilates. The thing that framed everything around here, women in leotards with sinewy muscles who could plank for hours, marching around the grounds of the Manor, searching, it seemed, for that elusive concave stomach, that toned behind. Mom taught the hottest class in town, her sixty-something-year-old body something of a legend among the middle-aged lady set who were hoping to bypass the Not Your Daughter's

Jeans—the ones with stretch—and head straight to the Free People or 7 For All Mankind areas at Nordstrom. "Yes, got up early, decided to take a drive. Trying to establish some work/life balance," I said.

"But it was a work errand," she pointed out.

Shoot. It was. "Stopped along the way and had a coffee," I said to underscore that I did have some pleasures in life.

"So that's what that smell is," she said. "To me, it almost smelled like marijuana, but then I thought, 'Not my Belfast.'"

"No, not pot, Mom. Coffee. That comes in a pot."

I had to get away from her, or the next thing you knew I'd be grounded. She'd take my keys and I would be stuck at the Manor until she decided I was allowed to leave. It sounds crazy. It is crazy. But it's my life now and I knew this woman; she was capable of anything.

"You should take my morning class," she said. "Might help with this work/life balance that you speak of."

"Me? Pilates?" I laughed out loud, not intending to. "I don't think so, Mom, but thank you."

I started for the kitchen. "Oh, and Belfast," she said before I went through the swinging doors. "You have visitors. In the dining room. Kevin and Mary Ann." Before I left, she called out one more thing. "Family dinner! Six sharp."

How could I forget? It was a command performance every week and usually resulted in the proverbial airing of grievances, decades old, and a few tears. Good times, I tell you. Good times.

I went into the dining room. Kevin Hanson and his bride, Mary Ann D'Amato-Hanson, were the last two people I expected to see on a Sunday, particularly since

I assumed that they went to Mass first, after which Mary Ann forced confession plus a round of Stations of the Cross on her husband. "I hope you haven't been waiting long," I said, even though I had no idea why they were there in the first place. They were sitting at the same table that Alison and Bobby Crawford had sat at, facing the big windows, looking at the Foster's Landing River in the distance. In front of Mary Ann was a thick book, the cover padded and white, their wedding album, if I had to guess. When I walked in, Kevin stood and sniffed the air around me.

"Coffee," I said. Before he could say it, I held up a hand. "I know. But it's not. Pot, that is."

"I was going to say patchouli, but okay," he said, the guy I had known since kindergarten and whom I had once loved. He smiled at me. "We got our album!" he said with much more enthusiasm than I would have expected from him. He had seemed terrified in the days leading up the wedding, but now that they were officially married he had returned to his old self: hapless, good-humored, a guy without a care in the world, all qualities at odds with his job as a detective with the Foster's Landing Police Department, working right under Lieutenant D'Amato, his new father-in-law.

We like to keep it close in Foster's Landing. All in the family. Among friends.

I gave Mary Ann a kiss and sat down at the table, holding out my hands. "Can I see?" I asked. I ran my fingers over the embossed initials on the front, the trim around the photo in the center of Mary Ann and Kevin, framed by falling leaves on the great lawn of Shamrock Manor. I remember the photographer's assistant in the tree, shaking branches as leaves rained down around the smiling couple, an optic that needed a little help in ex-ecution.

"We wanted to show you because they got some nice shots of your food," Mary Ann said. "The beautiful canapés. The hors d'oeuvres. The duck ballotine." She looked at me, wonder in her eyes. "It was amazing. The best food I've ever had at a party that big. How do you do it, Bel?"

I looked at her, a pediatric oncology nurse, someone for whom every day brought stress and sadness, won-dering how she could think that putting microgreens on top of mini-crostini even warranted the question. She was a saint. An angel. I was a cook. "It's my thing, Mary Ann. Always has been. And it was my pleasure."

"I'm recommending the Manor to everyone for any event they're having. Some of the nurses at work were here and they are talking the place up, too," she said.

I flipped through the wedding album and looked at the photos of her family, small but close, a shot of Kevin and his sister by the windows while his best man toasted him. There was a photo of the boys playing a particu-larly festive tune by the looks of it, Cargan's violin bow strings hanging off the end of his instrument, Feeney's mouth open in song, Derry mid-bang on his snare, Ar-ney jamming on an accordion. In another, I was hold-ing out a tray of duck ballotine proudly, the intricate dinner one that I hadn't wanted to make but to which I had finally acquiesced, making more duck than I ever had for one party. The guests had been floored and Mary Ann and Kevin had been thrilled. I had to admit that I had been proud of the accomplishment as well, think-ing that I was finally settled in at the Manor; I was cooking my food, my way, and that was something I never thought I'd live to see.

And there was Brendan Joyce, dancing by himself in the middle of the floor, a champion Irish step dancer whose irrepressible joy at flying through the air was caught in the still photograph. I turned the page quickly.

"It was a beautiful day, Mary Ann. You were a gorgeous bride," I said, flipping to the end of the album and pushing it back to her.

"Kevin and I wanted to thank you again in person and see if you and Brendan wanted to come to dinner," she said. "I don't want to let too much time pass before we all get together."

I looked from Kevin to Mary Ann; I hadn't told anyone what had happened, so how would they know? "Um, Brendan and I broke up," I said, pursing my lips in a grim smile. "Right after the wedding. I guess you wouldn't have known that."

Mary Ann put her hand to her mouth. "I'm sorry, Bel," she said, shocked. "I had no idea."

Kevin shook his head sadly, looking at his wife, willing her to stop talking. He was uncomfortable and I knew that from years of knowing him, watching him rock from side to side, something he had done since we were kids. "I'm sorry, too, Bel." He looked out the window. "He's a nice guy."

I didn't know why they cared that my short-lived romance had died a quick death. They seemed more upset than they should be, but maybe they were aware, like everyone else in this town, that there were exactly three single guys, Brendan being one, plus the guy who took tickets at the train station (eighty if he was a day) and the third, the shop teacher at the high school who was of indeterminate origin, but suffice it to say, Foster's Landing wasn't a place that bred warm-and-fuzzy people.

Maybe not, I thought, Brendan's lie of omission, the photograph in his wallet, something that I would find hard to forgive. He knew what Amy had meant to me and he had kept his feelings for her secret. What would it have taken to say, "Well, Bel, I had a crush on her in high school and I never really got over it"? Or, "I know it sounds weird, but I've always wondered where she went, so I carried a photo of her around hoping I would see her"?

Anything. He could have said anything except what he had said.

"I don't know where that came from."

Mary Ann and Kevin were looking at me and I realized it a beat before they started to worry why I had fallen silent. "Nothing makes me happier than to have you be so happy," I said, and to my own ears it sounded relatively convincing. It was still a shock to see them together, to know that they were married. I had known it in my peripheral consciousness, but every day, or so it seemed, I was reminded of them and their togetherness.

Today just underscored the fact that they were married, they always would be, and Kevin would never be mine again, even in friendship. He had married her and that had changed everything.

CHAPTER Thirteen

I was in the kitchen the next day when Dad called over from the office. I was bent over the stainless-steel counter, thinking about the proper proportions for a pudding that I wanted to make, knowing I could go to my phone to look it up but stubbornly trying to recall the specifics from the deep recesses of my recipe-packed brain.

"Belfast! Phone!"

There was an extension in the kitchen, an old-timey wall phone with a long, twisted cord, but I never picked it up because the call was never for me. This time, it was.

"Bel?" the person said when I answered. "Alison Bergeron."

"Hi, Alison," I said. "What can I do for you?" I realized that with everything that had gone on, my trips to Wooded Lake, I had never followed up with her about the booking for her stepdaughter's wedding.

"Listen, I know this is short notice, but my stepdaughter has a free afternoon and I'm not teaching today. Since she knows her father isn't all that excited about the wedding I thought we could—"

"Sure," I said, cutting her off from a long explanation as to why they wanted to come by. I welcomed the interruption, the distraction. Talking about a wedding and what we could do here at Shamrock Manor would be just what the doctor ordered. "Come on up. What time works for you?" I looked up at the big clock on the wall: ten thirty.

"How about noonish?" she asked. "If we leave now, that gives us plenty of time."

"Sounds good. I'll make us lunch," I said.

"Oh, no need!" she said. "We don't want to impose."

"It's not an imposition," I said. "It will give your step-daughter an idea of what we can do here. Any personal favorites?"

"Well, she loves chicken. Her fiancé, and I should have mentioned this earlier, is gluten-free, so we'll need to take that into account."

"Not a problem," I said.

"Lactose intolerant, too," she added.

"Still okay."

"And a vegan."

"Okay, now you're pushing it," I said, laughing. "Don't worry about it. I am a whiz with Brussels sprouts."

In the background, I heard the sound of crying. "Sorry," she said. "I have to run. See you later." I heard her call out to a child in the background before she hung up.

I went to the refrigerator and looked in to see what I had. I had some chicken cutlets that I would turn into a nice marsala, and with a few key ingredients that I happened to have I whipped up a nutty rice pilaf. A fresh garden salad completed the meal. I was working on a vinaigrette when Cargan came into the kitchen to check in.

"For me?" he asked, picking a nut out of the pilaf.

I slapped his hand. "No. Prospective booking. The couple that was here last week. The one where the father of the bride isn't terribly enthusiastic about this union . . ."

Cargan raised an eyebrow.

"Age. She's too young, according to him. But the stepmother is on board and wants to bring the bride here because the wedding is Memorial Day. She knows they need to book ASAP."

"I'll say," Cargan said. "Despite being a veritable house of horrors," he added, referencing one murdered guest at our cousin's wedding and a murdered groom at another, "we still seem to be of interest to some people. Crazy people, but some people nonetheless."

"Might have something to do with Dad's elastic billing policy," I said. "Have you spoken to him about being more competitive?"

Cargan's look said it all.

"All right, forget it," I said. "I know it's a lost cause."

"Baby steps, Belfast," he said. "Baby steps." He went into the walk-in freezer to see what was available, if I needed him to place an order. "Looks like you're all set," he said.

The newspaper that Alison had left behind was sitting on the counter, the page open to the story about Love Canyon. Cargan gave it a once-over and I steeled myself for the realization that was sure to dawn on his face when he saw the photo of Amy, very much alive, very much free, happier than I had ever seen her in Foster's Landing, the tilt of her head, the looseness of her body. When he looked up at me, though, there was nothing, just a blank look, a look that he had no doubt practiced for many years as an undercover, no recognition of our long-lost friend in the faded photograph in the wrinkled newspaper.

The phone rang in the office and Dad called out to me to pick up in the kitchen. At the other end of the line was the voice of someone I never expected to hear from again.

"Belfast McGrath? Chelsea Mertens."

CHAPTER Fourteen

I held my breath for a second, not knowing if she was going to reprimand me again for inadvertently pretending to be Francesca Dell'atoria or not buying one of her works when I visited her studio.

"I don't have long and I will deny this if it ever comes up or is revealed, but you seemed very upset about your friend."

"I was," I said. "I am."

"I did see her," she said.

I leaned against the wall, holding the phone against my ear so hard that it throbbed after I hung up.

"I saw Archie again about fourteen years ago. No one knows, not my husband or my brother or my daughter." She paused. "And I'd like to keep it that way. I just wanted to confront him. I had some outstanding issues with him. Nothing happened but I would rather that no one know."

"Of course."

"Your friend was there. She worked in the kitchen. It was more like a summer camp at that point than a commune, but I will tell you that she was safe. I never talked to her, but it was a safe place for her." She paused. "I'm risking a lot by telling you this and frankly, I'm not sure why she seemed scared and frightened. She was running from something."

"I'll never tell anyone, Ms. Mertens. I promise," I said, even as my stomach turned sour at the thought that Amy had been on the run.

"Thank you for saying that." In the background, I could hear the sound of a cat crying, low and mournful, the sound punctuating our conversation. "I don't know why she was there or what she was running from, but . . ."

"She was safe," I said, finishing her sentence.

"Yes." She let out a sigh. "Just so you know. Maybe you can have some peace now."

"Not until I find her," I said, but the line had gone dead. I hung up the phone and looked around the kitchen, wondering where this path would lead me, if I could get any closer to finding her. Behind me, the door to the kitchen swung open and May arrived, her hair pulled back into a tight ponytail, her chef's coat unbuttoned.

"You look like you've seen a ghost," she said, pulling on a pair of plastic gloves so she could begin her tasks for the day.

"Something like that," I said as I stood by the phone wondering what to do next. May, seeing that I was going to be useless without direction, gave me my marching orders which wasn't common but this was an unconventional kitchen. An hour later, we had a meal prepared for our tasting, one that never would have come together without my sous's artful direction.

In the dining room, after we served the entrée, it was clear that we would most likely get this booking.

"This is the best food I've ever eaten," Erin Crawford

said, polishing off the last of her chicken and rice pilaf. It really wasn't a very elaborate dish, but the flavors were spot-on; I knew that and now Erin Crawford knew it, too. The food at her wedding would be wonderful, and that, coupled with the view that she faced from the table in the dining room, meant her wedding would be perfect. The earthy Pinot Noir was the perfect complement to the meal and the two glasses Erin had drunk had probably swayed her toward a booking. I had resisted the urge to proof her. Her father was correct: If she wasn't too young to get married, she certainly looked too young. A baby, really. A little sprite of a person with long blond hair and a face that belied her twenty-four years.

Alison hadn't mentioned that Christine, Erin's mother and Crawford's ex-wife, would be with them, but there was no tension among the group. They all seemed like one big, happy family and I wondered how they had achieved that with what seemed like ease. Christine and Alison acted as old friends would, joking with each other and each deferring to the other when an opinion was needed on wedding meal details.

"Alison, this place is a find," Christine said, sipping her wine. "I would have leaned toward Connecticut, but coming up to the Hudson Valley makes perfect sense especially since Fez's family is up here, too."

"Yeah, Crawford and I went looking for an open winery last Saturday and hit upon this place." Alison turned to me. "Oh, speaking of that, Bel, I had a newspaper with me that day and I think I left it here. You don't happen to still have it, do you?"

My face caved in but not because I didn't have the paper anymore, but because I had saved it. And I wanted to keep it. I had been distracted and preoccupied most of this lunch, Chelsea Mertens' words still ringing in my ears, that dolphin charm on Tweed's wrist, being the only things I could think of.

"It's okay if you don't have it," Alison said. "It had a list of antique places that I wanted to keep, but I'll look them up online."

"I have it," I said. "It's in my apartment. I'll get it when we're done eating." I had brought it over there before they had arrived, stashing it for safekeeping. Dad was a vigilant recycler and Cargan was nosy. I didn't want it to go missing when I wasn't around or was not paying attention.

"Great!" she said. "There was also an article on some crazy commune that I wanted to finish reading. Love Canyon?" she said, looking at Christine. "Did you ever hear of that place? It sounded nuts."

Christine gave a little shrug. "Not that I recall. Love Canyon? Sounds interesting," she said, laughing.

"Sounds like the kind of place Crawford would *love*," Alison said. She turned to me. "He's not exactly what you'd call 'Mr. Romance.' And a commune? That would send him completely over the edge."

"Ew," Erin said, finishing her wine. "Can we not talk about my father and romance in the same sentence?"

The meal finished, I got up. "Save room for cookies," I said. "I'll be right back."

In the kitchen, before grabbing the cookies, I poked my head into the office. "Dad, Alison Bergeron is back with her stepdaughter, Erin. Erin's mother is here, too. You may want to give them the grand tour once we finish up in the dining room."

"Thanks for the heads-up, Belfast," Dad said, putting on a pair of large sunglasses. "Better?" he asked.

"Frankly, Dad, the black eye is better than the sunglasses. You look like a bad guy from a Bond movie." I walked over and took them off his face. "You can explain about the Christmas tree and the accident."

"And my lazy sons?" he asked. "Can I explain about them?" He pushed away from the desk and smoothed down the front of his shirt, a green polo that had a stitched representation of the Manor on the left breast, "Shamrock Manor" underneath it. As if there were any doubt. The Manor's architecture was pretty distinctive. "Okay. Showtime."

Dad walked into the dining room and proceeded to charm the pants off of the bride-to-be and her mother. Alison stayed at the table and watched them go off. "This is their moment," she said, looking at me. "Mother and daughter. Not mother, daughter, and crazy stepmother," she said, laughing. "I've got a few years until I might have to do this again."

"You have children?" I asked.

"A daughter. Bea. Named after Crawford's late aunt," she said. "She's four."

"Bea Crawford. Nice name," I said. "If you wait here a second, I'll run over to the apartment and get the paper."

"I'll go with you," she said, and before I could protest that that wouldn't be necessary we were on the front porch of the Manor and then climbing up the steps to my second-floor apartment above Dad's studio. "I'd love to see where a chef lives."

"You'll be disappointed," I said.

The door was unlocked and I steeled myself for the mess that would greet us. I stepped in. Not too bad. Not too great but not terrible. There was a wet towel hanging on the bathroom door; I grabbed it, threw it into the tub, and slammed the bathroom door before Alison could get a good look.

She walked into the living room. "I love what you've done with the place," she said, hands on hips. "You're not planning on staying, are you?" she said.

"What makes you say that?" I asked.

"Looks like a temporary residence," she said. She grimaced. "Man, that was rude. I'm sorry. I have this problem, see. I say the first thing that comes into my head."

"It's okay," I said. "To be honest, when I came back, it was a temporary situation. But the longer I'm here, the clearer it's become that I'm staying."

"You happy about that?" she asked.

I thought about it. "It's where I need to be right now."

"Then, that's your answer," she said. "But you need curtains. For privacy."

"That's the cop's wife in you talking," I said. "My brother Cargan says the same thing."

"He a cop?" she asked.

I wasn't sure I could say that he was and immediately regretted mentioning him. He had been deep undercover for years and I didn't know if his identity was still a secret. I didn't answer her question. "What kind of curtains?"

She eyed me before turning to the window. "A valance. And some sheers, maybe? Would really dress the place up," she said. "But what do I know? I still have old blinds in my daughter Bea's room that have been there since husband number one."

I spied the paper on the coffee table and handed it to

her reluctantly. "Here you go," I said, holding on to it a second too long.

She held it in her hand. "Do you want it?" she asked. "Is there something in there that you want to find?"

I looked at the window, the one without the curtains. "Not something."

She cocked her head. "I'm not following."

"Someone."

They had taken two cars, Erin traveling with her mother and Alison driving alone. After a quick call to Crawford to make sure he'd be home in time to get Bea from day care, I found myself in Alison's Subaru traveling the same highway that I had traveled a few days earlier, the two of us headed back to Wooded Lake. I had told her the whole story, start to finish including how I had been to Wooded Lake already, had e-mailed the author of the article but hadn't heard back from him, and had visited Chelsea Mertens in Farringville. How the artist had called me and told me she had seen Amy. I told Alison everything, but I wasn't sure why.

Her face lit up at the thought of a caper, a mystery. Hijinks. She was as excited by my discovery as I was and that alone made me feel a little less crazy, not as obsessed. She explained the thrill to me as we drove north. "It all started when my car was stolen, years ago, and one of my students was found in the trunk," she said in a way that made it sound like it was the most natural thing in the world. "That's how I met Crawford."

"Hmmm," I said. "Lucky."

"Yeah, I know it sounds creepy," she said. She thought for a moment. "Super creepy. But he turned out to be a nice guy, something my first husband was definitely not." She turned the heat down in the car. "Who knows where you'll meet your soul mate, right? Gotta keep an open mind."

My mind flashed on Tweed Blazer and I swept it away like an annoying mental dust bunny. The guy was lying to me and I still found him intriguing. Attractive. What was wrong with me? I had already had a lying fiancé; you'd have thought I had learned my lesson. Apparently not.

"Anyway, that whole thing started a few years ago where I couldn't take a step without finding a dead body or getting involved in something that I had no business being involved in."

"And Crawford?" I asked. "How did he feel about that?"

"Hated it!" she said, going silent as she listened to her GPS. "Anyway, we had the baby, I settled down into motherhood, and he and I tried to establish this thing called 'work/life' balance," she said. "Ever hear of it?"

I made a noncommittal sound.

"It's bullshit. I come home from work—"

"What do you do?"

"College professor."

"Huh. Right." I knew that, somewhere in the deep recesses of my brain. "Not what I would have guessed." In the deep recesses of my mind, I think I remembered hearing that had been her profession but it was at odds with her entire *gestalt*—the nervous energy, the trouble-seeking streak that seemed to run through her, the one that made her want to get in a car with a woman she barely knew to solve a mystery she knew nothing about.

"What would you have guessed?" she asked.

"I don't know. But I guess it makes sense," I said. Now that I thought about it, she had to do something that involved a lot of talking. *A lot* of talking. College professor was starting to make sense, particularly if stream-of-consciousness was on the curriculum.

"So that's me," she said, turning onto the exit. "What about you?"

"Nothing to tell," I said. "You know everything. The Monkey's Paw, back to Shamrock Manor, live with the family." I looked out the window. "That's about it."

"And this thing following you around since you were a teenager."

"And this thing following me around since I was a teenager," I said. "Yes. There's that."

"That's a lot, Bel," she said, coming to a stop at the end of the exit. "That's what they call 'baggage.'"

"I guess so," I said. "It's not like it's informed every day of my life, but it's always been there."

"But you feel responsible."

"I don't. But people think I am," I said. "Responsible, that is. I was her best friend. To lots of people, I must have had something to do with it."

She turned and looked at me for a split second.

"But I didn't. I didn't know where she went or why. A lot of people don't believe me."

"Well, that explains the obsession," she said, almost to herself.

We drove down the Main Street of the town; the holiday decorations—ecumenical and representing every creed on earth, or so it seemed—had exploded since my last visit. I pointed out The Coffee Pot, filled with people drinking coffee, on laptops, studying their phones. "That's Tweed Blazer," I said.

She leaned over and peered out my window. "I'm not big on the Amish beard, but that guy is kind of cute," she said, nudging me in the ribs.

"I hadn't noticed," I said. "Anyway, he's Archie Peterson's son. The guy who started Love Canyon."

"Or as I call him: 'the perv,' " she said, straightening up and driving slowly down Main Street. "Why do they have different names?"

"Blazer is his mother's maiden name. I think he wanted to distance himself from the father."

"The perv," she repeated. "I read enough of that article to form an opinion, obviously." She pulled over at the end of the street and threw the car into park, turning to me. "So, what do we do now?

"Do?" I asked.

"Yeah," she said. "Do you know where this Love Canyon is?"

I tried to remain inscrutable, but she was on to me.

"You do!" she said. "Isn't that why we came here? Why you wanted my help?"

I didn't recall asking for her help, but I did want to dig deeper. I had never met anyone so determined to be involved in something that had zero to do with her and I wondered just how I had landed here, sitting in her Subaru, Goldfish crunching beneath my feet, an empty juice box shoved into the panel of my door. I couldn't figure it out, so I asked her outright, "What's going on? How did we get here?"

"Here?" she asked.

"Yeah. Here. In your car. In Wooded Lake."

She looked away from me, out her window, toward a little cluster of shops that I would have loved to visit if I hadn't been sitting in a car with a virtual stranger who

I suspected might be just a little bit crazy. "Want the truth?" she asked.

"That would be great," I said.

"I'm bored. Out of my skull. Since I got married and had Bea, all I do is go to school, come home, clean, cook, and watch a little crappy television before going to bed. Make out with Crawford when he's around and doesn't fall asleep watching the aforementioned crappy TV." She looked back at me. "Don't get me wrong; I love my life. Wouldn't change a thing. But when you told me that story about your friend, well, I don't know, I just thought that this might give me the spark that I've been missing." She rested her head on the steering wheel. "I love a mystery," she said, sighing.

"The wedding planning isn't enough?" I asked.

She shook her head. "It's complicated. I know we look like a very cohesive unit, but I have to tread lightly. I'm not Erin's mother and I think I may have overstepped a bit by bringing Crawford to Shamrock Manor on a lark like that."

"Got it."

"And frankly, sister, you look like you need something to break your way for once."

"What does that mean?" I asked. I thought I looked pretty healthy, mentally and physically.

"I've been there. Where you are. You know, not being in a place you want to be professionally, personally." She smiled sadly and put a hand on my shoulder. "I've been you." She picked her head up and arranged herself in her seat, ready to go further.

"You've been me?"

"I've been you," she said. "And just like that, it all

turned around. I wouldn't recommend finding love the way I did, but while it shouldn't have worked out, it did."

"I'm happy for you," I said. And I was. I believed what she was saying and hoped that I could find the same contentment, either with someone or on my own.

She smiled. "So, let's do this."

"So, you're not a crazy person?" I asked. "Don't make me regret this."

She shrugged. "I may be a little crazy but I own it."

I considered that. A little crazy may have been just what I needed. "Let's go."

CHAPTER *Sixteen*

"What are we hoping to find?" I asked Alison as we circumnavigated the property.

"Hmmm?" she asked, looking around, not paying attention to me or the task at hand. "What does an acre go for up here? A nice little log cabin?"

"You're thinking about real estate?" I asked.

"Why are you whispering?" she asked. "There's no one here."

She was right; there wasn't. All there was were some bare trees, the sound of chilly water lapping the lake's edge, a bird or two circling, some poor, unfortunate field mouse in our midst being surreptitiously preyed upon. There was the log cabin where Tweed lived and the barn that he had taken me to, but other than that, there was nothing.

No one.

She walked over to the barn and slid in between the rickety doors. "This place is cool!" she called from inside. "I'm just thinking that it might be a good idea to snap up some land before it gets too expensive." I heard her let out a cough. "Dusty in here."

I circled the barn. "You know, I don't think there's anything here," I said, a certain anxiety gripping me, suddenly making my toes tingle. I hadn't had this feeling in a long time, like something would happen that would be out of my control and that it would be bad. I wish I had had that feeling the night at The Monkey's Paw, but all I felt that night was rage. Pure, unadulterated rage. I hadn't felt it since and that was a good thing.

In the distance, I heard the rumble of a vehicle.

A motorcycle.

"Alison," I said. "There's someone coming."

"What?" she called. "Do you know how much this reclaimed barn wood would capture at a flea market? I wouldn't say that this Tweed guy could retire, but we downstaters are always looking for a bit of rustic authenticity. It's amazing."

"We've got to go," I said, but it was too late. The motorcycle roared down the deserted lane toward the log cabin, a long way from the road and a rutted path with only one destination.

Her Subaru parked prominently in front of the cabin, there was no time to pretend we weren't there, to try to head down that lane ourselves. The Irish are consummate storytellers; just hearing my dad tell stories of life in the "old country," probably made up or, at the very least, exaggerated, and you knew that it was part of him. And now it had to be part of me.

A man pulled up in front of the cabin, a shiny black helmet only partially masking a head of long white hair that grazed his shoulders. Wraparound sunglasses covered his eyes and a scarf wound around his neck hid the lower portion of his face. I looked around, but my partner in crime, one Alison Bergeron, was nowhere to be found.

"Help you?" the man asked, taking one wary step toward me.

"Yes!" I said, a little too brightly and with a faux cheer I didn't feel. "My friend and I," I said, looking back over my shoulder toward the barn, "are looking for reclaimed wood to put in our new house." I stayed where I was, as did the man. "Downstate. Westchester County."

"Oh, I figured you'd say 'Brooklyn,'" the man said. "That's where all of the lookie-loos come from."

"Yep, that's us," I said. "Lookie-loos. But not from Brooklyn."

"How did you find this place? Did you come for Breath and Body?" he asked.

When I didn't answer, he elaborated.

"Breath and Body. Yoga. Breathing. Some meditation. My class?" he asked. "You just drove down the road and found a barn?"

"Yes! Breath and Body, too. We have heard such wonderful things. Restorative things." I put a hand on my midsection. "Breathing. I need that."

He took one more step toward me. "You know you're trespassing, right?"

"Not trespassing at all. The class. The barn," I said. "I'm not sorry now that I know that we're in the right place." I wondered how we were going to do yoga in jeans but as other cars started to approach realized that we'd have to figure it out.

I couldn't see the man's eyes, but by the way he was standing I could tell he was thinking. "So tell me. How much does this reclaimed wood go for?" he asked. "In other words, how much would you be willing to pay?"

I had no blessed idea. "Maybe one hundred and fifty a beam?" I asked. This was taking "fake it till you make it" to a whole new level.

Alison emerged from the barn and I wasn't sure how

much she had heard of our conversation, if she knew that we were suburban prospectors on the hunt for reclaimed wood and that we'd soon be doing breathing exercises with a group of middle-aged, yoga-panted women who were assembling. "Hi!" she said with enthusiasm. Before she could go so far as to introduce herself, I put my arm around her waist.

"This is my partner." I pulled her close, the air going out of her with the force. "I'm sorry we trespassed. Lovely place you have here."

"Wait," the man said. "Before we get into class. Do you have a card or something? Somewhere you can be reached?" he asked.

"Um, no," I said. "But if we're interested, we know where you live."

"I'm sure my son would be interested in talking to you," he said as Alison and I walked toward the Subaru.

"Your son?" I said.

"Yeah, my son. He owns this place. And a coffee shop in town that he practically lives at."

CHAPTER *Seventeen*

And that's how we found ourselves sitting in a circle on the dusty floor in the aforementioned barn, eyes closed, hands on our thighs, listening to the silence in the room of twenty people.

Or the sound of our breath. That's what we were instructed to do by the man on the motorcycle who still hadn't officially introduced himself to us but who seemed to be a known quantity to the group of people who had assembled, men and women, young and old, all with a singular focus on listening to their own breath. I had heard his name whispered and figured out that this was Tweed Blazer's father or Archie Peterson, alias Zephyr. I opened one eye and found Alison sitting across from me, her eyes wide open, looking around the room and flashing me a smile that told me that she had no idea how we had gotten here and or how we were going to get out. She jerked her head to the right, directing my gaze to a long table filled with brownies and cookies, mouthing the word, *Edibles?*

Motorcycle man was speaking softly, his eyes still closed, his body relaxed. "I feel as if some of us aren't focusing on our breath."

He was right. Some of us weren't, and if this continued

much longer the shaking I saw in Alison's shoulders, the suppressed giggles, were going to come spilling out, blowing our cover as a renovating couple from Brooklyn. I closed my eyes tight and went inward, thinking that after the few months I had endured, a little introspection wouldn't be a terrible thing.

I did what I was told. I focused on my breathing, on the "soul living inside." The soul was tired, though, and it was only when I slumped over, hitting my head on the dirt floor and knocking into the person next to me on the way down, that I realized that introspection, for me, equated boredom and boredom eventually led to sleep. I righted myself and tried to stay awake, but it was hard. Across from me, Alison seemed to have taken Archie's advice and was stock still, her face placid and serene, her body relaxed.

What was wrong with me? Why couldn't I do yoga or mediation without going through a laundry list of my every failing, every humiliation, every error? Was it the Irish in me, constantly self-flagellating for transgressions that most people wouldn't even remember? Or was it that lethal combo of Irish and Catholic, two identifiers that eschewed self-reflection of any kind and made sure that a hearty helping of guilt accompanied every joyful experience I might have? I didn't know, but I worried this in my brain, wondering how long it would take to end this torture, the idea that I would never reach anything approaching Nirvana depressing me in a way that no other thought could.

"Namaste," Archie finally said even though we hadn't done any yoga. I looked over at Alison and realized that her serenity was really a cover for a deep sleep and it was only when she let out a little snore that she awoke and looked around the room, momentarily confused as to where she was and why.

We got up and met at the snack table. Alison picked up a brownie and surreptitiously sniffed it, looking at me and saying, "Bottoms up!" before stuffing half of it in her mouth.

I grabbed her by the arm and dragged her to a corner of the barn. "How are we going to get home if you are as high as a kite?" I asked, whispering.

"You know how to drive, right?" she asked. She held her hand out in front of her and studied it. "Nope. These are just brownies. The one and only time I smoked pot, it looked like I had five hands."

"Just five?" I asked. "And pot may be different now than when you were——"

"Please don't say 'young.'" She looked sad. "It *was* 1895, but it feels like yesterday."

"We really should get out of here," I said. "It's getting late and I have a cramp in my hip from sitting on the floor with my legs crossed."

"Who sounds old now?" she asked.

Archie was standing by the front door as we departed, and I stopped, my one chance to get a little more traction, answers to my questions.

"Excuse me," I said.

"Did you like my class?" he asked, smoothing back his hair. Yep, the guy was definitely on the make. Alison hung back and took in the surroundings; if I didn't know better, I would have believed that she really did want to do some kind of renovation with reclaimed barn wood.

"I had a friend," I said. "And I think she lived here."

"I have lots of friends who lived here," he said, smiling. "This place used to be a commune."

Well, that was easy. "Yes, I am aware," I said. "My friend's name was Amy. She was about eighteen when she came. Tall, blond. Really pretty. Do you remember her?"

He tapped his head. "The old brain isn't what it used to be. But you've just described about twenty percent of the girls who lived here." He looked up, thinking. "Nope. No Amy."

"Are you sure?" I asked. "Amy Mitchell."

He shook his head. "Sorry, doll. I can't help you."

With nothing left to ask and nowhere else to look, Alison and I slipped out the front door, nodding at our fellow meditators, and got into her car.

"Sounds like we've got ourselves a mystery," Alison said as we headed back to the Manor. "And I love a mystery." For the first fifteen minutes of the trip, I wasn't convinced that she wasn't stoned, but now that we were cruising smoothly along the highway it seemed like she was in full possession of her faculties and I was able to relax a bit. With her, it was hard to tell the difference.

"*Another* mystery," I said. "I am more concerned about Amy's connection to this place than reclaimed lumber, a father who is supposed to be estranged from his son, and a failing coffee shop in a hippie town."

"Yeah, but they are all connected," Alison said. "Trust me on this one."

"Trust you?"

"Yeah, I'm an expert, remember?" she said. "I've solved more mysteries than Nancy Drew." She stared straight ahead, watching the road, but I could almost see the wheels turning in her head. "That guy was lying. And why do you lie?"

"To protect yourself," I said.

"Or someone else."

There had been someone else in Amy's car when it had sunk to the bottom of the Foster's Landing River; their identity was still unknown. I had been so focused on wondering where Amy went that I hadn't considered the question that I really needed to ask: *why* Amy went.

CHAPTER *Eighteen*

I was still thinking about that question—Why?—when I found Mary Ann D'Amato-Hanson standing in the foyer, her hands on the Bobby Sands plaque. There was a time when I could have asked her husband a lot of questions, questions like Why? and How come? and Who did it?, but those days were over. I was looking for Amy and maybe he was, too. Our purposes, however, may have been crossed and I had to watch out for that.

"I noticed this on my wedding day, but I don't think I realized who he was. What he stood for," she said.

"Yes. He went on a hunger strike for freedom," I said. "Heck, if I miss breakfast, I can barely function."

"What a terrible story. A terrible situation," she said.

"Yes, we Irish are full of them. Lots of joy in our heritage but lots of tragedy, too."

She changed the subject, not interested in walking down the Irish memory lane, a road pockmarked by war and disease and, yes, hunger. It still astounded me that as a people we were known for our humor and joviality. "I stopped by because I was talking to my father last night and he reminded me that he wanted to have the department's Christmas party here this year," she said, holding up a hand. "I know. It's short notice. I'm hoping you have the Tuesday before Christmas open. I'm sure your weekends are all booked."

They weren't, but it was kind of her to think so. We did have a post-Christmas-themed wedding, but it was a slow month for us. My hesitation made her think we were really booked when we weren't.

"I know it's short notice, Bel, but I'm hoping . . ."

"It's fine, Mary Ann. How many people are we talking about?" I asked.

"About fifty," she said. "You know, all of the officers and staff and their significant others." She brushed a lock of hair off her shoulder, all the better for me to see the honking diamond stud in her ear; Kevin had clearly upped his game in the gift department. For my seventeenth birthday, he had given me one ticket to a Mets game in the nosebleed section; I never did go, not wanting to venture to Queens by myself. "It's not a big crowd, as you know."

"Let's go into the office and just confirm the date," I said. "I want to let Dad know."

My parents were in the office in a romantic clinch, Mom with her arms wrapped around Dad's neck, Dad kissing the top of her head. My parents—even after forty-six years of marriage—were still lovebirds, and while it made Cargan want to heave, he being the one who worked most closely with them, it made me jealous and a little sad. I had never had that kind of connection with anyone, had never had the time to let love grow into something so sustained and constant. They didn't even flinch when we came in, separating as naturally as they had come together, Mom smoothing down her blond coif and beaming when she saw us, but mainly beaming at Mary Ann, the daughter she wished she had sometimes. Perfection in business casual.

"Mary Ann Hanson!" she said, using her married name. "To what do we owe this pleasure?"

"So good to see you, Mrs. McGrath," Mary Ann said.

"How many times have I told you to call me Oona?" Mom asked.

Exactly zero times, I expected. This was as big a girl crush as I had ever seen.

"Hello, Mr. McGrath," Mary Ann said.

"Please, girl, sit," Dad said, motioning to a chair in front of the desk. "What can we do for you?"

"Lieutenant D'Amato wants to have the staff Christmas party here," I said, going around to the desk and opening the reservations book. No online tracking for Shamrock Manor; Mom and Dad wrote each individual booking in a ledger, crossing out those that were canceled and penciling in new events as they booked. "Looks like we're free on that date, Mary Ann." I picked a pencil out of the mug on Dad's desk and wrote in the information that she had given me. "Let's talk menu."

Mary Ann pulled a list out of her purse and read from it. "Three choices: chicken, fish, beef. Your delicious mashed potatoes, Bel. Two vegetables, your choice. Buffet-style."

"Well, that makes it easy," I said. "Dessert?"

"Can we do an assortment of cakes and cookies?" she asked.

"Of course," I said. "And can I surprise you with what they are?"

"Your surprises are the best, Bel," she said.

"Flattery will get you everywhere," I said, the choices

already flashing by on the Rolodex of recipes in my head.

"And the Manor will be decorated beautifully, Mary Ann," Dad said. "We are still in the process of decorating the exterior, but everything will be perfect for the event. We're stringing lights on the trees that lead down to the river."

"It will be a winter wonderland," Mom said.

They were laying it on a little thick; we already had the booking. I went over a few logistics with Mary Ann, wondering the whole time why it was she, and not Kevin or her father, here planning the FLPD Christmas party.

I decided that the answer was as it always was: because she was perfect.

After she said good-bye to my parents, I walked her out into the foyer, where she admired the giant tree. "It's beautiful," she said, touching one of the crystal ornaments. "I have no idea how you get it in here and get it decorated, but I give you a lot of credit."

I flashed on my fighting quartet of brothers and the work it had taken to get the tree upright. "You don't want to know," I said.

She turned and looked at me. "Bel, tell me if I'm prying. . . ."

If you have to ask, you probably are.

"But what happened?"

"Oh, you mean Dad's black eye?" I said.

"Well, that," she said, "and Brendan. What happened?"

"Dad rode the Christmas tree like a bucking bronco and Brendan and I broke up," I said. I thought it was obvious.

"I know," she said. "But why? He's such a wonderful

guy. And you're equally wonderful. You should be together."

It was my turn to focus on the tree, an ornament, anywhere but on her sad face, her eyes, big and brown and full of compassion. Where did I start? "It's a long story, Mary Ann."

She grabbed my hand. "I'm so, so sorry."

"Me, too," I said, and, using every ounce of strength I had, put a smile on my face as if to say "it's not a big deal." I was sorry, too, sorrier than I had been when my engagement had ended, than when I had lost my job. It was maybe the sorriest I had been since Amy's disappearance but I didn't want her to know that.

Her face suddenly brightened. "Listen, a group of girls and I go out once a month. For drinks," she said, as if I thought they went swimming at the Y. "Our next date is Friday. Will you join us?"

"Oh, I don't know, Mary Ann," I said. "But thank you."

"Think about it? Please, Bel? I think it would be great for you to get out and meet some new people." She smiled. "Well, they aren't exactly new. They're girls from our high-school class."

I steeled myself. I couldn't count on one hand a group of "girls" from high school whom I would want to see again.

"Like Hallie Gatter," she started.

Jesus. Gatter the Chatter? She had been the biggest gossip in our class and the reason I had spent one entire Saturday cleaning the rectory after she told her mother—who told my mother—that she had seen me drinking a beer on Eden Island.

"And Margaret Dunleavy."

Okay, she was nice. Even though I knew the only reason she talked to me was because I could help her do
the geometry proofs she couldn't.

Mary Ann named a few other innocuous sorts whom
I could tolerate but whose take on me I wasn't sure of. I
had a history here and it wasn't necessarily a good one.
She stood there, looking at me expectantly. "These
other girls may or may not come."

"I'll think about it," I said. "Thank you. It's very nice
of you to ask."

"It's fun," she said. "It's never a really late night
because they all have kids and have to get up early."

"Sounds like my kind of crowd," I said, thinking
about my new rising time of 6:00 a.m. and how it was
totally at odds with my internal body clock. Dad hit the
studio beneath my apartment early and didn't care who
he woke up with his banging and sawing and melding,
all in the name of art. I walked her to the front door.

"I hope you come, Bel," she said. "And as for Brendan?"

"Yes?"

"He really . . ."

Loved me? If that's where she was going, she needed
to leave. I didn't need to be reminded. I practically
pushed her out the door and slammed it shut, leaning
against it and taking a deep breath to rid myself of the
feeling that told me she was right.

CHAPTER *Nineteen*

The next day, I called Tweed Blazer.

I thought he might ask if I and a friend had visited Wooded Lake the day before, but doing so would reveal that we met Archie Peterson, or whoever that guy was. Sure, Tweed could have come up with a different way of knowing we were there, but I think my call caught him off guard, which was exactly how I wanted him. He knew me as a fake, part-time historian; how hard did he think it would be for me, even a fake, part-time historian, to find out that he was probably not estranged from his father, a guy who taught a kick-ass Breath and Body class in Tweed's barn? I was leaning onto the stainless-steel counter, holding my phone to my ear, and looking out into the foyer, where I saw Feeney pass through, a set of old golf clubs slung over his shoulder. Why he would need golf clubs in the middle of December was beyond me. And come to think of it, I had never seen him actually play golf; that was Arney's pursuit. I didn't think about it again, though, as I listened to the phone ring, just about to hang up when I heard Tweed's voice.

"Hi, Tweed. This is Belfast McGrath," I said, sounding far more confident than I felt.

He was surprised to hear from me. "Belfast." It was

in that one word that I knew he was aware of my visit
to Wooded Lake, his house included, the day before.
"How are you? Any closer to finding what you're looking for?"

"Not really," I said. "But that's not why I'm calling."

"It's not?"

"No," I said. "You mentioned getting together. On my
'home turf,' I think you said?"

"Yes, to talk about your friend. Amy was her name,
I think?"

"Yes. Amy. But let's put that aside for a little while.
I'd like to cook for you," I said. "Show you what we can
do here. Downstate, so to speak."

"I was never not convinced of the culinary hotbed
that downstate represented," he said.

The double negative in the sentence took me a moment to decipher.

"You still there?" he asked after a long pause.

"Yes!" I said, a little too brightly. "So dinner. I can
cook something here at the Manor, if you're interested."

"Interested? In a Belfast McGrath meal?" he asked,
letting me know that he had done more than a little research on me in the intervening days since our first
meeting. "I'm more than a little interested in that."

Although it had been a while since I had been in a
professional kitchen—a *real* professional kitchen, not
the Manor kitchen—I didn't feel rusty in the least. I already knew what I would make, what it would taste
like, what it would make him feel like when he put one
luscious forkful of *boeuf bourguignon* into the mouth
behind the bushy beard. I wasn't sure about this guy,
who he was, what he represented, if he was telling me the
truth, but I knew one thing for sure: He would be putty

in my hands after the meal I would make. He would tell me everything, unable to form another lie.

"Can I bring dessert?" he asked.

"I have a better idea," I said. "Bring some me of your coffee and I'll make a chocolate cake."

"Do you want the coffee with or without the marijuana in it?" he asked.

I paused again.

"Kidding," he said. "Just kidding."

We settled on the next evening at seven. I'd be done with my work for the day, and presumably so would he.

Feeney was back. As I hung up, he came into the kitchen, a forty-something—I never could keep my brothers' ages straight—boy/man, whose dream of becoming a professional musician took a detour and ended with him at the Manor. He was the band's lead singer, a good one at that, but he would never be Bruce Springsteen, picked from tri-state obscurity to become a rock god. A legend. Nope, he was Feeney McGrath, the self-appointed head of The McGrath Brothers, and playing weddings would be his milieu unless Clive Davis wandered into Shamrock Manor and offered him a recording deal.

When you know someone your whole life, you know when they are up to something. I looked up from my phone to find him rustling around in the cupboards, checking out the contents of the refrigerator, going into the walk-in. "Help you, Feeney?" I asked.

He turned around, seeming to have forgotten that I was there. Where else would I be? I practically lived in this kitchen. "Huh?"

"Do you need something? A sandwich? A drink?"

He looked at me blankly. "No. Not hungry."

That was a first. "So what are you looking for?"

"Do you have any chicken fat? Or lard?"

Now it was my turn to stare back blankly. "For what? You're not cooking something, are you?" Last I heard, his "apartment" was one step above a cardboard box under an overpass. It surely didn't have a stove.

"No. I need it for something else," he said. "Got any?"

I tried to figure out what his motives might be. Here's the thing: My brother is gorgeous. I'm not just saying that; he really is drop-dead handsome in a way that few men are. He is the best looking of my brothers but also the most mercurial, the wildest of wild cards. It was no surprise that despite his good looks and kind of feral charisma, he was still single, since his most recent paramour, a woman much younger who seemed to adore him, had flown the coop. Seems the adoration had worn off after a bit, her introduction to my family probably playing a role in her departure, and her recently conferred Associate's Degree maybe waking her up to the fact that yes, although my brother was a babe as well as a ton of fun, he was also a ne'er-do-well with a Peter Pan complex. That made him the kind for dating but not marrying.

"No. Not cooking." We stood across from each other, the counter between us. "I need to grease something up."

"What needs greasing?" I asked, figuring I would ask that one question, get an answer, and then let it drop. I walked over to the refrigerator and pulled out the crème de la crème of animal fat: duck. He didn't respond to my first question, so I asked the most reasonable of second questions if you were a member of my family and didn't really want to know the answers. "How much do you need?"

I could see the wheels turning in his head, his mind measuring the length and width of something, his hands spreading apart and creating a space that was more than a foot in length.

"I don't have a foot of duck fat, Feen," I said. I pulled out a plastic container and scooped a bit into it. "Use it sparingly. It will grease what you need to grease and then some."

"I need more," he said.

I pulled the original container close to my chest. "Nope. That's it. That's all you're getting. That's gold right there," I said, pushing his container toward him.

He picked up the container. "Well, thanks." Before he left, the container under his arm, he asked, "Do you know where I could get more fat?"

"A restaurant, maybe?" I said. "Joe's Chicken Joint on Route Thirty-Six?"

Again, the wheels spun furiously behind his furrowed brow. "I just don't understand why you don't have chicken fat."

"For the record, it's called schmaltz and I am sorry I have disappointed you," I said.

He grumbled a few more unintelligible words, storming off before I could ask him why he had left earlier with an old pair of golf clubs. He was gone, though, so I remained with my own thoughts. What would I serve Tweed Blazer for dinner? But more important, how would I get the information I needed before he figured out that I was in this a little deeper than I had let on? I decided that his lies were now what was keeping me going, more than finding Amy in a way. This was a mystery wrapped in another mystery and at this point I needed to answer one question first: What was he hiding?

CHAPTER Twenty

I work with my family. Therefore, whenever someone is coming to the Manor to see me specifically and not for a booking, I have to let them know so that they don't do the hard sell the minute my guest walks through the door.

"Welcome to the Manor! We're running a special! Everything is free!" would be some of the things a person walking through the big double doors might hear. Although Dad hadn't gone to offering completely free weddings, it sometimes seemed that he was headed in that direction. It was only through Cargan's strong and steadying hand that the business hadn't gone completely under.

I decided that texting them was the best way to go. Dad hates texting, thinking that it's the "work of the devil"; Mom only texts if there is a change in the Pilates schedule; and my brothers—Cargan excepted—wouldn't respond unless it had something to do with them specifically, like decorating the Manor during business hours when they all had much more pressing matters to attend to. It didn't. I was just letting everyone know that I was hosting someone in the Manor that night, the kitchen specifically, for dinner, so not to be alarmed if they heard voices coming from my work domain after hours.

It took Cargan all of ten seconds to come into the kitchen after getting my text; he had been in the office next door and I heard the *DING!* of his phone just moments before he came through the kitchen door.

"So, who is it? Your new friend, Mrs. Crawford?" he asked, an eyebrow raised.

"Not that it is any of your business, but no, it's not my new friend. And her name is Alison Bergeron. Crawford is her husband."

He waved a hand. Too much information. "Brendan Joyce?"

The noise I made in reply was somewhere between a gag and a snort. It was certainly not becoming and probably a little more vehement than it should have been. It had been my decision to end the relationship, not his. It had been my decision not to believe him when he said that he didn't know how Amy's photo had ended up in his wallet. Sometimes, late at night, when I can't sleep and I'm thinking about recipes, I wonder if I was wrong, if I had let the wall that had formed around my heart keep out a kind and tender soul.

"So who, then? If not Mrs. Crawford and not he-who-shall-not-be-named, who is coming over?" Cargan asked.

The question was pointed, although he didn't mean it to be. I had few friends in Foster's Landing.

"I didn't mean it like that," Cargan said. "I know you'll get out of this kitchen eventually and get a social life."

"Glad you're confident of that, Car," I said. "No, it's not Mrs. Crawford or Brendan Joyce. It's a man I met. In Wooded Lake."

"What the heck were you doing up at Wooded Lake?" he asked.

"Looking at some vintage stuff for my apartment."

"I thought it was knives?" he asked, catching me in my previous lie. When I didn't answer, he continued. "That would mean you're staying?" he said, a little lilt in his voice to indicate that he thought that was a splendid idea.

"Maybe so, Brother," I said, turning my back so he couldn't see the lie written all over my face. I didn't know if I would stay, but I certainly hadn't gone to Wooded Lake for antiques.

"What did you get?" he asked.

I went into the refrigerator and pulled out a ham and the remaining pieces of a rye bread that I had baked a few days earlier. I turned back around and put the items on the counter. "Where?" I asked, already having lost the thread of the conversation, my mind on Tweed and how I was going to get from him what I wanted. If he indeed had anything to give me.

"Wooded Lake," Cargan said, eyeing the ham as if he were going to the chair and this was his last meal.

"Oh, no," I said. "This trip was basically reconnaissance. To see what kinds of stores they have."

"And what kinds of stores do they have?" he asked.

"Stores. Big stores. Little stores. Antique stores."

"Names of these stores? Maybe just one or two?" he asked.

It took me a minute to realize I was being interrogated. I put some ham between the two slices of bread and handed the sandwich to my brother. "Stores. Different kinds of stores. Stores with merchandise. Stores that sell things. I didn't get names."

He was taken aback, but he grabbed the sandwich from my hands anyway. "What's gotten into you?" he asked.

"Nothing," I said. "Just don't ask me a hundred questions."

"I think I asked you three." He took a bite of the sandwich. "And now I know that you didn't go to Wooded Lake to buy antiques. Or knives. At big stores or little stores."

I stood in front of my brother, my best friend really, and stared him down. He ate the sandwich quietly, going to the refrigerator for a tin of horseradish mustard and slathering some onto the bread with a knife I handed him. When he was done, he washed his hands at the sink and then took his place at the counter again, the whole set of tasks done in silence, until he reached into his pocket and pulled out a folded-up piece of paper. He slapped it down on the counter and looked at me.

It was from the same newspaper that Alison had left behind and the same page that I had kept.

He looked at me, his eyes looking tired and sad at the same time. It took him a few minutes to speak, but when he did I didn't know whether to laugh or cry.

"I see her, too."

Where I had been had always been clear to him. Now he knew why.

CHAPTER *Twenty-one*

I don't know why, but I texted Alison Bergeron just mere minutes before Tweed Blazer arrived that night. Maybe it was Cargan's inadvertent insinuation that I had few friends—he was right, by the way—or maybe it was the kinship I felt to her, another amateur sleuth with a burning desire to see wrongs righted and questions answered.

Instead of texting me back, she called me, out of breath. "Hey. So you've got the hottie Amish guy coming over for a little dinner, huh?"

"He's not Amish."

"Might as well be with the beard and the barn. And all that potentially reclaimed wood! If that's not Amish, I don't know what is."

I didn't want to get into the finer points of being Amish—heck if I knew what those points were—so I just let her continue.

"Amish wouldn't be terrible. You'd have to give up the cell phone, though, and you probably have to cook on an open flame every night. Maybe? Not sure. But if anyone could do that, you could."

"Are you finished?" I asked, forgetting that I was

talking to a potential customer and not a friend. A real friend with similar interests, in this case, finding Amy.

"That's all I've got," she said. "I don't know a lot about the Amish, I must admit."

Man, she had a tough time focusing. I didn't know if she was qualified to be the Bess Marvin to my Nancy Drew. "To answer your first question, yes, I'm having Tweed to dinner."

"What are you making?

"Hanger steak. Fingerling potatoes. Roasted Brussels sprouts." I had decided that *boeuf bourguignon* was a little pretentious, a bit show-offy. He looked like a meat-and-potatoes guy—or a vegan, it was hard to tell—so I went with the old standby.

"Would it be weird if I showed up for dinner, too?"

"Yes. Yes, it would," I said.

In the background of our call, I could hear people talking, moving past her in whatever open-air setting she was in. Finally, she got into her car, the thunk of her car door sealing her off from the outside noise. "Sounds good. Do you think he knows we were up there the other day?"

"I think for sure he knows," I said.

"How are you going to handle that?" she asked.

"It all depends," I said. "If he admits that he knows about our visit, he'll also have to admit that his father is still in the picture." I opened the oven door and peered in at my Brussels sprouts, which were roasting to perfection. "And I don't know if he wants to admit he lied."

"Hmmm," she said. "I can't wait to hear how this goes. Will you call me tomorrow and tell me everything?"

Sure," I said. "But won't you be at work?"

"I suppose," she said. "But if you call when I'm in class, I'll just assign a writing project. That will keep the kids busy for a least a whole class period."

"Sounds good," I said before hanging up. I looked around the kitchen. I had dragged in a small table for two that was normally in the coat check room and draped it with one of Mom's pressed-linen tablecloths. I found a pair of old sterling silver candlesticks in the basement and pillaged the supply room for some long tapers, which I lit a few minutes after my Brussels sprouts were done, a signal that my guest—if he was a punctual type—would be arriving soon.

I heard Dad coming down the front stairs, his heavy footfalls announcing his presence. He still had a black eye and was hurting from the Christmas tree debacle, but he was in a better mood than he had been. I heard his feet hit the marble in the foyer at the same time as a loud rap on the front door announced my date's arrival. I raced from the kitchen into the foyer, hoping to way-lay Dad, unsuccessful in my attempt. As I skidded to a stop next to the bust in the foyer, Dad opened the door, letting in a gust of wind and my date for the night. Dad took in the sight of Tweed Blazer, a man bigger and more imposing than even my father, a giant in his own right . . . or at least his own mind.

"Can I help you, sir?" Dad asked.

"Dad, this is my friend, Tweed. I texted you about him coming over tonight."

"Groom?" Dad asked.

"Coffee shop owner," Tweed said, mistaking Dad's utterance as a guess at his profession rather than his marital status. "I'm allergic to horses."

"A friend of Belfast, you say?" Dad said, giving him the once-over.

"Well, I didn't say, but yes, I'm a friend of Belfast," Tweed joked trying to infuse a little levity into the situation.

I walked over to my guest and got between him and my father. "Dad, meet Tweed Blazer. He's a friend of mine from Wooded Lake. I met him recently when I was driving around."

"Driving around?" Dad asked. "Why are you driving around?"

To get away from you. To get away from Mom. To make sure I don't go completely insane. "I was looking for some antiques for my apartment, so I went for a drive." To find Amy.

"And I'm glad she did, sir," Tweed said. "I was happy to meet your daughter."

Dad stood in silence, assessing the man in the foyer. "So what are you doing? Going out?"

"It was all in the text, Dad," I said. "We're going to have dinner in the kitchen."

"The kitchen?" Dad said. "The kitchen? No one eats in the kitchen!"

Cargan appeared out of nowhere. "Dad, there's a problem with the printer. I need your help." He held out a hand to Tweed. "Hello, I'm Cargan, Bel's brother. Nice to meet you," he said even as he was grabbing Dad by the forearm and practically dragging him out of the foyer, soothing Dad with assurances that only he, the head of the house, could fix the printer, that it needed his special brand of technological skill, of which we all knew he had none. He had once accidentally rewired

Mom's landline in the Pilates studio so that every time she dialed out she got 911 instead, which I don't think Lieutenant D'Amato minded; he seemed a bit sweet on my gorgeous mum.

Once they left, Tweed handed me a bag. "You promised me some kind of coffee dessert."

"I did, didn't I?" I said. "Come on, let's go to the kitchen."

He took a seat at the little table once we were inside the kitchen and looked around. "You do event cooking in here?" he asked, taking in the unimpressive space.

I nodded. "While I would love a complete renovation on this space, it's unlikely to happen. Unless we book a royal wedding or something like it." I pulled the fragrant coffee out of the bag and pulled down a mixing bowl, throwing together a quick batch of coffee-infused brownies that we could share. The rest of our meal had stayed hot under the warmer, so I put together our plates and placed them on the table. "Wine?" I asked.

"Sure. May I?" he asked, picking up the bottle and after a quick nod from me pouring me a glass. "Your dad seems . . ." He searched for the right word. "Protective?"

"Or crazy?" I said. "I haven't lived here in a long time, so it's odd for him to see me actually living my life. I think in his head I was a teenager at sleepaway camp the whole time I lived in the city and other places."

"That sounds like a pretty normal reaction for a father," Tweed said. "Not that I would know."

I took a sip of my wine. "Meaning?"

"I don't know why I said that. I wouldn't know actually. I didn't have a normal father. Or a normal childhood.

Or a normal life," he said, before shutting down, something that I saw happen as his eyes went blank and his face hardened a bit.

I let it go.

We ate without talking for a few minutes, the scent of the brownies filling the room. "Your food is delicious," he said finally.

"Thanks," I said. "I'm lucky that I get to do what I'm passionate about . . ."

". . . and get paid to do it," he said, finishing my sentence.

"Well, that's not exactly how it works around here, but someday, maybe, I'll return to getting a real paycheck."

"Your parents don't pay you?" he asked.

"They do," I said. "Just not a lot." I got up and checked on the brownies, which still needed another ten minutes or so to be done.

"Tell me, Belfast," he said, pushing his plate aside and picking up his wineglass. "Are we still talking about your friend or is this more of a casual thing, friends getting together?"

I didn't want to answer too quickly, to show my hand. When I took the time to think about it, though, I thought I might be a little interested in him as a friend, but the lie about his father held me back. "It would be nice if we were friends," I said. "I don't have a ton of friends here in the Landing."

"But you're from here, right?" he asked. "Don't some of your old friends live here?"

"I didn't have a lot of friends after . . ." I trailed off.

"Your friend, Amy, left?"

So he had done his due diligence, finding out about

me the one thing I didn't want anyone to know. That I had been the last to see her, that I had no idea what had happened or why. I don't know how he knew, but he did.

I looked into the oven again, willing the brownies to be done so that we could move on to another portion of the meal and go back to talking about culinary things. The oven timer was set and was due to go off shortly, but I stared at the brownies, waiting for the top to crisp sufficiently. While I wanted to know everything he knew, another part of me trembled with profound discomfort at knowing anything about his life—and Amy's part in it—at all.

Out in the foyer, someone knocked at the door, someone new, unexpected. I heard Dad tear himself away from the broken printer and lumber to the front door, where raised voices and Dad's begging for calm were all I heard, one voice besides Dad's coming through loud and clear.

Brendan's.

Brendan Joyce burst into the kitchen, holding a side-view mirror that I recognized as the right size and color of his car. The glass was cracked and had wires dangling from it; it was covered also in a thick, viscous substance that was also smeared across the front of Brendan's shirt.

Chicken fat? Definitely some kind of grease.

Schmaltz.

Or, more specifically, duck fat. Liquid gold.

Brendan brandished the broken mirror like a slick sword, waving it about. "Want to tell me what you know about this?" he asked. In his current state, he looked sexier and more attractive than I had ever seen him look; unbridled anger suited him.

The oven timer went off and I put on two oven mitts to take the pan out. "I don't know anything, Brendan," I said.

"You're lying," he said. "We weren't together that long, but I know when you're lying, Belfast. And you're lying." He was out of breath and red in the face. He looked at Tweed. "She's a terrible liar."

"Good to know," Tweed said.

"This isn't your style, but if I had to bet, I wouldn't put it past one of your brothers."

Feeney's handsome face popped into my head, but I cast the image aside. "I don't know, Brendan. I'm sorry for what happened, but I have no idea how it did."

Behind him, the kitchen doors swung open and, like an episode of *Boyfriends of the Past,* Kevin Hanson popped in, his tie askew and his pants bearing a smear of their own. He looked at me and then at Tweed. "Sorry to interrupt, Bel, but do you happen to know where Feeney is?" He moved toward Tweed. "Kevin Hanson."

"Tweed Blazer."

I could see the corners of Kevin's mouth move in a way that let me know that a case of the "church giggles" was imminent. The last time I had seen Kevin's face do that, we were in the seventh grade and we had both been thrown out of a penance service. And all because Karen DiLuzzio said "ton-gay of fire" instead of "tongues of fire" while reading a Bible passage aloud. "Well, nice to meet you, Mr. Blazer." He took in Tweed's appearance, the bracelet of wooden beads on his wrist, now missing the dolphin charm. "Nice bracelet."

"Thanks, man."

Kevin turned to me. "Bel? Feeney?"

"I haven't seen him, Kevin. Is there a problem?"

Brendan waved the mirror again. "I'd say there's a big problem."

Tweed got up from the table. "Bel, I think I should go. It seems like you have some things to work out."

Brendan looked from Tweed to me and then back to Tweed. "Listen, man, let me give you some advice: Stay away from this family. They are a bunch of lunatics." With his hair sticking out at all angles and his clothes covered with duck fat, his eyes wild, he was one to talk.

"That really is unnecessary, Brendan," I said. "Whatever happened between us doesn't give you the right to denigrate my family."

He turned and looked at me. "They're not crazy?"

I thought about that but didn't answer. Maybe they were. And more than a little bit.

Tweed grabbed his jacket from the back of his chair and put it on, starting for the door. "Bel, I'll call you," he said.

"Tweed, wait," I said, following him into the foyer, but I wasn't fast enough. The big double doors clanked shut and I was left with two *schmaltz*-covered ex-boyfriends in the kitchen, one with an ax to grind and one with one of my brothers to arrest.

CHAPTER Twenty-two

Alison listened to my tale patiently before saying, "Okay. Saturday. I'm coming up and we're going back up there."

"Wait. What?" I pulled the towel off of my wet hair and shook it out, spraying water all over the bathroom; my hair wasn't quite as dry as I thought it was.

"Up there. Saturday," she said. "Crawford has the day off and so do I, obviously."

We didn't have a wedding, so I was free, too.

She continued. "The big drama notwithstanding, from everything you've told me that Tweed guy is hiding something. Besides the fact that his father is definitely very much around." She groaned. "Hey, does your back hurt from that yoga class?"

"No," I said, returning to the conversation we had been having before she decided that her muscles ached. "What do you think he's hiding?" I asked.

"That's what we're going up there to find out."

"What about your husband? Your daughter?"

"You're in luck: They have a birthday party at some trampoline park."

"You don't have to go?"

"I took her to see the last Disney movie in three-D.

It's his turn," she said. "I had a headache for a week after that one."

"Sounds like he drew the short straw," I said, putting the phone on speaker and placing it on the bathroom vanity while I dabbed some foundation over the dark circles under my eyes.

"He loves it," she said. "At least that's what I tell myself. What fifty-year-old guy doesn't want to be at a party with a bunch of four- and five-year-olds?"

"Tomorrow afternoon it is, then." I didn't know what she thought we'd find, but it was worth a try. I had exhausted every other avenue, even going so far as to spend the morning on my computer, looking up everything I could about Wooded Lake and Love Canyon and finding one story after another that was long on speculation and short on facts. Before I finished, though, I sent another e-mail to Dave Southerland, the author of the original article, hoping that he would eventually write me back and tell me something I didn't know, something that would help me close the chapter on Amy once and for all.

Something that would give me peace or at least something that would tell me why Tweed would lie about his father's presence in his life and on this earth.

On the family front, Feeney was on the run, or so it seemed. Vandalism and criminal mischief—especially when you had a bit of a record—came with a hefty fine and, in Feeney's case, possibly jail time. It all depended on how far Brendan Joyce wanted to take this whole thing and last night, with him covered in duck fat, it seemed that he wanted to take it as far as it would go. I hoped to get a glimpse of my AWOL brother while I was running errands this morning, knowing that I was better equipped to find him than the Foster's Landing Police Department. Right before Kevin had left the night before, he had given me a look that told me that when it came to Feeney he wouldn't be looking very hard for him, and for that I was immensely grateful. Justice, in the Landing, is meted out according to relationships and Kevin's and my relationship definitely had its advantages in this case.

I was out most of the day, running here and there, but there was no sign of him at his apartment, no sign of him at any of the local watering holes, and no sign of him at any of the places I frequented—the egg farm; the Whole Foods in the neighboring, swanky town; the local wine store; or even the Goodwill store, where I stopped in to see if they had any old serving dishes that I could repurpose for use in my own home. I was sitting down to a plate of dumplings at the better-than-average Chinese place in the middle of town, the one in the one five-store strip mall that had slipped through Foster's Landing's iron-fisted zoning board, when I saw not my brother in the parking lot, as I had hoped, but someone—and something—much worse. I bent my head over my dumplings, hoping that I hadn't been spotted behind the big window that fronted the place, but it was too late.

Brendan Joyce saw me. And Brendan Joyce saw me seeing him hug Janet Grace, a girl who had been in our high-school class and who now, like Brendan, taught at the high school. French, I thought. It had to be. I remember her wearing a scarf wound around her neck and holding a long, unlit cigarette most of our senior year, her attempt at looking "cosmopolitan" almost succeeding.

The beret was just too much.

Janet Grace got into her car, a sensible Honda Civic, and drove away; it seemed she hadn't spotted me. Brendan turned and looked at me, moving into Janet's vacated parking spot, his hands in his pockets. He jumped when a car behind him, waiting for a coveted space in the small lot, honked, breaking his reverie and making him move to the sidewalk.

He stood out there for a few minutes while I alternately stared at my dumplings and back at him until he finally walked into the restaurant, greeting the hostess behind the counter by name; he was a regular even though we had never been here together. A post-breakup haunt? Dumplings to soothe the brokenhearted? Who knew? I watched as he strode over to my table and pulled out a chair, turning it backward and sitting down, almost as if he wanted the chair to provide another barrier between us.

"Your brother is an asshole," he said.

"Nice to see you, too," I said. "And how do you know it's my brother?" I asked, stopping myself before acknowledging that yes, it was my brother Feeney, in some misguided sense of justice, who had gone out with a set of golf clubs and a container of duck fat, hell-bent on making Brendan Joyce's life miserable, at least for a few hours.

Brendan looked at me and in that instant I was sorry for everything that had happened between us, between him and Feeney, between him and my family, who now hated him with the heat of a thousand burning suns. The McGraths are a pretty genial lot . . . until they're not. And they weren't so genial when it came to Brendan Joyce. Heck, Kevin Hanson and I had broken me over fifteen years earlier and they still hadn't forgiven him.

He picked a dumpling off my plate and popped it in his mouth, his growling stomach always taking precedence over any other emotion he might be feeling. "Listen," he said around mouthfuls of pork dumpling. "I am going to tell you this one more time and then I'm not going to tell you again."

I waited, the preamble taking the wind out of his sails, his voice dropping to a whisper at the tail end of the sentence.

"I don't know how that photo got into my wallet. I'm telling you the truth, Bel. I knew Amy about as well as I knew you in high school—that is, not really at all." He put another dumpling in his mouth, warming to the story and my lunch in general. I noticed that the angrier he was, the stronger his brogue. Right now he had not a trace of it, defeat making him more American and less Irish. "I wish you'd believe me."

"So how did it get there? The photo?"

"I have no bloody idea. How many times do I have to say that?" he asked. The brogue made another brief appearance. "Yeah, Bel, you know. I'm a coward. I left you by the river that day when they found her stuff after all these years. But I'm not a liar. I'm not someone who has been carrying a torch for a girl I barely knew for all this time." He looked at the dumplings but decided against another one. "I had a crush on a girl once." He looked up.

Now it was my turn to look at the dumplings, anywhere but at him. The chalkboard with the various kinds of sake was interesting, too.

"That girl was you, Belfast." He got up and my eyes trained on the chalkboard; all I could see were his khakis, which also bore a smear of grease across the right front pocket. Duck fat was insidious and nasty; it was everywhere once it was somewhere. "But it seems like you've moved on."

"So have you," I said quietly. "Janet Grace? Really, Brendan?"

"She's teaching me French."

"I bet she is," I said, chuckling sadly.

"I'm taking my ma to Paris for spring break."

"That's an unusual spring break choice," I said.

"Not for a seventy-year-old woman and her bachelor son," he said. "She's teaching me French. Janet Grace, that is."

"And you hugged her in gratitude? It looked like a very close embrace." Ever hear of Rosetta Stone? I wanted to ask.

He made a sound, disgruntled, impatient, exasperated. "Not that you'd understand, but I think she has a little crush on me," he said, his cheeks turning red. "Just remember something, Bel."

I finally looked up, making eye contact with him, his blue eyes watery and sad, eyes that I used to love looking into. "What's that?"

"I'm a coward. I admit it. But I'm not a liar. There's a difference."

CHAPTER Twenty-three

The last thing I wanted to do was go out with Mary Ann D'Amato-Hanson and her gaggle of women, but I had committed, responding with a thumbs-up emoji before I could think about it when Mary Ann had texted me the time and place. I don't know why I did except that I hadn't done a ton of socializing with my own gender since returning home and hanging around with my brothers and my parents was getting old. Even the driving up and back to Wooded Lake had lost its luster, and if the other night was any indication I'm sure I had seen the last of Tweed Blazer. After seeing the spectacle that was my enraged ex-boyfriend preceding my dopey high-school cop boyfriend into the kitchen, and hearing about my ne'er-do-well older brother, he had probably run for the hills.

It made his lie about his father seem like small potatoes in the scheme of things, even if he was equally embarrassed by his paternity. That whole thing with the duck fat and Brendan's car was something out of a surrealist drama, and if I had been Tweed I would have lost my number and any thought of pursuing even a casual relationship with me, the deliciousness of my dinner, barely eaten, notwithstanding.

We were going to a local craft-beer place down by the river. I had never been there, but it sounded like just the kind of place that newcomers to Foster's Landing enjoyed and that old-timers, natives as it were, eschewed. I put on a pair of clean jeans and a long sweater, winding a scarf around my neck before putting on a leather jacket. I couldn't compete in the Mary Ann D'Amato-Hanson beauty department, but I could rock this vintage leather jacket like it was no one's business. I looked at myself in my bathroom mirror and wondered aloud.

"Why do you care?" I asked. "After all these years. You're a grown woman. She's a grown woman. So what if she's thin and gorgeous and married to your ex-boyfriend? Who cares? So what?" It sounded convincing, but it wasn't. There was something about that woman that had always left me feeling like a bull in a china shop, Hummels and little teacups and sugar bowls all around me, waiting to be toppled.

Mary Ann, Hallie, and Margaret were all there when I arrived, and by the look on Hallie and Margaret's faces you'd think that I had just returned from battle. They both leapt from their seats at the little table by the window that they had secured and encircled me in a warm embrace that I wanted to hate and make fun of but couldn't. It was sincere and kind and they seemed truly happy to see me.

After all these years and the circumstances under which I had left, I was shocked but tried not to let it show.

We sat down and I caught up with them, ordering a beer. "So, how are you both?" I asked. "Mary Ann and I have had a chance to catch up since I got back home, and of course I was at her gorgeous wedding."

"She told us," Margaret said. "We were both at the wedding with our husbands, but we didn't get a chance to talk to you, Bel. It sounds like you've had an amazingly successful career."

Well, up until this point, yes, I thought. "It's been fun," I said.

Hallie took a dainty sip of her beer, looking as if it were her first and she was twelve. "You must have stories to tell."

"I do," I said. "Lots of stories." There was that one time a former president almost died in front of me, but you already know about that, right? I didn't say it. It didn't have to be said. So I launched into a story about my time in Paris, describing the little apartment that I lived in, how the rooftops looked from the window that cranked open and didn't have one thing to obstruct the view. I regaled them with stories of Italy and how I learned to make a branzino that became a staple at The Monkey's Paw. It was after a breathless fifteen minutes when I didn't come up for air that I realized I was dominating the conversation. I stopped abruptly. "Tell me what you've been up to."

"Nothing like that!" Margaret said, clinking her glass against mine. "I don't know. Law school. Partner in a white-shoe firm by thirty. Gave it all up to come back to the Landing and be a stay-at-home mom."

"Do you miss it?" I asked. "The big-city life?"

The look on her face told me she didn't, but she smiled mischievously. "Every freaking day." She hoisted her glass, pointing it toward Mary Ann. "Just waiting for this one to procreate so I have someone to hang out with during the day. Drink wine with before my husband gets home." She turned back to me. "So, tell me. Are you dating?"

"Are you interested?" I asked, trying to deflect. The last thing I wanted to talk about was my love life, or lack thereof.

"Well, I read *Vashti* every day, so I know what it's like for a single gal out there," Margaret said.

"*Vashti*?" I asked.

"Oh, yeah," Margaret said. "It's an online magazine named after a kick-ass woman in the Bible. All sorts of stuff on dating, being single." She raised her eyebrows suggestively. "Sex."

"Ah," I said. "Sounds like something I should be reading if only to find out what sex is." I was hoping that the discussion of my love life was over, but I was wrong.

"So, you. Any guys?" Margaret asked.

It was clear what had made her a partner at her law firm before the age of thirty. The woman really didn't know how to let anything go.

Under the table, I felt movement as Hallie Gatter, who was uncharacteristically not chatty, kicked Margaret, who tried in vain not to wince.

"Sorry," Margaret said. "I remember now that you had a broken engagement."

"And that I recently broke up with Brendan Joyce?" I said, figuring they had heard from Mary Ann but filling in some, but not all, of the blanks. A heroine in a Harlequin Romance I was not.

Margaret grimaced a bit and that's how I knew that she knew, that she had access to the town's gossip pipeline as only a stay-at-home mom could. All those hours at playgrounds and at playdates must have yielded the juiciest tidbits, and even if I didn't think that my love life was fodder in any way, let me remind you that Foster's Landing is pretty sleepy. Not a heck of a lot going on here, if you didn't count the two murders at the Manor.

Margaret's brief line of questioning brought the conversation to a halt and after talking about the great view from the bar, the controversy surrounding the new blinking stoplight in town (many thought it should be a traditional light and that had given birth to the "Light Movement" in the village), and the lack of water fountains at the river walk, we settled into an uneasy quiet, which led to another round of beers and then another. None of us, it would seem, would be driving home.

I looked at my phone, thinking that we should wrap this up. "Do we have Uber in this town?" I asked.

Hallie, mostly silent to this point, decided that now would be the perfect time to bring up the one subject that I tried never to discuss outside of the Manor: Amy. Without any preamble, she just let it fly. "A lot of people still think you know where she is. Where she went."

I didn't feign surprise or confusion. The "she" in the sentence was always there, a memory that I carried and that prompted others' memories as well. There was a time I was in the dark about where she went, but no longer. She went to Love Canyon. Where she was now was still a mystery, though. "A lot of people would be wrong, Hallie," I said, holding her unwavering gaze. Whoever blinked first was going to lose; that was clear.

"Just telling you what I know," she said. "What I've heard."

"Thank you," I said. "That was a delightful public-service announcement." I grabbed my bag from the floor and found some bills in my wallet to throw on the table. "This has been fun. Thanks for inviting me, Mary Ann."

I got up and went outside, the cold air hitting my face. I decided that texting Cargan would be my best bet; I was no longer in any shape to drive. I'd come back in the morning for my car. I was mid-text when Mary Ann appeared, looking chagrined.

"Bel, I'm sorry," she said.

"It's okay," I said. But it wasn't. I didn't know why I would be forever attached to this story, why being Amy's best friend made me suspect and not at all sympathetic.

"I believe you," Mary Ann said. "I always have."

"Thank you," I said. "That makes one of you." I hit send on the text to Cargan, adding *No questions please* in a follow-up message.

"I thought this would be fun," Mary Ann said. "I'm sorry it wasn't."

"Me, too," I said. "On both accounts."

She crossed her arms, warding off the chill. "Do you think she'll ever be found? That we'll ever know what happened?"

The beer loosened my tongue, and although I didn't plan on responding, the words fell from my lips. "I do," I said. "I think we will figure it out, sooner rather than later."

"You do?" she said, shock registering on her face. "That would be amazing. What makes you say that?"

I had enough presence of mind to shut up. I didn't want Mary Ann to know because I didn't want Kevin to know . . . yet. "Just some feelings, Mary Ann. Things I have heard since I got home."

"Like what?" she asked, a flush coming to her cheeks

from the cold or the thought that this mystery might soon be solved.

Cargan's timing was impeccable, letting me off the conversational hook. He pulled up in the old Vanagon and motioned for me to get in. "Thanks, again, Mary Ann," I said, giving her a quick hug. "This was fun." I don't know why I said it, but she had been kind enough to invite me, so it seemed only reasonable. My mother hadn't raised a rude daughter and I hoped she knew that.

In the car, Cargan stared straight ahead at the road. "Did you have fun?"

My silence was enough of an answer for him.

CHAPTER *Twenty-four*

Saturday afternoon rolled around and Alison pulled up in her car, looking as if she had just been sprung from a penitentiary. "You really didn't want to go to that trampoline park," I said, getting into her car.

"Have you ever been to a trampoline park?" she asked. "It's the seventh ring of hell. There's screaming, jumping, more screaming, some tears, myriad injuries, and then at the end crappy pizza. And worst of all: no booze."

"Your husband must be thrilled to be going," I said as I directed her out of the Manor and toward the highway.

"Here's the thing," she said. "We're old for having a kindergartner. We know that. He's older than I am. So, he wants to enjoy every minute." She pulled onto the access road. "Now if I could just get him to retire, we'd be good."

"Is he ready?"

"Not quite," she said. "Almost but not there yet. Tried it once and it was a disaster. Guy's a cop. It's hard to go from that to . . ." She waved a hand around in the air. "Nothing."

I thought of Cargan, whiling away his days in the

Manor, managing bookings and doing some general up-
keep of the old place, at loose ends. He needed to go
back to work but wasn't ready; that was clear. If Alison's
husband was anything like my brother, he'd be hard-
pressed to find purpose outside of the police department
and its blue world.

"So how did the dinner with Tweed go?" Alison
asked. "Get any juicy details?"

"That didn't go exactly as planned."

"How so?"

I filled her in on the evening. "Now my brother is on
the run from the Foster's Landing Police Department, my ex thinks that my family is crazier than he
thought . . . and he'd be right . . . and I am no closer to
finding out anything about Amy or Tweed or anything
else, for that matter." I looked out the window, noting a
little traffic ahead, unusual for a winter weekend. The
traffic came to a complete stop. "I e-mailed that reporter
again because he hasn't written me back, either."

"You've been busy," she said.

"Yeah, and I went for beers last night with Mary Ann
D'Amato—"

"Remind me who she is?"

"Wife of my high-school boyfriend?" I said. "Remember?"

"Right."

"Anyway, there were two other women there and we
got a little drunk. One of them told me that people think
I know where Amy is. What happened. Still. After all
these years."

"Hey, some people think I'm a murder magnet. It's
hard to shake these things," she said. "And whoever said
that to you may be right. She just doesn't know it yet."

She looked at her phone, accessing her GPS. She pulled off the highway at the next exit. "One thing I've picked up from my husband is an inability to sit in traffic. We'll go the back way."

We wound through parts of the county that I had never seen, but it was scenic. At least there was that. I knew that it would take far longer to get where we were going, but we wouldn't be sitting on the highway, where, according to the report on the news radio channel playing in the car, there was a four-car accident blocking the road. A sign on the two-lane road that we were traveling indicated that it was Route 54, practically a backwoods trail that snaked through some pretty villages.

We pulled up to a stoplight and Alison pointed to a building on my side of the road. "Well, lookie here," she said.

I tried to follow where she was pointing, but all I saw was a chain drugstore, a gas station, and a discount clothing retailer.

"Isn't that the name of the newspaper that I was carrying when Crawford and I stopped by that day?" she asked, and I followed her finger to the building to which she was pointing: the *Hudson Courier.*

"It is," I said. "Pull in."

She was way ahead of me, putting the turn signal on with such force that I was sure it almost came out of the console. "What are the odds?" she asked, her face flush with excitement.

"I e-mailed the guy who wrote the article, but he didn't write me back," I said. As we got closer, I got a little nervous. "We don't know what we're going to get from him, if anything. . . ."

"If he's even there," she said. "Maybe he's out doing

a hot investigation on rigged scales at the local apple or-
chard or something like that." She pulled into the parking lot. "So, what's our game?"

"Our game?" I asked.

"Yeah, the plan. What are we going in with?"

"The truth?" I said.

She looked surprised and then accepting. "Yep.
That'll work," she said, getting out of the car and trudg-
ing across the parking lot, her clogs making her slip
and slide on the little patches of snow that dotted the
path to the front door.

"You should have worn boots," I said, pointing at my
own duck boots with a heavy tread.

"Wrong shoes. Bad weather. The story of my life,"
she said. "It's kind of my trademark."

We entered the office, which was comprised of two
desks, one on the left, the other on the right, with a big
opening between them that led to a table, a copy machine, and a paper cutter. The whole operation was very
low-tech, down to the old-fashioned coffeepot, a perco-
lator, that was bubbling away, and the presence of a
beehive-wearing woman in polyester pantsuit separates
that dated back to the Johnson administration.

"Help you?" she asked, her cats'-eye glasses dangling
from a sparkly rhinestone chain.

"Hi," I said. "We're looking for Dave Southerland. Is
he available?"

The woman turned her head slightly and called out
to a back room, "Dave! Ladies here to see you."

Based on the woman's sartorial homage to the sixties and the vintage feel of the office, I was expecting a
guy with similar style, but the guy who came out of the
back room was young, hip, and not to mention hand-

some. Alison gave me a quick chuck to the ribs with her elbow and let out a little snort. She had noticed, too. It was hard not to.

"Yes, I'm looking for advertisers, but it has to be the right kind of product for the *Hudson Courier*," he said as he walked toward us, talking about something that had nothing to do with our visit. Alison had gone into a semi-trance state, staring at the body that rippled beneath a crisp blue dress shirt and a pair of pressed khakis. His light brown hair was cut short and stylishly, and his blue eyes were highlighted by the color of his shirt. "No Web start-ups, no fly-by-night farmers' markets that open for one weekend a year and then disappear. Definitely no gym franchises. They come and go." He stopped in front of us. "Sorry," he said, putting out his hand. "Dave Southerland. I should have started with that."

I took his hand. "Belfast McGrath. And this is my friend Alison Bergeron."

He gestured toward two seats in front of the desk on the left; he took a place behind it. He gestured toward the woman at the desk on the right. "And this is my mother, Barb Southerland, founder and editor in chief of the *Hudson Courier*."

Barb waved from her desk, her head bent over a magnifying glass and a large piece of paper.

"So, what can I do for you?" he asked.

"Do," Alison said, still a little mesmerized by his looks. "Do."

"Yes. Do for you? Your company? Product?"

"That's not why we're here." I leaned forward in my chair. "You ran a story a few weeks back about . . ."

"Love Canyon," he said.

"Yes," I said. "How did you know I was going to ask about that?"

"Lots of interest in that story. I thought it would be a one-off, but it's turning out to have legs," he said. "What's your connection?" He put his hands behind his head. "Belfast McGrath. You wrote me about this."

"I did," I said. "You never responded."

"Yeah, sorry about that. It's been a little crazy since the story ran."

Based on the lack of activity in the office, I had a hard time believing that that was the reason he hadn't responded.

Alison came back to life. "How so?"

He gave her a quizzical look.

"How has it been crazy since the story ran? What's been happening?" she asked.

"And you are?" he asked.

"Alison Bergeron," she said. "Friend of Belfast."

He paused, looking at a spot over our heads, out the picture window to the parking lot. Try as he might, there was no way anyone else was going to drop by unexpectedly to this little hole-in-the-wall tabloid office. "There has been some local interest in the story. People wondering why we chose now as the time to run it."

"And why now?" I asked. "Why did you pick this time to run it? Because of the anniversary?"

Barb spoke up from the next desk without taking her eyes off of her magnified copy. "Yep. And circulation. Lack thereof. We're barely staying afloat. I thought now might be a good time to do a story like this. Clearly, the apple crops and local DUI reports aren't getting us new subscribers."

"Your paper is free," I said.

"Yeah, that, too," she said. "We're trying to keep this rag alive after fifty years, but it seems like time is running short."

"So you did a story about Love Canyon. Thinking that it might give your son a good byline, an interesting story to garner interest."

"Bingo," she said.

"Seems like you should be taking any advertisers you can get, then," Alison said.

"We get burned a lot," Barb said. "People wanting ads backing out." She looked up. "Not paying."

I didn't really care about the ins and outs of running a small newspaper, so I tried to steer the conversation back to our reason for being there. "Let me cut to the chase. One of the photos you ran in the story had a young woman in it. A blond woman. She's next to a horse?"

He pulled open a drawer and took out a fat file folder; it was stuffed with photographs, all old, all black and white. He dug through the stack and pulled one out, placing it on the desk. "Is this the one?"

In person, up close, it was clear, not blurry like it was in the newspaper. It took my breath away, seeing the young woman, Amy for sure, standing next to the horse, her head turned slightly, a little smile playing on her lips. She looked happy.

And alive.

I pointed to her—to Amy—with a shaking finger. "That's my friend. My friend who disappeared a long time ago. Her name was Amy Mitchell."

Alison reached over and put a hand on my shoulder.

Dave sat up a little straighter. "Huh," he said. "Well, that's funny."

"Funny?" I said.

"Yeah. Funny. Not ha-ha funny but funny. Odd. Weird." He leaned across the desk. "And probably not true."

"Why wouldn't it be true?" I asked, the words trapped in a thick cluster of emotion in my throat. I cleared the feeling. "Why wouldn't it be true?" I repeated.

"Because that's my wife, but her name's not Amy."

CHAPTER *Twenty-five*

Not a wife, per se.

Ex-wife.

Her name wasn't Amy.

But she was Amy.

I was sure of that.

My heart raced at the thought that I had found her, but Dave was quick to let us know that she was gone and that he didn't know where she was.

"What was her name?" I asked. "If it wasn't Amy?"

"Bess," he said. "Bess Marvin."

Alison let out a sound that was part guffaw, part snort.

"Why is that so funny?" he asked.

"Bess Marvin was Nancy Drew's sidekick," she said. "Did she have a family member named Ned Nickerson?"

"Um, no," he said, his face going red. "That was her name. It was on her license and everything."

It was my turn to ask some questions. "Did she show you a birth certificate?"

"Why would she do that?" he asked. "Has your husband seen your birth certificate?"

Alison laughed again. "I'm sure mine has it reduced to card size and laminated. Probably carries it around in his wallet just in case I go missing." She took in Dave's and Barb's incredulous looks and explained further. "He's a cop. As far as he's concerned, we're all in danger all the time."

"So, Bess Marvin," I said. "What else?"

"She left me," he said. "Wasn't interested in being married to a local newspaper magnate." He had a sense of humor about it. She must have been gone a long time for that to come to the fore.

Barb let out a derisive laugh.

"When? When did she leave?" I asked when I got my voice back.

"Five years ago." he said. "Let's just say that she was leaving long before that."

"Told you not to marry her," Barb said, going back to her print copy.

"And you have no idea where she went?" I asked. "None at all?"

"Not a clue," he said.

I looked at the photograph again. "Tell me about her. What was she like? As an adult?"

He smiled, the memories good ones. "She was gorgeous and funny and smart as a whip."

That was Amy.

"She was the reason I did the story. Because after she left, I thought about what she had told me, how she had come here as a kid and gone to Love Canyon. I thought I would write something finally, something with a journalistic bent that would revive this rag." He looked at beehived Barb. "No offense, Mom."

"You didn't think to write this while she was still around?" Alison asking the question I was thinking.

"I did. But she wouldn't have any part of it. Would clam up when I asked too many questions."

"About her past?" I asked.

He nodded. "Particularly about her past and the time before Love Canyon. She disappeared a lot. For a day. Maybe two. But not this long. This time, though, she's gone for good."

Alison backed the conversation up. "Where did you meet?"

He laughed out loud. "A bar, of all places."

"Not exactly what you'd call a 'meet-cute,'" Barb said.

"How long ago?" Alison asked.

"Ten years ago."

"Married too young," Barb said.

She sounded like Alison's husband. Dave and Amy would have been just a little bit older than Erin and Fez would be when they got married.

"Do you have any wedding photos?" I asked.

It was Barb's turn to laugh. "Nothing. Not a one." She hooked a thumb in her son's direction. "Burned them all."

"Anything? One photo?" I asked.

He crossed his arms over his chest. "Let's just say that this didn't end well for me, so I erased all evidence of what turned out to be a really tragic mistake."

"Where did she say she was from?" I asked.

"Canada," he said. "Said her family was in some rural area east of Quebec City and that they weren't close."

"And none of this seemed suspicious to you?" Alison asked.

"Love, sister. It was love."

Barb chimed in. "And maybe a little lust?"

I wanted to know more, but my head was so flooded with thoughts and emotions that I wasn't sure I could adequately voice everything that was left unsaid. "She was my best friend. She disappeared a lot of summers ago and I need to find her," I said, my voice small with the idea that they had seen her, that she had had a life. "All these years, I was sure she was dead."

Barb, hearing my emotion, got up from her desk and came over to me. "Oh, honey. She is very much alive. And if you find her, tell her her ex-mother-in-law has a bone to pick with her."

"And what's that?" Alison asked.

"She broke my boy's heart," Barb said. "Isn't that enough?"

CHAPTER Twenty-six

Sitting in the stacks of the Foster's Landing library, Amy and I pored over every new Nancy Drew mystery that the library procured, hoping one day that we would find ourselves embroiled in a mystery, with our own sporty blue coupes and Ned Nickersons to help us along the way.

I had my mystery now, but without the cute car or the cute boyfriend. My sidekick was a bored middle-aged college professor, and although the mystery deepened with every step, the two of us were as in the dark as ever.

We were back in the car, on our way to Shamrock Manor, the meeting with Dave Southerland not reaping what I was expecting, but much more.

"She's alive," I said, watching the browns and taupes of the winter landscape whiz by. "Well, she was at least five years ago. I can't believe it."

"Do we believe this guy?" Alison asked. "I'm starting to get the sense that everyone north of the Tappan Zee Bridge has a very tenuous hold on the truth."

"Like who?" I asked.

"Like your friend Tweed. Like Archie Peterson."

"Technically, Archie didn't lie."

"Okay, point taken. But I don't know how much I

trust this Dave Southerland guy. And that Barb is a piece of work, too. The narrative is a little too neat, a little too well constructed." She scratched her head as if trying to solve the riddle of what we had just heard. "And Bess Marvin? Really?"

I didn't care about the riddle. All I could think of was that she hadn't died that last night or any night after that. She was still alive, and if anyone could find her I could.

What was I hoping to do? Reunite her with her family? Her father was in a mental-health facility after attacking me and Cargan, another person convinced I knew where Amy had gone all those years ago, and her brother was a local cop who wasn't too happy with me, either. Would they welcome her back with open arms? Was I even on the right track with that or had she left a situation I knew nothing about and had no business getting involved in?

I should stop, I thought.

But I can't.

I'm obsessed and it's not healthy. It wasn't that I had to clear my name; or was it? I couldn't figure out what was driving me to do the things I was doing, but in my heart I wanted to find her because it would make everything right again.

Alison recited back some letters and numbers to me: a license-plate number. "I don't know what that might help with, but I have this thing about memorizing license-plate numbers. Call it my gift. There was only one other car in the parking lot, so we've got a fifty-fifty chance that it's Dave Southerland's car. Maybe we can find out something about him." She passed a slow-moving Dodge in the right lane. "I'll have Crawford run it on Monday when he goes back to work."

"You really think we'll find something out about a small-time journalist from his license plate?" I asked.

"Hard to tell, but we can try, right?" she said. "Or rather, Crawford can try."

"If he's survived the trampoline park party," I said, punching the numbers into a running list of items I kept in my phone, putting it right after "ham," a reminder to myself to buy pork for the next wedding, a post-Christmas extravaganza that was coming up in a few weeks.

We were almost to the Manor, having ridden in silence the whole way, when I turned my attention to a question I could get an answer to, something I could control. "A question for you."

"Yes, I think we try to find Archie Peterson again and I think we stop pussyfooting around this whole thing and ask Tweed Blazer what the truth is and why he lied."

"That's not the question."

She pulled into the driveway of Shamrock Manor. "What else do we have?"

"Are Erin and Fez any closer to making a decision on Shamrock Manor?"

She burst out laughing. "Just driving into this place changes your whole perspective." She pulled up into the driveway in front of the Manor. "Before I left today, I told Crawford that we need a decision. Memorial Day weekend is popular, and if they want their wedding here I don't want them to lose it while they dillydally on the venue."

"The truth is if that I go inside and don't have at least a kind-of answer from you, Cargan will hammer me until we get an answer. This is the kind of thing that keeps him up at night," I said.

"Wow, he takes his job seriously," Alison said. "Let

me go home, see how the trampoline park party was, and then I'll get Crawford liquored up. That's a good way to get him to get on it and get an answer from Erin." Alison narrowed her eyes. "She's a bit of a pill, if you want to know the truth."

"She wouldn't be the first bride to be a pill," I said. "So, you'll be in touch. And so will I if think of anything else."

I went into the Manor and stood in the foyer, the place quiet, the smell of pine from the giant Christmas tree filling my nose. Cargan appeared on the second-floor landing, taking in my face and rushing down the stairs.

"Where have you been? What's going on?" he asked.

"Alison and I had lunch," I said, heading toward the kitchen.

"Where?"

"Grand Mill," I said, mentioning a restaurant not too far from the Manor.

Cargan followed me into the kitchen. "That garbage is smelling pretty ripe," he said.

"That's *your* job," I said, peeling off my coat and hanging it on a hook next to the door. I opened the oven and pulled out a sheet pan.

"What did you eat?" he asked. "At the Grand Mill?"

"Burger," I said.

He waited a beat before his reveal. "You were also in Hudsonville."

He was right; I was. "How do you know that?"

"Don't worry about that," he said.

But I knew. My phone had gone missing a few days earlier for about an hour and mysteriously reappeared right where I thought I had left it. He had engaged the location device and was following my every move.

"Want to let me know what you were up to?" he asked.

"Gosh, Cargan, you are worse than Dad sometimes," I said.

"Don't change the subject," he said. "You're up to something and I want to know what it is."

I oiled the sheet pan, not sure what I was going to cook, but trying to buy myself some time.

"Your new friend? Mrs. Crawford?" he said.

"She goes by 'Bergeron.'"

"Whatever. She's got a bit of a past, poking her nose in where it doesn't belong."

"She's okay," I said. "Her heart is in the right place."

"She's seen her share of dead bodies. More than any one college professor should." He softened his tone. "Her ex-husband was *dismembered*," he said. "They found pieces of him in two different jurisdictions."

"Gross."

"Please don't let her be your Holmes."

I didn't answer. The proverbial train had left the station.

"Bel, I'm on your side," Cargan said. "Tell me what's going on. You know I can help you."

I put my hands on the counter and took a deep breath; he had loved Amy, too. "Amy's alive, Car. Well, at least she was five years ago." I told him what we had discovered, that the person in the photo from the *Hudson Courier* had been Amy for sure. "We can find her. I know we can."

My brother is contemplative and not the least bit impulsive. But I saw something flare behind his eyes, a spark that anyone rarely saw, no one really knowing what made him tick, what got him excited. I saw it now. This had him excited even though his face was a mask of composure. It confirmed for me that something was there, that we had something to go on. "The only thing I've got is the word of her ex-husband and a license-plate number."

"Whose license-plate number?" he asked. "And what made you think to get it?"

"We're not sure whose it is but probably Amy's ex-husband." I shrugged and smiled. "And Alison has a thing about license-plate numbers," I said. "Not sure why, but she took it down and gave it to me. Maybe it will be helpful?"

"Text it to me," he said. "Who knows?"

"She said she'd get her husband to look into it, too," I said.

Cargan grimaced. "I'm sure he'll love that. Nothing cops like more than civilians trying to play sleuth."

"Does that happen a lot?" I asked, not believing that there was a cadre of middle-aged women running around New York trying to solve cold cases.

He started for the door. "You'd be surprised."

"Hey, brother!" I called after him.

He turned.

"Any word from Feeney?" I asked.

He smiled. "That's one thing you don't have to worry about, Bel. He's fine."

"I have visions of him on the run. On the lam, as Dad would say."

"We'll get this sorted out," he said, going through the swinging doors that led to the foyer.

I wasn't sure what he meant, which part of the story he was referring to, but I hoped he meant both parts, for my other brother's sake and for Amy's.

CHAPTER Twenty-seven

Tweed's voice let me know that he was happy to hear from me, and I was glad about that, our last meeting having taken such a weird turn. I told myself that whatever idiosyncrasies my family had, his was much stranger by a lot.

"I'm hoping we can get a do-over on our last meeting," I said.

"I'd like that," he said, his voice somewhat tentative but agreeable nonetheless. "Here's the thing, Bel."

And here it comes, I thought.

"Can we do it up here?" he asked.

I let out a mental sigh of relief. "Of course."

"It's just that I'm in the midst of my end-of-year accounting and inventory and things are crazy-busy right now."

"I understand," I said, and I did. Although we didn't have anything approaching formal end-of-year accounting or inventory, there was sort of a buzz in the air at the Manor signifying that the year was coming to a close and a rethinking of some of our practices and habits needed to be reassessed. Or maybe that was just me. Everyone else seemed content to coast into the New Year with nary a thought of "best practices" or even the odd New

Year's resolution. "What works for you?" I asked. It was just past noon and I had completed my work for the day; I would head out in a bit to go to the egg farm, but otherwise my calendar was wide open.

"You're not free tonight, are you?" he asked, his tentativeness simmering down, his voice becoming more relaxed.

"Well, I know there are some rules that say I shouldn't say 'yes,' but yes, I'm free," I said. According to *Vashti,* which I had skimmed after learning about it at the craft-beer place from Margaret, I learned that I should most definitely not immediately accept when a guy asked me out. The reasons were still unclear to me, but doing so was apparently a no-no.

"Screw the rules," he said. "I close at seven. Let's meet at my house and then we can decide where to go from there. Do you remember how to get there?"

"Give me the address again," I said, jotting down the information.

There was a long pause after that and I wondered if he had hung up, the plan set and our meeting time and place arranged. He finally spoke.

"I know you met my father," he said.

Now it was my turn to be quiet.

"It's okay. I can explain," he said. "I will explain."

"I'd like you to explain," I said. I realized I had some things that needed to be clarified from my side, too. "I can explain, too," I said.

"Great. So seven thirty tonight. And we'll both explain why . . ."

"We lied," I said. Might as well call a spade a spade. I hung up. I was getting closer.

I did my errands and returned to my apartment to get cleaned up and dressed for a night in Wooded Lake. The door was unlocked, which wasn't concerning because Mom came and went at her pleasure, leaving me "healthy" foods, which meant "things Bel would never eat," and putting a new toilet brush beside my bathroom sink every two months, like clockwork. I walked in and looked around, my eyes finally settling on my bedroom, where I found Feeney on top of my down comforter scrolling through my iPad.

"To what do I owe this honor?" I asked, taking the iPad from him and stowing it in my nightstand drawer. The last show I had watched on it had been a show about high-class call girls, and if he saw that he would most certainly tell the rest of my family and then my life would be over for good, any respect I had garnered since returning to the Manor evaporating in one fell swoop.

"High-class call girls, Bel?" he asked, getting up. "And you have no food. What kind of chef are you?"

"What are you doing here?" I asked. "Aren't you on the lam? Shouldn't you be hopping a train west to avoid the law?"

"That's why I came here," he said. "I'm hiding in plain sight."

Kind of like Amy.

"Good plan, Feen," I said. "Now why did you cover my ex-boyfriend's car in duck fat and break his mirrors?"

If I didn't want to kill him so badly, my heart would have melted just a bit at the umbrage he took at Brendan's . . . well, what? Carelessness where my feelings were concerned? Lack of a backbone? It was hard to say. He looked at me, his eyes filled with sympathy for my situation, my two most recent loves failing to live up to any standards, let alone mine. "Well, I care about you, Bel," he said. "You're my favorite sister."

"I'm your only sister."

"That, too," he said. I was touched nonetheless. And then, shattering any illusion that his heart remained firmly rooted in the right place, added, "Can we order a pizza?"

"I'm going out," I said. "Does anyone know you're here besides me?"

He shook his head. "I don't think so." He followed me into the bathroom, where I started brushing my teeth. "So can we? Order a pizza?" he asked.

"Feeney, I'm going out and I won't be back until later." I knew that he couldn't order himself, nor could he greet the delivery guy or girl at my door. Foster's Landing was a small town, and by now anyone with a Twitter account who followed the police department—and that was just about everyone in the Landing, a town of nosy parkers if there ever was one—knew that they were looking for Feeney McGrath, middle-aged vandal. I finished brushing my teeth and ran a brush through my hair. "Look in my freezer."

"I did. You've got a bottle of vodka," he said. "Well, you did have a bottle of vodka."

"Thanks," I said. "When you're out on bail, you can go buy me a new one."

"You can't buy booze when you're out on bail," he said, the two of us in my bedroom, me picking out clothes from my closet.

"And you would know," I said, giving him a pointed stare. "Can you please get out of here?"

"I can't," he said. "I have nowhere to go."

"No, not here," I said, sweeping a hand around to indicate the larger space. "*Here*. My bedroom." He stood, rooted to the floor. "And if Cargan has had access to your phone, he already knows you're here. He's tracking our every movement, apparently." Based on our previous conversation, I was almost certain that Cargan knew where Feeney was, and while I would have expected him to find Feeney other accommodations, he had chosen to leave him right here, hiding in plain sight, as Feeney pronounced.

"He doesn't know where I am," Feeney said. "I have a burner phone."

That took things to a whole new level. I had one brother who spied on all of us and another brother who was duplicitous enough to know that and take precautions against it. To what depths did my family's insanity go? I wasn't sure I wanted to find out.

When he finally left my bedroom, I hoped to follow my suggestion that he cook up some of the pasta that was in the cabinet to the left of the refrigerator, I pulled out a black turtleneck and a pair of jeans from the closet, adding a pair of black boots. I grabbed a scarf from a hook on the back of the door and went into the kitchen, where Feeney had managed to put together a meal that looked appetizing enough to make my stomach growl.

"You can't stay here forever," I said as he shoveled bow tie pasta into his mouth. "You can't outrun the police department."

He arched an eyebrow in my direction. Sure he could. He was slick and the cops weren't. An image of me and my brother—both old and with gray hair, still living in this apartment—flashed in my mind's eye and I shuddered. This roommate situation could go on for a very long time indeed.

"Tomorrow," he said, his mouth full. "Could you go to my place and get me some clothes?" When I didn't respond, he added, "Please?"

"Maybe," I said, when the answer was really no. I picked up my keys from the table next to the door and headed down the stairs to my car, never happier to leave Foster's Landing and my family home.

CHAPTER *Twenty-eight*

I called Alison Bergeron on the way up to Wooded Lake. In the background, I could hear a child in full high dudgeon, something about the preparation of her macaroni and cheese not suited to her delicate palate.

"Add a little milk," I said. "Sounds like she wants it thinned out a bit."

"Bea! Hold on!" Alison said. "She can wait. It's not life threatening."

"You may have a future chef on your hands," I said, thinking back to my own protestations about my mother's meals of the past. "God help you, if that's the case."

She went to a quieter location, the sounds of her daughter, accompanied by the barking of what was definitely a large dog, fading into the background. "What's happening?" she asked.

"I'm headed to Wooded Lake. To see Tweed."

"Huh," she said. "And how did this come about?"

"He invited me up," I said. The long highway stretched before me, the drive still boring, but with the promise of good food and conversation at the other end. Maybe some information about Amy. Maybe not. I had to calibrate my hopes where she was concerned; knowing she was alive possibly had quelled some emotions, aroused others. It was a lot to think about, more to process.

"Will you call me on the way home? Let me know what happened tonight?" Alison asked. "Oh, wait, you're younger than me and can probably stay awake after ten. I'll never be awake. Call me tomorrow. God forbid Detective Crawford not get his beauty sleep. I'll never hear the end of it."

"How was the trampoline park party?" I asked, seeing the sign for the Wooded Lake exit.

"Oh, you know. Just how a four-year-old's birthday should be. Fifty of the little special flower's best friends, a bunch of parents, no booze, stale pizza." She let out a gusty laugh. "He had a ball."

"Sounds like a blast," I said.

"Did I mention no booze?" she asked.

"You did. Twice," I said. "I'll call you tomorrow. I'll let you know if I find out anything further, but somehow I think we've hit a plateau." Although I had been excited when I left Foster's Landing earlier, I felt now as if I was wasting my time on both the mystery front and the romance front. I don't know why, but I had a sinking feeling.

"How so?"

"I don't know," I said. "Just feels to me as if we're going to be spinning our wheels for a while." I remembered Amy. I knew Amy. If she didn't want to be found, she wouldn't be found. She had been right under our noses, practically, and still no one had located her.

I was smart. She was smarter.

I had to pull over and put Tweed's address into my GPS, something I had forgotten to do before I left Shamrock Manor. According to my phone, I was exactly three miles from the cabin in the woods, and I followed the directions, missing one dirt road turnoff and having to double back to pick it up. Eventually, I was on the right road and followed it to the front of Tweed's house. Behind it, the lake sparkled, a little sliver of moonlight hitting the still, mirrored surface of the water. I approached the house, one lamp lit in the front window, a floodlight coming on automatically as I approached the steps to the porch.

The front door was ajar, and when I knocked, it swung open, its weight giving it motion. It banged against the wall behind it, a wall at the bottom of a long staircase, startling me. I called out to my host, "Tweed? Are you home?"

When he didn't answer, I entered the house, taking in its beautiful, rustic styling, the well-worn leather sofa, the Shaker-style end tables and stained-glass shaded lamps, the neatly stacked issues of *The New Yorker* on the coffee table. I called out his name again and got no response. I passed a credenza outside of the kitchen, photos artistically placed, a photo of his father, Archie Peterson, featured prominently. My eyes grazed over the other ones, a mix of old and new, his mother, presumably, the focus of a few photos, a tall, gorgeous woman with light hair and azure-blue eyes, a woman from whom Tweed had inherited his prominent yet finely planed nose. The resemblance couldn't be denied, Archie a more rough-hewn sort, a man who looked like he would be equally at home on a farm or in a seedy biker bar.

One photo, pushed toward the back, caught my eye and I picked it up. In it, a young Tweed, barely out of his teens, or so it appeared, stood beside a woman in a long white dress, a ring of flowers on her head, the two of them standing beside the body of water that sat right in back of the house in which I stood, my feet refusing to move, my limbs frozen. They looked happy. Healthy. Beautiful and free.

Alive.

A noise behind me broke my paralysis and I turned, taking in the sight of Tweed, a guy I didn't know at all really but who I now knew had lied to me, again and again. I had been right: In some ways, this was a waste of time and I would never get the whole truth, the truth being a ball of yarn that kept unraveling, end never in sight.

"You married her," I said. "Amy. She was your wife." She had been busy since leaving Foster's Landing, with two marriages behind her and maybe another one on her marital résumé. Who knew what she had done, what she was doing. It was a mystery that couldn't be solved. Not without the truth from the man in front of me, someone whose blood had drained from his face.

He reached a hand out to me. "Help me," he said, a mere whispered croak.

"Help you what?" I asked, my ire rising at an alarming rate, the thought of sweeping my hands across the credenza and knocking the photos to the floor prominent in my mind. "Help you? You lied to me. Over and over."

He stumbled forward and it was only then that I saw the pool of blood at his feet, starting back at the stairs, a maroon handprint on the wall. He came at me, falling into my arms, the two of us crashing back into the credenza, the photos that had my attention a few seconds earlier falling to the floor in a hail of shattering glass. My back hit the large piece of furniture, going numb right before the pain flooded my body. We ended up on the floor, Tweed on top of me, my eyes catching sight of the reason for the blood, the knife sticking out of his back. His body convulsed at the same time that I heard footsteps on the stairs and the door slam against the wall again.

It took some effort, but I managed to get out from beneath the man on top of me, pulling the knife out of his back with some effort, the sound it made as it slid from his body not unlike what I heard when I yanked a blade from a hunk of meat. A gag rose in my throat as I saw the giant wound from which the blood flowed and I thought back to the time when my mother had encouraged me to be a nurse and forget culinary school. I didn't know what to do with a wound like this, something so big and gaping that it seemed it could never close, so I pulled off my scarf and pushed it down, hoping to stanch the river of blood that seemed to come from his body.

I found a vintage-looking wall phone on which I dialed 911, breathlessly asking for help before hanging up and heading outside. I hadn't passed another car on the road in, nor had there been a vehicle besides Tweed's in the driveway. Whoever had done this was on foot.

I got outside, my eyes taking in the number of hiding places that there were on a large wooded lot, finally landing on the barn. I hesitated, the only thing breaking up the soundless night a bird overhead letting out a sharp caw. I approached the barn, knowing I was in over my head now, but there was no turning back. Amy had brought me here, and now I was devoted more than ever to solving this mystery.

I thought of Amy, of our life before and my life after. This wasn't how it was supposed to end with me

bumbling around a dark lot and her out there, somewhere, maybe living a better life than I could ever
imagine. This wasn't the script. We would find out that
she had died and we would move on. Or I would find
her, happier than she ever been. But this wasn't it, lies
on top of lies, with no end in sight, no truth to be told.

We still didn't know whose DNA was in Amy's car,
unearthed by the drought. We knew it wasn't her, but
the identity of that person was still an unknown. Did she
have something to do with that person's death? Is that
why she had run? The questions swirling in my brain, I
started for the barn, leaves crackling beneath my feet.
Finally the sound of sirens broke up the silent night and
gave me hope that it wasn't too late.

My hand on the barn door, I thought of a few things
before the night went completely black and I with it.

My parents.

My brothers.

Even Brendan Joyce.

The last time I had seen Amy, her smile a betrayal of
me and everything we had ever had.

CHAPTER *Twenty-nine*

"Wrong place at the wrong time or part of the problem here?"

Swimming back to consciousness and not having a lot of luck, I listened to the voices around me, not one of them familiar.

Or friendly.

I opened my eyes, but the lights were too bright, red, blue, white, spinning around me.

"She's awake."

"Great. Let's get her up."

"She's not ready yet. Give her a few minutes."

Coffee breath, sharp and pungent, washed over me, the person kneeling beside me having ingested a strong brew.

"Wonder if she can tell us anything?" a female voice said.

"Wonder if she's the one who did it?" a male voice replied.

At that, I bolted up, not wanting the conversation to go on any longer. Suspecting me of stabbing Tweed was not part of this script and I had to let them know that. A wave of nausea flooded my body as I sat up and I swallowed a few times, the cool night air having no effect on the sweat breaking out on my forehead.

Did what, exactly? I had to assume that things hadn't worked out for the best, that Tweed Blazer was dead, but I had watched enough cop shows to know that I should keep my mouth shut and maybe even ask for a lawyer, even though in my addled brain I thought that doing so might imply that I was guilty. All of these thoughts floated through my head as my consciousness swam to the surface, my eyes adjusting to the pitch black punctuated with bright light.

"What's your name, sweetheart?" a guy wearing a puffy down coat asked me as he helped me to my feet. He looked vaguely familiar, but I couldn't place him, like someone I had met once or a long time ago, or both. White hair billowed around his head like a silky halo.

"Is he dead?" I asked.

"Well, that's an odd name," he said. He looked up at the woman beside him. "Must be a nickname."

A regular comedian. Just what I did not need right now.

"Tweed. Is he dead?"

"Why don't I ask the questions and you give the answers?" he asked. "What's your name?"

"Belfast."

"Belfast?" he asked. "What kind of name is that? That's not a name. That's a place. And just how hard did you hit your head?"

"My parents are Irish. I'm Irish. We're Irish," I said, bending over at the waist and taking in a few gulps of chilly air.

"Huh," he said, an older man with a wispy gathering of last remaining gray hairs covering his shiny pate, glasses that magnified his kind eyes hovering on the tip of his nose. "Interesting. Glad my parents didn't follow suit and name me Kraków."

"You're farsighted," I said, wondering, too, just how much damage that hit to my head had done. "And I didn't hit my head. Someone hit it for me."

"Well, that wasn't very nice," he said, holding out his hand after I stood up straight. "Larry. Larry Bernard."

The woman whose voice I had heard in my state of semi-consciousness stood behind him, clarifying just who he was. "*Detective* Larry Bernard."

"You have detectives in Wooded Lake?" I asked. Kevin Hanson was a detective, and not a very good one, which mattered not a whit in Foster's Landing for the most part.

"Just one," he said. "Me. Been doing it for nearly forty years. But this is a new one on me."

"What's that?" I asked, not wanting to give too much away.

"Why don't you tell me?" he asked, leading me to the back of an ambulance and helping me sit down on the steps. He grabbed a blanket from inside the vehicle and placed it over my shoulder. An EMT appeared out of nowhere and handed me an ice pack for my head, which I gingerly placed as close to the injured spot as I could without pressing on it. It hurt like hell and I was going to have quite a bump.

The detective repeated his question. "Why don't you tell me?" He pushed his glasses up on his nose and his eyes, cornflower blue behind thick lenses, grew larger from the magnification.

I figured there was no harm in just starting with arriving here, leaving out any mention of previous visits or mysteries to be solved. "I came to have dinner. With Tweed."

"And how did you meet?" he asked.

"At the coffee shop. I'm a chef. I was driving around, looking for places to buy locally sourced food. Vegetables. Meat. Eggs."

He held up a hand. "I know what food is."

"I guess you do," I said. I moved the cold pack to a spot closer to the bump on my head. "That's how we met."

"And tonight?" he asked.

"I got here around seven thirty." I looked around. "What time is it now?"

"A little after eight," he said.

So I hadn't been unconscious that long.

"Tell me more." I watched as the female cop talked to one of the EMTs, a cup of coffee in her hand, a cigarette in the other. In all, there were two police cars with two uniformed cops in attendance, one ambulance and two EMTs on the scene. I wondered where Tweed was—if Tweed *was*—but knew I wasn't going to get anywhere until I told Detective Larry Bernard my story in full.

"We had a date to meet and then we were going to decide what to do. Once I got here," I said. "But there was no answer at the door, which was open, so I let myself in and . . ." I stopped, fluttering my hands to indicate what I had found without having to actually say it. "Blood," I said. "Lots of it."

"And you saw no one else?" he asked, dropping his hands between his legs, rubbing them together to keep them warm.

"I didn't see anyone, but I heard someone leave. I

suspect they hit me over the head, but I can't be sure." I pulled off the ice pack. "Too cold."

"Yep. All of it," he said. "Way too cold."

I knew he wasn't talking about just the weather. "Can I go?" I asked. "If I give you my name and contact information?"

He still hadn't told me about Tweed and I didn't see another ambulance, so I went with the assumption that he was gone, if not just from this place then from the world. I wasn't sure where to put that emotionally, as I was numb, both physically and emotionally. In shock. Shut down until such time as I would power on again and make sense of everything that had happened, beginning with that newspaper article about Love Canyon and culminating with the death of a guy I barely knew but had wanted to get to know better, if only to get closer to the truth.

My truth.

Larry Bernard rubbed his hands together some more, thinking of his choices. "You know, I don't think you should go anywhere for the time being, the biggest reason being that you're a little concussed, in my humble opinion." He waited while an EMT attended to my head, looking on silently. "Looks like a leftie hit."

"How would you know that?" I asked.

"Been doing this a long time." He fell silent.

There was more.

"And?" I asked, waiting.

"I feel as if there is more to this story than you're letting on," he said.

"There's not," I said, a little too hastily and without conviction.

He let that sink in, an old detective with a lot of experience being lied to by someone he could only imagine had a lot to hide. "Well, you're my only witness to an attempted homicide," he said, giving me the answer that I had been hoping to hear but wasn't expecting.

"Attempted" was good. "Homicide" was not.

CHAPTER *Thirty*

When my parents had five children and the oldest had exceeded all expectations by going to law school and becoming the only divorce lawyer in the town of Foster's Landing—a hundred Hail Marys for his soul, please—they thought they had knocked it out of the park both genetically and in terms of child-rearing. But then came the rest of us: lazy Derry, who was only too happy to marry a woman who kept him in a lifestyle to which he wasn't born but quickly acclimated; Feeney, who didn't meet a petty crime he didn't like; and Cargan, who was the smartest of us all but odd in the way that most geniuses are.

And then there was me. Belfast McGrath. The chef with a temper. The girl who couldn't leave well enough alone, who was now involved in something and way in over her head, sitting in a small police station in an upstate town, Larry Bernard giving me half of his pastrami sandwich and a splash of Diet Coke while he asked me more questions about what I had seen.

In between bites of some of the best pastrami I had ever eaten, I asked the one question I swore I wouldn't. "Do I need a lawyer, Detective Bernard?"

He shrugged. "Meh. What do I know?" he asked,

chomping away on his sandwich. "Do you think you'd feel more comfortable with a lawyer present?" He handed me a napkin and pointed to the side of his mouth. "Mustard."

I dabbed the side of my mouth and, true enough, there was mustard on the napkin. Nice guy, this Larry Bernard. Did they make him in a younger model, one that would attend to my every need and bring me pastrami on rye just when I needed it? "I think I might," I said, realizing that my only option was Arney and, well, he was a pain in the ass as well as a not-so-great lawyer.

"Then you should call a lawyer," he said. "And if you can't afford a lawyer, one will be provided to you."

"Those sound like my Miranda rights," I said.

"Nah," he said, throwing down his crumpled-up napkin. "I just have to tell you stuff like that so that you know . . ."

"My rights," I said. "My Miranda rights."

"Right. Your rights," he said. "Do you have a phone?"

I checked my coat pocket and there was my phone. At least one person knew where I was—Cargan—but instead of calling him and trying to explain what had happened and why I needed a lawyer who was anyone but Arney, I called someone else.

"Hello?"

"Alison? It's Bel." I looked at the detective while I spoke.

"Bel? That was fast. That can't be good."

"It's not," I said. "Hey, do you know a lawyer? A good one?"

"A lawyer?!" Her voice was so loud that the detective moved back from the table.

"Yes. Unfortunately, when I got here," I said, attempt-

ing to sound casual and failing, "well, you'll never believe this, but Tweed had been stabbed." And married
to Amy! I wanted to scream but didn't. I smiled at Larry
Bernard, pointing at the remains of my sandwich and
giving him a thumbs-up.

"That's horrible!" she said. "A lawyer. Yes. I have
one. And he owes me."

I couldn't imagine why a lawyer might owe her something but figured I would ask later, after I had been let
out of the Wooded Lake Police Department's conference room.

"Got a pen?" she asked.

I mouthed, *Pen,* and wrote some doodles in the air;
the detective handed me a pen, a little slippery from
being in his pastrami-covered hands. I wrote down
"Jimmy Crawford" and a phone number. "He's Crawford's brother. Crazy as a loon but a good lawyer. The
best, really. I'll call him and tell him to expect your
call."

"I'm all the way up in Wooded Lake," I said. "And
it's late."

"I was his kid's French tutor for six solid months.
Without me, she'd still be in French One and ordering
beef heart instead of a hamburger during her study
abroad. He won't mind," she said. "And if he does, he'll
never let on to you. Me, maybe. Crawford, for sure. But
not you."

"Thank you, Alison. Really. You're a lifesaver."

"You're the first person who's ever said that," she said
before hanging up.

I waited ten minutes before calling Jimmy Crawford.
In the intervening minutes between my punching his
number into my phone and his picking up, the detective

had produced a brownie, which he cut in half, placing my piece on a napkin and sliding it toward me.

"Is this Belfast McGrath?" Jimmy asked.

"It is."

"Hear you've got a bit of trouble," he said.

"I do."

"Can you keep your mouth shut for about an hour?" he asked. "You're in luck. I'm at some mountain resort with my wife about a half hour away. If I were downstate, you'd be chilling in Wooded Lake all night."

"Guess I'm just lucky," I said.

"Guess you are," he said. "No surprise that you're friends with my sister-in-law. She has a habit of getting arrested, too."

"Really?"

"Well, just once, but she's been in her share of scrapes. You two had better be careful. I'm thinking of retiring soon."

I looked over at the detective, focused on his brownie, pretending not to listen and not doing a very good job of it.

"Thanks. And hurry?" I asked before the phone went dead. I looked at Detective Bernard. "I have a lawyer coming."

He shrugged again, his go-to nonanswer.

"He'll be here soon."

"Huh."

"Tell me, is Tweed going to make it?" I asked. "Live?"

"Hard to know. He lost a lot of blood," he said, looking chagrined.

It hit me then. His hair was shorter now and he wasn't quite as nattily dressed as the first time I had seen him, the first time I had come here. "I know you."

"You really don't," he said.

"You were the man who told me that Love Canyon was a sore subject around here."

"Yep."

I sat back in my chair, let that sink in. "Did you recognize me?" I asked.

He rubbed a hand over his head, pushed back the unruly strands that crisscrossed his pate. "Yes." He leaned forward. "And that's why I need to talk to you a little longer."

"With my lawyer," I said, everything coming together. I was a suspect and not only because I was the only "witness" to the crime. Because I had been here, been seen. Been poking around.

He nodded. "With your lawyer."

CHAPTER Thirty-one

Jimmy Crawford wasn't what I was expecting but was exactly what I needed. He came into the conference room in a whirlwind of expensive cologne, pants dotted with whales, and a pink polo shirt that would have looked more at home in one of the tonier suburbs south of here. He told me where he lived, and there wasn't a home that cost less than a million dollars. Jimmy, as Feeney would say, was clearly a "baller," even if the belly hanging over his fabric belt and the wild mess of black hair belied that fact. He was as loose and feral as his brother was buttoned up and tame.

"Hey, Detective. Any reason why this young woman can't go home?" he asked, pulling out a chair at the conference table and whipping a worn leather briefcase onto the table.

"This young woman is the sole witness to an attempted murder," Detective Bernard said. "I think that's reason enough."

"I didn't witness anything," I said to Jimmy. "I came after the fact."

"A moment with my client, Detective?" Jimmy said.

Larry Bernard left the room, closing the door behind him. Jimmy turned to me. "Tell me everything."

I started at the beginning, years ago when Amy disappeared, and ended up at tonight, a few hours earlier. "That's it."

He studied my face. "When I said 'tell me everything,' I didn't mean literally everything." He wiped his hands across his face. "Wow. That's quite a story."

In spite of his editorializing, it felt good to tell him everything, to reveal the real reason I had come to Wooded Lake again and again.

"And my sister-in-law is helping you?" he asked.

I nodded.

He blessed himself. "God save the queen." He took a moment to think. "So you didn't stab this guy?"

"No!" I said. "I couldn't do something like that. Besides, I liked him. Well, until I found out just how much he had lied to me." What was it about my face that made every eligible man I met want to tell me half-truths or, better yet, no truths?

Jimmy opened the door and called to the detective, who reappeared so quickly that I knew he had been right outside the whole time.

"Case closed," Jimmy said, standing up and offering the detective his hand. "You know where to reach us."

"Actually, I don't," the detective said.

Jimmy whipped a card out of his pant pocket and handed it over. "Here you go. So, I am assuming Ms. McGrath has told you everything she knows and you have asked her every question you wanted, in multiple forms." Jimmy leaned over and smiled at me, whispering, "Not my first rodeo."

"I have, Mr. Crawford," Detective Bernard said. "Haven't gotten much information from her. Hoping she'll remember something that might help us." Bernard smiled. "Not my first rodeo, either, Counselor."

Jimmy smiled but it wasn't friendly. "A good night's sleep, a nice cup of tea in the morning, maybe some eggs, and she'll regroup and call you if she does remember something."

Detective Bernard knew that there was no reason to keep me here, so with a resigned shrug of his shoulders, he stood as well. "Thank you for your time, Ms. McGrath. And please take care of that head wound." He looked at Jimmy. "She refused treatment at the scene, but she has a pretty big bump on her head."

"Yes, she mentioned that," Jimmy said. "So perhaps the person you're looking for is someone who goes around stabbing people and then hitting others on the back of the head."

"Ms. McGrath?" Detective Bernard said before I left the room. "Here are your keys. I took the liberty of having one of our officers drive your car over here. If it were up to me, though, I'd prefer you left it here. I don't think you're in any shape to drive."

"Thank you, Detective," I said, taking the keys.

Outside, the cold air, mixed with fine, icy crystals, hit my face, and with a new wave of nausea hitting me I decided that the detective was right. I looked at Jimmy. "I'll call an Uber."

"To take you back to Foster's Landing?" he said. "No way. Get in."

"But what about your wife? Your getaway?" I asked.

"Don't worry about that," he said. "It's been thirty years. She's used to me by now."

His car was a low-slung, two-door sports car, black and sleek. I lowered myself into the passenger side and sank back into the soft leather seat, closing my eyes. "I can't thank you enough, Jimmy."

He started the car. "Ah, it's nothing. Despite the trouble she gets in, I love my sister-in-law. Would do anything for her."

"Because of the French tutoring?"

He let out a quick snort. "No, not that."

"Then what?"

"For bringing my brother back to life."

He pulled onto the highway and gunned the engine. If he drove this fast all the way, I'd be home in no time.

"You'll send me a bill, right?" I said.

He snorted again. "This is one of my pro bono cases."

"How many do you do a year?" I asked.

"Exactly zero. You'd be my first."

CHAPTER *Thirty-two*

It's hard to be in one's thirties yet still be answering to your parents, both of whom stood in the foyer of the Manor, their repeated texts to me and my cryptic answers only infuriating them more.

"Where were you?" Dad said, enveloping me in a bear hug as Mom stood silently seething behind him. His concern always outweighed his consternation.

At the sound of the front door or Dad's voice, Cargan appeared. His face was its usual inscrutable mask coupled with a glimmer of relief. "Yes, where were you?" he asked.

"I had a date," I said. "It didn't go very well."

Mom and Dad had no idea why I would have gone to Wooded Lake, but Cargan did. He eyed me warily as I told my parents about this nice man I had met and whom I was casually dating—Remember? I wanted to say. He came to the Manor one night?—but who had met a grisly fate. No one knew why. Maybe it had been a burglary gone bad, him interrupting whoever had plans of ransacking his house.

But in my mind, I knew the truth, something I wouldn't voice: This had something to do with Amy, her disappearance, their marriage. It was all there and not at all random.

"They think it was a burglary," I said, touching the back of my head. "I got hit in the head."

At that, Mom rushed forward, lifting my hair off of my neck. "You've got quite a bump there. Let me get some ice. Mal, put on some water for tea."

Left alone with Cargan, I averted my eyes as he studied the space over my head, seething like Mom. "You're in over your head, Bel," he said finally. "You're always in over your head, come to think of it."

"I'm not, Cargan," I said. "I'm this close to finding Amy and I'm not going to stop."

He considered that for a long time, but I was used to my brother's forays into himself, his own fertile mind. "We should tell Kevin. Maybe he can help. Reciprocity with Wooded Lake PD and all."

"I don't know, Cargan," I said. "It's been months and they still don't know who was in Amy's car. Who they actually found."

"That takes time."

"Still, you expect Kevin to be able to help me?" I loved Kevin, as a friend of course, but I had never had much faith in his investigative abilities. I couldn't see how he could help me besides giving me information before the fact, like just who was in that car in the river?

He turned and started up the stairs. "Give it some thought."

Before he got too far, I called out to him, "The license plate? Anything on that?"

"The car belongs to David Southerland. Just like it should."

In the kitchen, I heard the kettle blaring, the water boiling away. I would have a cup of tea and let my mother minister to the bump on my head. I would allow Dad to bluster about how nowhere in the world was safe anymore, and then I would go to my apartment and pull the covers over my head and figure out a cake I could make for Jimmy Crawford to thank him for tonight's bailout and any future bailouts in which he might be involved.

While making tea, my mother had made some kind of poultice that she put in a big piece of cheesecloth, poultices and cheesecloths two things that don't really exist in the modern world but which for us were commonplace. I took a few sips of my tea and held the wrap against the back of my head, feeling better instantly, whether from the poultice or the tea I couldn't be sure.

"Thanks, Mom," I said.

"I don't like the sound of this new guy," Dad said. "Sounds like he has enemies."

"It was a burglary," I said. "A burglary gone bad."

"I've never heard of such a thing," Dad said.

Mom let out a jaded laugh. "Sure you have, Mal. Horrible things like this happen all the time." She leaned on the counter and looked at him, her eyebrows raised. "And sometimes they happen here, if you recall."

Dad shook his head as if to dispel the memories of two deaths at the Manor since I returned home. "Belfast, stick to Foster's Landing. Stick to the Manor. Stick close to us," he said, and I saw real fear in his eyes, the thought that I could have been part of something much more deadly written on his lined face.

I felt my shoulders droop and could see that Dad took that as a sign that I was acquiescing. He didn't know that it was just exhaustion coupled with the knowledge that in between preparing for weddings and pretending I was focused on work and family, I was heading up north first chance I got to figure this out, once and for all.

The lie fell easily from my lips. "I will, Dad. I promise."

CHAPTER Thirty-three

Kevin agreed to meet me for breakfast the next morning. There was one authentic Greek diner in town that had been here since before I was born, and while the prices went up steadily every year, one thing remained the same: The food was good but the coffee tasted like windshield-wiper fluid. The place was special to us, though, because back in high school, when we weren't hanging around Amy's father's bar, we were here, eating pancakes and eggs and, if we had gotten paid from our part-time jobs, the occasional greasy cheeseburger. I fingered the laminated menu and thought about how far my culinary horizons had expanded.

Kevin came in, dressed for work in his usual sport coat, khaki pants, and lace-up shoes, a regular gumshoe's outfit, the outline of his little notebook, the one he carried everywhere, in his shirt breast pocket. "Did you order?" he asked. "Sorry I'm late."

"No problem," I said. "And no, I didn't order. You know I like to wait to see what everyone else is having before I commit."

"Right," he said. "I had forgotten that." He looked at the menu and then up at the waitress when she stopped by the table; if I remembered correctly, she was the same waitress who had been here since I was a kid, and the thought of that made me both happy and sad at the same time. "Coffee, Swiss-cheese omelet, rye toast."

I closed my menu. "Make that two," I said. When she walked away, I said, "See? Same as it ever was."

"Hey, where's your brother?" he asked casually.

"Which one?"

He smirked. "Okay, Bel, you know which one. Feeney."

"Not a clue," I said. He had been asleep on my couch when I left and I expected he was still there.

"If you hear from him, will you let him know that I need to talk to him?"

"I'm pretty sure he knows that," I said. "And no, I won't tell him."

"Blood running thicker than water and all that?"

"Yep," I said. "And all that."

"You don't want an aiding-and-abetting charge."

"You're right. I don't."

He could see that he was getting nowhere. "You have two choices, then. You can have Feeney turn himself in or you can convince Brendan Joyce to drop the charges."

Two unlikely, if not impossible, scenarios.

That subject out of the way, he pulled over the little ceramic holder of sugar packets and shook a few in preparation for his coffee. "So to what do I owe this pleasure?" he said, quickly revising, "I mean, honor?"

"Just a catch-up," I said. "I know you'll be at the party at the Manor next week, but I'll be working, so we won't have a chance to talk."

"Yeah, the big party," he said. "Should be a good time."

"We'll make sure of that," I said. The waitress

dropped off our coffees and we focused on those for a few minutes. "Listen, Kevin . . ."

"I hate sentences that start with 'Listen,' " he said. "That usually precedes some kind of bad news. A negative statement." He smiled. "A breakup."

That last one was a little out of left field, but I let it go. "It's been over two months. Do they know who it was? Who was in Amy's car?"

His face fell at the realization that this wasn't really a social call, two friends catching up.

"I'm sorry," I said. "I just want to know."

"We still don't have a positive ID, but we're thinking that it may be a girl who disappeared from that town up the river, you know, the same day that Amy did. It just seems too coincidental," he said.

"I guess," I said. "But it could be anyone, right?"

"Sure. Tests aren't back yet, so nothing is conclusive." He sipped his coffee. "Obviously."

"Obviously," I said.

"Why are you asking?"

"I don't know. It was just on my mind and I thought I'd ask you."

He leaned across the table. "Bel, I know you better than that. You don't ask random questions."

"Sometimes I do."

"Never." He pushed his coffee toward the center of the table, pulled it back. "What's going on?"

"Listen . . ."

"Oh, there you go again," he said.

I leaned in close, brought my voice down to a whisper. "I think Amy is still alive."

The coffee in his hand made an arc across my head, splashing hot liquid on my neck and landing on the floor beside me. At the same moment, Mary Ann slid onto the bench next to Kevin, having successfully sidestepped the mess that he had made. She kissed his cheek, nonplussed by the flying coffee cup. "What's going on?" she asked. "Coffee too hot?"

Kevin ran a shaky hand over his forehead. "Yes. Scalding."

A busboy scurried over and cleaned up the spill.

"I'm sorry, man," Kevin said. "And I'll take another one when you get a chance."

"Hey, Bel," Mary Ann said. "How is everything? Flying coffee cups aside?"

I didn't tell her, or him, anything, and just went with "fine." The last thing I needed this model of perfection in front of me knowing was that I was involved in something way bigger than I should, with a giant bump at the nape of my neck to prove it. Thank God for long, unruly curls to cover the injury.

"Do you need any more information from me regarding the party?" she asked. "Dad has been all over me to make this the 'best one ever.'" The waitress placed a paper bag in front of Mary Ann, a check stapled to it. "I don't know why it's so important to him, but it is."

"Everything is set, Mary Ann. Don't worry about a thing," I said.

"The holiday decorations? The lights?" she asked. "All good?"

"The best," I said. "If you haven't seen the Manor at Christmas, you're really missing out. We're getting ready to put the lights on the trees that go down to the river."

"I will this year," she said, pulling the bill off of her take-out order. "Honey, I'll see you later," she said, kissing Kevin full on the mouth, taking him by surprise, his anxiety over my revelation still the only thing on his mind. "Bye, Bel. Have a good day!" she said, scampering off, the sound of her rubber-soled nursing clogs mixing with the din of silverware scraping plates, cups clattering onto saucers.

Kevin's face was ashen, his look confused yet horrified. "I thought you'd be happy," I said. "About Amy."

"I . . . I-I am," he said, his stammer belying the statement. "What makes you think she's alive?"

I ran through the various aspects of my amateur investigation.

"Who's Alison?" he asked at one point in the story, stopping me from going any further.

"A potential Manor client."

"A bride?"

"A bride's stepmother."

"That makes even less sense."

"It doesn't matter who she is," I said. "Just follow the story." As I finished the tale, ending with the night before, his face regained some color, but it was a deep flush rather than a normal hue. "What's wrong?"

"Nothing," he said. "It's just that you've put yourself in so much danger. In harm's way. For Amy."

"Right. For Amy," I said.

He gazed at a spot in the distance, a place over my head and out the window but, if I was reading him correctly, gazing at a point in time that was long gone. "You always had such a blind devotion, Bel. You always thought she was much, much better than she really was." He stayed where he was for a few more seconds before returning his attention to me, to the present. "She betrayed you. You forget that."

"No," I said. "I'll never forget that. But we were young, and anyway, if you recall, so did you. Betray me, that is."

He regrouped, changed his tune. "It was just a kiss," he said, but right there on his face was the fact that it wasn't just a kiss; it had been much more.

It didn't matter what had happened, but it did matter how he had felt at the time. So that close bond that I thought we had, that I had almost given up my true self for, had been all in my mind. As with Brendan Joyce, it had never been about me; it had always been about her.

He pulled out his notebook, casually writing down a few notes. "What did you say those names were? The people up at the *Hudson Courier*? In Wooded Lake?"

"I didn't," I said, digging into my purse and throwing a twenty on the table. I slid out of the seat, my mind going in a million different directions but landing on one thought, a memory that I had suppressed for the last couple of months, not wanting to believe he had been standing in the middle of the Foster's Landing River, the water gone and the earth below cracked and barren, looking out toward the spot where we had found Amy's car.

But he had. He had been standing there a long time, and while I wondered then why he would, I was starting to think I now knew.

CHAPTER Thirty-four

When I got home, I put together a list of things I knew and things I didn't know. Feeney was still asleep on the couch, now seemingly a permanent fixture in my home.

I knew that Archie Peterson was in Wooded Lake and that Tweed had lied to me about that. Estranged, my ass.

I knew that Amy had married two men in the span of fifteen years—Tweed first and then Dave Southerland— and again, Tweed had lied to me about that.

I knew that Kevin loved Mary Ann D'Amato but at one time had loved Amy, too, just like Brendan had and Cargan as well, even though he would never reveal anything of the sort to me. There was no talk of love in the McGrath family; you just had to assume it was there.

I knew I could only trust a few people, and they were a disparate, ragtag group that consisted of the guy on my couch (who now owed me big-time), Cargan, and Alison Bergeron. I couldn't think of anyone else with whom I could trust the information that either I had been given or I had learned over the last several days. There was a lot outside of my control, but there was maybe one thing I could control, could change for the better, and Feeney's loud snoring reminded me what that might be.

I texted Brendan Joyce and asked if he was available for lunch, saying that I had something to talk to him about.

His response was immediate and positive, suggesting a quick sandwich at a local place that would ensure he could get back to school for his afternoon classes. I guess he was naïve enough to think that this was a step in the right direction for our relationship, and I felt a pang of guilt that my intentions weren't pure. This was about Feeney. Not us.

There was no "us" anymore and he was going to have to get used to that.

I went over to the Manor, where I found Mom and Dad huddled together in the office, Mom in a formfitting one-piece catsuit that a woman half her age would have trouble pulling off, but when you're a Pilates-practicing denizen of a small Hudson-river town, I guess you can wear anything you like. That woman had muscles on top of muscles. As I often did when she was decked out in a skintight getup, I sucked in my stomach, even though my flesh was hidden beneath a long turtleneck sweater with a leather bomber jacket on top of it.

Dad jumped up when I arrived. "Belfast, how's the head?" he said, pointing at his own as if I had forgotten just where my own head was.

"It's okay, Dad. Thanks for asking," I said.

"And how are you?" he asked, giving me the once-over.

I mumbled something noncommittal. He was going to get more out of me; it was just a matter of when and how. He had his ways.

"Out for breakfast?" Mom asked, ignoring the fact that there was lot unsaid in this conversation.

"Yeah," I said. "I wanted to touch base with Kevin about the party."

"Any new developments?" Dad asked. "I've told Lieutenant D'Amato no fewer than eighty-five times that we'll be finished decorating by the time the party rolls around."

I had convinced his daughter of the same thing not an hour before. It hadn't occurred to me to ask Kevin about Mary Ann's sudden appearance, if she knew we were together and decided to drop by or if her showing up was as big a surprise to him as it was to me.

"I'm going to work in the kitchen and then I'll be out running errands," I said. "Talk to you later."

As I turned to leave, I saw Mom grab a hunk of Dad's muffin top and squeeze it; that was a bad sign. Old guy would be on one of those Pilates contraptions faster than he could say "plank."

In the kitchen, I took off my jacket and threw on a clean apron, wondering just what I would do with the intervening hours until I had to meet Brendan. Craft Feeney's apology, one that he would never give? Beg for his forgiveness of my brother's rashness? Or hit it straight: Feeney's crazy and so are the rest of them. Take some pity on me, please.

You owe me: You're the one who broke my heart and not the other way around.

In the end, as I walked into the sandwich shop where we agreed to meet, I decided to play it straight. I asked him outright, the look on his face showing that this was not what he was expecting.

Before I had arrived, I had stopped at the bank and taken out a thousand dollars, more than enough, I was sure, to cover the damage. I pushed an envelope across the table like we were engaged in illicit activity, resting my hand on top of it.

"Are you trying to bribe me, Bel?" he asked, aghast.

"Bribe you?"

"Yes. Bribe me. With money."

"Well, I sure ain't bribing you with sex," I said, not getting the uproarious response that I was expecting; his face remained a mixture of confusion and hurt. "It's not a bribe. It's the money to cover the damage."

"I had to have my windshield replaced," he said.

"Which is free if you have insurance." I had seen the commercials; no one paid for a new windshield these days.

"And the rest of the car detailed because some of that . . . stuff . . ."

"It's called schmaltz," I said. "Well, technically schmaltz is chicken fat and this was duck fat so it's not really schmaltz. . . ."

He held up a hand. "Bel. Stop." He pushed the remains of his sandwich, one bite taken, into its wrapping and crushed it, his appetite gone. "I used to find you hilarious. The funniest girl I had ever met. But now, you're just insulting me." He couldn't look at me. "So, just stop."

I closed my mouth, my lips tight together.

"I will drop the charges against Feeney," he said. "Deep in my heart, there is a place where I find what he did admirable, protecting his baby sister against a horrible guy like me."

"You're not horrible, Brendan," I said.

"I know I'm not," he said. "But that's what Feeney thinks. That's what they all think." He looked at me, forlorn. "I would appreciate it if you could disabuse your clan of my wrongdoing, even if you don't believe what I told you. I've said it once and I'll say it again: That photo was never mine and I never put it there."

I had heard this story before and I had been too hurt to believe it. Something about his look and demeanor today, though, was swaying me a bit, and while it might have been the familiar smell of his body wash—Jungle Prince, a scent made for middle schoolers that he just couldn't get enough of—or the way his tie was just slightly askew, as if he still couldn't figure out how to tie it himself, or his acknowledgment that my brother's heart was in the right place, I started to thaw just a little bit inside.

And he could see it.

"Yes, I'll drop the charges, Bel. Just tell them the truth. Tell them that I haven't given Amy another thought since that day she disappeared, that I would never betray you in that way." He shook his head. "I would never be with you if I loved her. Even after all these years." He turned his head to the side, unable to look at me. "Never."

"Hey, Mr. Joyce!" some kids called as they grabbed their sandwiches and exited the sandwich shop.

"Hi, Brody. Carl," he said. "See you in a few minutes."

"That your girlfriend, Mr. Joyce?" another kid asked, a cheeky girl in a "Nasty Woman" sweatshirt. It was the onset of winter and yet not one of the little ragamuffins wore a coat. I remembered those days.

"Shouldn't you be working on your self-portrait, Celine, instead of questioning me about my personal life?" Brendan asked, a big smile on his face. When the kids were gone, he answered her question, looking at me with those blue eyes that I used to love looking back at. "She used to be. My girl, that is."

He stood up, pushing the remains of his sandwich into the garbage bin by the door. We walked out to the sidewalk, teeming with students going to and from their lunch destinations and back to the high school again, a loud, boisterous throng jockeying back and forth, bumping into one another and us, the smell of pizza and Chinese food and deli meats wafting through the air. One of Brendan's colleagues passed by, Mr. Malloy, the guy who coached swim team when I was in high school.

"Hey, Belfast," Mr. Malloy said. "Hey, Brendan."

"Dan," Brendan said. He looked at me. "Coach here says that we have a potential record breaker in the one-hundred-meter fly."

"Impressive," I said. "I was a freestyle girl myself. A little backstroke. Never could get the rhythm of the fly."

"And we tried, right, Bel?" the coach said. "It's a tough stroke."

"The toughest," I said.

"So what brings you two here? Into the middle of the lunchtime fray?" he asked.

Brendan pointed at the sandwich shop. "Sandwiches," he said, as if it were obvious.

"Right! Sandwiches," he said.

When it was clear there was nothing else to say, that he had interrupted a tense encounter, the coach waved as he walked off. "Gotta go. See you at school, Brendan."

"Poor guy," I said. "Doesn't know what he walked into."

"He's a nice guy," Brendan said. "Bit of a ball buster these days. Not as cool as he used to be. Swim team is doing well, though."

"I had him for PE," I said. "Nearly failed me because I forgot my sneakers."

"For one day?" Brendan asked, incredulous.

"Well, it was actually two months." My mother had threatened to tie my shoes around my neck after getting my progress report that semester.

Brendan repeated his promise. "I will drop the charges, Bel," he said. "But there's one thing?"

I wasn't sure I would like what I would be agreeing to, but familial loyalty always won out, to the detriment of my own personal emotional health. It was the way of the McGraths.

"Sure. What is it?" I asked.

"You have to believe me."

CHAPTER Thirty-five

I waited for the official word from Kevin, who must have had a bit of an idea that I was involved in Brendan's decision, on the dropped charges before I sent Feeney on his way. The money that I gave Brendan couldn't have covered all the damage, but the next morning when I went down the stairs behind my apartment to the parking pad below, the envelope was tucked under the windshield wiper, all of the bills still intact, a note from Brendan asking if we could try "this" one more time, "this," I imagined, being our relationship, the whole falling-in-love-all-over again thing. I was nothing if not stubborn; the blood of a thousand intractable Celts ran through my veins and it was a hard habit to break, being the one who held fast and stern in the face of the obvious.

In this case, it was that the guy loved me and hadn't lied. But that raised a larger question: Who put that photo in his wallet? It wasn't something even one of my squirrelly brothers would do as a joke; they weren't that cruel. So who was? Who was cruel enough to make it seem like he had carried a torch for my best friend all of these years, just to break us up? I didn't think it was the French teacher at the high school, but who knew? Maybe she had a vindictive streak. Eligible bachelors weren't a dime a dozen in this town; rather, they were like unicorns: rarely seen and maybe nonexistent. He was back on the market now at least, but it seemed his mind was elsewhere, still on someone else.

Me.

Feeney's belongings were everywhere in my apartment: a comb that went straight into the garbage can and a toothbrush that looked as if it were suitable for cleaning grout and nothing else. I was bagging up the trash at the end of the day when my cell phone rang; it was Alison Bergeron.

"How are we feeling today?" she asked. "Oh, and you'd be proud of me! I'm making chicken soup."

"Good for you!" I said.

"But it's got a ton of fat on the top. What do I do with that?" she asked.

You don't use it to vandalize your sister's ex-boyfriend's car, I thought, but I went with the straight answer. "Cool the soup down, put it in the fridge, and then skim the fat off the top."

"That makes sense," she said. "How's the head?"

With all that had gone on for the last twenty-four hours, I hadn't even thought of my head. I touched the lump at the back of my neck; yep, still there. "Head's okay. Heart, not so much."

"Uh-oh."

I told her the whole story about Brendan. When I was done, she started talking immediately. "Went through something similar with Crawford. I was stupid. Don't be so stubborn that you can't let this go, Bel. The guy sounds like a complete doll and why would he lie about this? He wants you back."

"Sure seems that way."

"Think about that."

I did. She was right.

"Did you tell him about Amy?" she asked.

"I didn't."

"You going to?"

"I'm not sure," I said. "If this does come together again, I may. But I'm going to take it slow." I put her on speaker while I tied up the garbage. "You've been there since the beginning. You just didn't know it. That night at The Monkey's Paw. That was the night my engagement ended and a part of my life as well."

"Hey, if anyone knows heartache, it's me," she said. "But I'm here to tell you that there are good ones out there and they should be found. And once they're found, they will never leave you." She laughed. "Heck, next thing you know you'll be at birthday parties at trampoline parks with little ones."

"Let's not get ahead of ourselves," I said.

"Why do you think I'm making this soup?" she asked. "I'm also going to try to bake bread. Make it up to the poor guy." She let out a long sigh. "What in the hell is happening to me? I used to have a refrigerator that held a jar of olives and a bottle of vodka."

"Times change," I said. "We change."

"Wow. Far out, sister. Don't get all existential on me now."

"I won't," I said, picking up the garbage and lugging it to the back door. "Talk to you soon."

I opened the back door and was surprised to see

Larry Bernard from Wooded Lake standing there, the sight of him making me gasp.

"Most women just say 'ugh' when they see me," he said. "Gasping out loud? Now that's a new one."

I opened the screen door and let him in. "Do I need my lawyer?" I asked.

"You do not," he said. "This is a friendly chat."

How could that be when I was the witness to an attempted murder—or the aftermath of one—and he was a cop? His Jewish-mensch-Columbo thing may have been an act and may have been designed to put me off my game, but he didn't seem like he had an agenda beyond figuring out what happened to Tweed and why.

"I was going to call you," I said, that thought floating into my mind as I had struggled to consciousness that morning. "I wanted to find out how Tweed was." I had hesitated making contact with anyone associated with what had happened; it all fell into an area in which I had never traveled, violence and harm the signposts I could see and wanted to avoid.

"Poor guy," he said. "He had surgery to repair a punctured lung and hasn't been conscious since."

"Is he going to make it?" I asked, the same question from the other night.

"My brother Saul is the doctor. I'm just the cop," he said. He smiled. "I couldn't tell you, Ms. McGrath. It's hard to know."

"Would you like a cup of tea?" I asked. Tea in an Irish family is the go-to refreshment. Before five o'clock anyway. Despite the hour, it didn't feel appropriate to offer him a drink, and my alcohol stash was depleted after Feeney's stay. I didn't wait for his answer, putting the kettle on and taking two mugs down from the cabinet next to the stove.

"More of a coffee guy myself," he said. "But I'll try this tea you seem to have an affinity for."

"It's the Irish in me, Detective. We love our tea."

"The Jews, we're not about the tea," he said. "But when in Rome . . ."

He went to the front window of my apartment and pushed the curtains to the side. "This is quite a place you have here, this Shamrock Manor. Sounds hokey, but it's much more beautiful than the name would suggest."

"Yes, my father picked the name. Thought it sounded like a piece of the old country. I'm with you: I think it sounds hokey."

"But everyone knows it by that name now, so too late to change it."

"Yes," I said, dropping a tea bag into each mug. "Sugar?"

He shook his head.

"Anyone who comes here with a preconceived notion of what it should look like is blown away when they actually see it," I said.

"Speaking of preconceived notions . . ."

The kettle began to blare. I poured water into both mugs and steeped the tea until it was the color I liked. I carried them into the living room and placed them on my old, scarred coffee table, a table better suited to a suite of college-aged boys than an adult woman with an actual job. Those sorts of thing didn't matter to me, though; I would much rather have a four-hundred-dollar cleaver than a coffee table that suited my stature in life.

"Yes?" I asked, sitting down in a chair next to the couch.

"I assumed when I found you out at Mr. Blazer's house that you knew more than you were letting on," he said, immediately contradicting his assertion that I didn't need a lawyer. This wasn't a friendly visit at all; why would it have been? I didn't think this older Jewish detective was interested in Shamrock Manor for his daughter's wedding or grandson's bar mitzvah. No, he was only interested in finding out what had happened that night.

I didn't answer, letting those thoughts play out all over my face.

"I can see you're suspicious," he said. "You should be. But I can help you, too."

"You can?" I asked. "How?"

"I did a little digging, Ms. McGrath. I know you're looking for someone."

"You do?"

He nodded. "I do. Wooded Lake is a small town. And I've lived there all my life." He let out a small chuckle. "Right, I can tell you're wondering. What's a nice Jewish boy doing in a place like that?" He took a sip of his tea, grimaced. Not to his liking. "Well, that's a story in itself."

"I'd love to hear it," I said, buying time in my head, thinking about how much I wanted to tell him about my visits to his hometown.

"Communists," he said.

"Who?"

"My parents. My whole family, really. My father was a screenwriter for MGM in the fifties." He rattled off a few films that I had heard of but never seen, films that any casual moviegoer would know of but that only a true cinephile would have taken the time to view. "We left the West Coast to protect him, so that he couldn't be found. Ended up in Wooded Lake." He pulled off his glasses, wiped the steam from his mug of tea that had gathered on the right lens on his sweater. "It was as good a place as any."

"That's quite a story," I said.

"It is. Name used to be Goldschmidt. First name, Leonid." He put the tea on the coffee table, placing it carefully on the one coaster that I owned. "Kind of like you. Belfast. It's a dead giveaway for our parents' sympathies."

"And now you're Larry Bernard."

"Since 1952. Had a renaming ceremony and all. I was three. Don't remember a thing about it but I'm sure there was a nice kiddush afterwards."

If he was trying to disarm me, he was doing a pretty good job with talk of Communists and post-renaming-ceremony feasts.

"So that's my story, Ms. McGrath. Belfast," he said, testing out whether or not we were on a first-name basis. "I know you know from heartache. I also know that you lost a friend a long time ago."

"You're a good detective, Larry," I said.

"I am," he said. "Years of practice."

"Amy Mitchell. She was my best friend," I said. "And she disappeared."

"And she reappeared in Wooded Lake," he said.

"I just found that out. Married two different men, one of them Tweed. Went by the name Bess Marvin."

He wrinkled his nose. "Why do I know that name?"

"You have kids, Detective? A daughter perchance?"

"Yep. Three girls."

"Do they like to read?" I asked.

It dawned on him slowly. "Used to read those Nancy Drews to the oldest. Bess was the plump sidekick."

"Bingo."

"This Amy has a sense of humor. As well as a couple of ex-husbands."

"I just learned that the other night." I braced myself for the answer to the next question. "You know Tweed. Did you know her?"

"I didn't," he said. "I knew of her because of course I've known Tweed since he was a little boy, but she was on the scene and then she was off. Not sure what happened there. It was a quickie wedding and even a more quickie divorce, it would seem. Would have been impolite to ask what happened, so I didn't."

"So you're a gentleman and a detective," I said.

"I'd like to think that. Sometimes being a gentleman goes out the window when you're trying to get to the truth."

"I haven't seen her, Larry, since that night when we were teenagers. Honestly, I thought she was dead all these years and was trying to make my peace with that."

"That must have been hard," he said.

I noticed that he hadn't touched his tea since that first, probably awful, sip. I was used to drinking tea, had started when I was a child. But if it wasn't your beverage of choice, it took some getting used to. He was a kind man; I could tell. I felt bad for not having coffee in the house. Whether my sympathy toward him was part of a calculated move on his part of just because he seemed to be such a kind guy I couldn't tell. I could tell, though, that he was shrewd and smart and it didn't hurt to have him on my side.

"Now that you know my whole story, do you have any other questions?" I asked. "You must want to know something else."

"I do," he said. "I want to know where she is, too."

CHAPTER *Thirty-six*

Everyone was a suspect.

Even me, I was sure.

And now so was Amy.

Larry Bernard didn't have any answers—at least any that he would share with me—about why Amy would suddenly want Tweed Blazer gone, but knowing what he knew about her and her disappearance from Foster's Landing, and hearing my story about her, what she was like, he had moved her to the top of the list of suspects. She was a woman who wanted to stay gone and the fact that I was poking around, had learned a thing or two about her whereabouts, was making her desperate. That seemed to be Larry Bernard's thought process, as far as I could surmise.

The one thing that didn't make any sense was how she knew. Was it that she, too, had seen the *Hudson Courier*? Knew that I had seen it? Knew that I would try to find her?

She couldn't know those things. There was no way. Maybe, like Feeney, she was hiding in plain sight and could see my every move, knew that I was in the mix now.

Knew that I would stop at nothing to find her.

I sat on my bed; I had hit a dead end. Sure, Larry Bernard was a kindly old guy, the kind of guy who, if he wasn't a cop, you'd confess everything to because behind those eyes was a world of sage advice, of wise counsel just waiting to be dispensed. And lord knows, I was in need of some wise counsel right about now.

I was in a deep reverie when Cargan appeared in the door of my bedroom. "Don't you have some cooking to do or something?" he asked.

"That cop from Wooded Lake was just here. Had some more questions," I said.

"What kinds of questions?"

"Questions about Amy."

Cargan took that in, not at all surprised, though. "So does the detective know everything?"

"I told him what happened, from the beginning. Now she's a suspect. That I know."

"Did you ask him why?" Cargan said.

"I did and he wouldn't say much." I came out of the bedroom and picked up the two mugs of cold tea that sat on the coffee table.

"Amy was always smart, Bel. And shrewd in a way that teenagers shouldn't be. There's a lot more to this story and I'm not sure you should go any further with it," he said. More wise counsel.

Not that I would take it.

He was tense, refusing to sit down in his favorite spot on my well-worn Ikea sofa, the one that was held together with duct tape and string on one corner because this particular piece of furniture hadn't come with all of its requisite nuts and bolts. "I do have one piece of news, though."

After his insinuation that this entire investigation was

over, at least where I was concerned, I wasn't expecting
anything else related to Amy. "Did my tenderloin finally
show up?" I asked, my beef vendor having a spotty delivery record.

"No," he said. "I heard something."

Cargan's inscrutability, his inability to get to the point
in any reasonable, timely fashion, had been a point of
contention between us for years. "Cargan, you're driving me crazy." I came back into the living room. "What
is it?"

"I was out last night. For a bit. At The Dugout."

"And?"

"I ran into Jed Mitchell." Amy's brother and I had a
very tense relationship stemming from a few incidents.
One involved his bar-owning father and his accidental
shooting of Cargan a few months earlier and the other
was related to Jed's matrimonial strife stemming from
his relationship with a girl who had worked here for
years. I didn't know how I had been given the blame for
both of these acts of violence and betrayal, but Jed carried a real grudge against me, thinking that my return to
the Landing had wrought all of this pain and hardship.
Wrong. It was his screwed-up family, which was screwed
up long before Amy left. I knew the stories about the
Mitchell family, how Oogie, the sole proprietor and
owner of The Dugout, had a slippery moral code and
maybe more than one or two screws loose, and how
Amy's mother turned a blind eye to her own husband's
dalliances. Amy had triumphed in spite of a family low
on emotional and maybe intellectual intelligence, the
bright star among a family of misanthropes, Jed sometimes included.

He was a cop in town now and newly single, thanks to his wife's own departure with their kids, and he lived above the bar that his father had founded.

"Does he actually talk to you?" I asked. "Because he hates me, for some reason."

"For some reason?" Cargan asked. "I think we know the reasons."

I rolled my eyes. "I feel as if I was collateral damage in all of that."

"Do you really want to be friends with Jed Mitchell?" Cargan asked.

All of a sudden, and without warning, I had lost the thread of the conversation, something that wasn't hard to do where my brother was concerned. "Wait. Let's back up. You went to The Dugout. You saw Jed Mitchell. You heard something." I waited, but he didn't answer. "What was it?"

"They know who was in Amy's car," he said.

CHAPTER *Thirty-seven*

Kevin was right: It was a girl from up the river just a ways who had disappeared the same night as Amy. But why she had been found in Amy's car and who she was to us was still a mystery. I had never heard of her and googling her disappearance, complete with photo, could say with certainty that I had never seen her, either. Her name had been Kelly and she had looked a lot like Amy.

A new wave of sadness came over me when I realized that there was another family out there who had been missing their daughter for as long as we all had been missing Amy. I wondered, in the midst of what was now their dulled grief, if there was any measure of comfort in knowing where she had been, how she had been encased in a watery tomb for all these years. Or was the grief still knife sharp and piercing, this revelation just succeeding in making it more acute, if that was even possible?

The news, despite my not knowing this girl, took my breath away, making the mystery of that evening more complicated. The things I had been certain of once—that Amy was gone and that she was dead—were things I only thought I knew and now everything was new again, just another piece of a complex puzzle.

I had been keeping what I knew close to my heart since I had found out that Amy was alive, but the time for secret keeping was over. Cargan was right behind me as I grabbed my keys, leaving my purse behind, and got into my car, him barely able to secure a hold on the passenger-side door as I started to drive away, jumping into the seat, one foot dragging along the gravel path in front of the Manor. I drove straight to the police station, not a word spoken between us, and parked the car illegally before going inside and striding over to Jed Mitchell's desk, where he sat, a cup of coffee in front of him, the steam rising in curly tendrils. Amy's brother was intent on his work when I walked through the front door, something taking his whole attention.

Of course I had seen Jed throughout the years, more so in the months since I had been home, but I had never really looked at him closely, taken in his face. Though he had been handsome and athletic back in the day, the years had taken their toll, deep lines around his eyes and mouth, once a smoker's mouth, but no longer. The nicotine gum on his desk was a testament to that. He looked up when I arrived, wariness turning to confusion turning to our old bond, our friend: resentment. "Bel McGrath," he said. "To what do I owe this distinct non-pleasure?"

"She's alive, Jed," I said. "Amy is alive." I could tell by his reaction to that news that Kevin hadn't told him about our conversation at the diner and I wondered about that.

There were a few people in the station house that morning, including Kevin, who emerged from Lieutenant D'Amato's office looking uneasy at my presence.

"Bel?" he asked.

Jed stood up. "If this is another one of your . . ." He searched for the right word before settling on, ". . . disruptions, you have to go. Please. I can't take one more thing from you, Bel."

"It's not a disruption," I said.

"That's not even the right word," Cargan chimed in.

"It's the truth, Jed. I know for a fact that she left here, went to Wooded Lake, and then disappeared from there again." I pushed him out of the way and sat at his computer, pulling up the story from the *Hudson Courier,* which, oddly enough, existed online, despite the fact that the newspaper was a mom-and-son operation. I moved to the side and brought him closer, pointing at the photo of Amy.

He stared at it closely, his breath leaving little wet marks on the monitor. Finally, he stood back and looked at me. "That could be anyone," he said, defiance in his voice.

"Then why are you crying?" Cargan asked.

Jed straightened up and turned toward the long bank of windows that ran along the western wall of the station. He put his hands in his pockets and stared out the window for a long time, the station having gone silent as if in respectful mourning for this broken man and the sadness he had carried, along with many of us, for years. He coughed loudly, clearing his throat, turning back around. "Let's go," he said. "Outside."

I had been wrong; he hadn't quit smoking. Once in the parking lot, he pulled a pack of cigarettes from his pocket and lit up, but not before proffering the pack to me and my brother, an offer we both declined. "Tell me everything."

I went through the story: the commune, the two marriages, the bad feelings she left behind. The Coffee Pot. Dave Southerland. Tweed Blazer.

"You're making that up," he said.

"Which part?" I asked, happy to be out in the sunshine, away from the prying eyes of the other officers and the smattering of staff in the station.

"Tweed Blazer?" he asked. "What kind of name is that? Who does that to a kid?"

"Some pot-smoking, commune-loving hippie," Cargan said.

I looked at Cargan. "Hey, 1950, we need our adjectives back."

"And this Tweed guy is in a coma?" Jed asked.

"He is," I said. "I didn't see anything that night and whoever did that to him hit me over the head and knocked me out, too. I can't even remember what I did remember, if that makes any sense."

"Nope," Jed said. "It makes no sense at all. And the cop's name up there? In Wooded Lake?"

"Larry Bernard."

He took a deep drag off of the cigarette and looked up at the blue sky, still vivid in the winter light. "She's alive," he said to no one, shaking his head. "You know we ID'd that girl? The one in the car?" He looked at Cargan. "I guess that's something you couldn't keep to yourself."

"Wouldn't want to. It confirms what we know about Amy."

That seemed to bring up another emotion in Jed, something none of us had considered. "She'll be a suspect. In that girl's death."

In bed that night, the day having washed over me like a sooty, dirty rain, I thought about those words and the ones we didn't speak.

She'll be a suspect.

Because she may have killed that girl.

And that would certainly explain why she left.

CHAPTER *Thirty-eight*

It seemed only fair to tell Brendan Joyce the identity of the girl in the car. After all, he had been with me that day when the car had been discovered, the drought dredging it to the surface of our small river, his first betrayal being that he had left me there by myself, too scared to confront what it was or why. We had worked that out, sort of, and then the photo had turned up.

We had made a deal, though, and that was that I would believe him in return for him letting Feeney go free to do whatever it was that my brother did in his spare time. I didn't really want to know, Feeney's life a mystery I wasn't interested in solving.

I met Brendan the next evening at a small pub in the next town. He was already sitting at a table, nursing a beer, when I arrived my customary five minutes behind schedule. "Some things never change," I said, sliding into the chair across from him.

"And what's that?" he said.

"You're early and I'm right on time," I said, smiling.

"You're actually late," he said, his brogue all of a sudden sounding like music to my ears, a soft and gentle lilt that took me back to all of the reasons I had fallen for him in the first place. A waitress dropped a glass of wine in front of me. "It's a Malbec," he said. "Your favorite, right?"

I laughed. "Well, one of them."

"Will it do?" he asked.

"It will," I said, and took a sip. "Hey, you sprung for the expensive one."

"I did," he said. "There was only a fifty-cent difference and I figured why not? You're worth it."

The light banter felt good. Normal. I took another sip of wine before saying, "I have a lot to tell you."

He leaned in, his elbows on the table, his hands around his pint glass.

"They know who was in Amy's car." I filled him in on what I knew. "And I think—actually I pretty much know—that Amy is still alive."

His face paled, his hands tightening around the pint glass. I had discovered that everyone had a different reaction to Amy's photo and her potential existence in the world. His was not out of the norm, based on what I had seen from others, but it was curious nonetheless because it made him uncomfortable.

"It's a long story as to how I know and I won't bore you with the details. . . ."

"Oh, please. Bore me," he said.

I told him about the *Hudson Courier* and Tweed Blazer, a revelation that made his face go dark, his eyes narrow. I had nothing to hide and nothing to be ashamed of and continued with the story until I got to the present day, to the part where I let Jed Mitchell know about his sister and how we were going to find her, once and for all.

"So this Tweed guy—" he started before I cut him off.

"That's your concern in all of this? The one thing that you want to know more about?" I asked.

"Well, no," he said. "If you had let me finish, I was going to ask how he was, if he was going to survive."

"Nice cover, but no you weren't," I said. "And to answer your fake question, I don't know. He had surgery and I haven't heard anything else about him. I have to keep my distance for now. I'm not entirely sure that I'm not a true suspect in this."

"I'm sorry, Bel," he said. "It is all awful. Too awful."

A few inches separated us, but there was still some distance. We sat in silence across from each other, studying anything but each other's faces. Finally, he put some words together. "What are you going to do next?" he asked. "How are we going to find her?"

"I really don't know," I said. "I keep thinking about it but can't gain any traction in my mind."

"Might be the bump on the back of your head," he said.

"Might be."

"So, we know she had these two husbands. That she went by some crazy made-up name."

"Bess Marvin."

He laughed. "My sister Francine loved those Nancy Drew books. Me, I was more of a Hardy Boys fan." He opened his menu, perused it for a minute before closing it again. "She was funny. Amy," he said, thinking back.

I thought about that for a minute. "Kind of. Not slapstick or laugh-out-loud funny. More wry than anything. Observant. Whip smart."

"The kind of person who could disappear, make up a new life, and stay gone?" he asked.

"I guess. She's done it for a long time."

"Did you look into her alias?"

"I'm not sure I can."

"But Jed can. Kevin can."

"Can they?" I asked, laughing.

"You've got a point," Brendan said. "Had I not fingered your brother, they never would have figured out who had done that to my car. I basically figured the whole thing out before they had even gotten out of the police station to respond to the call."

"I told them both," I said. "Hopefully they can take it from here."

"You're done sleuthing?" he asked.

"We've got the Foster's Landing Police Department on the case as well as Detective Bernard in Wooded Lake. Actually, he seems like the real deal, despite the fact that he's been doing investigations in a tiny upstate town his whole professional life." I looked around the restaurant, seeing families dining together, servers scurrying to and from the kitchen, hot plates of food on their arms, the din of the place lively and comforting. "I'm tired, Brendan. I think I'm going to let the professionals handle it for a while."

He exhaled, relieved. "You don't know how happy I am to hear that."

"I need to make some room in my life. For other things," I said. I had been home less than a year and had found myself embroiled in a variety of unsavory activities including two murders. It was time to hang up my investigation hat and get to the place where I started living again, the distractions of mysteries and murders and mayhem keeping me from doing just that.

"What other things?" he asked, hopeful.

"The things that make me happy," I said.

"I can make you happy, Bel. If you give me a chance, I can make you very happy."

I smiled. We would see about that, but I was open to trying. We still didn't know who had put that photo in his wallet or why, but I wasn't sure I had the energy anymore to figure that out. I wasn't sure it even mattered anymore.

"She was so close," Brendan said.

"Funny, right?" I said, oven though it wasn't.

"And no one could find her."

A random thought went through my head: How hard had they looked?

CHAPTER *Thirty-nine*

The winter wonderland that we had promised Mary Ann D'Amato-Hanson was not coming together as quickly or as smoothly as I had hoped or as Dad had promised. This prompted me to call my brothers together again, the ragtag group that they were, in an effort to get the Manor ready for the holidays. It was five days before Christmas and we were behind. Shocker. Thank God we didn't have a wedding today or else we would really be in the weeds.

We sat in the foyer, all of us, on the cold marble floor doing our best to untangle the lights that we would eventually wrap around the big evergreens that dotted the back lawn and that would illuminate the grounds all the way down to the Foster's Landing River.

"You think this year we could convince Dad to put these back in the containers in some kind of orderly fashion?" Feeney asked, strands of white lights wrapped around his neck and both arms.

"I'll give it my best shot," I said. "Cargan, maybe we should order some of those things that you can wrap lights around? So we don't have to go through this again?"

Derry piped up. "I saw something on the DIY Network where you can cut cardboard and fashion it so you can wrap the lights and they won't be tangled the next time you want to use them."

Arney found this hilarious for some reason. "I think you've just found your reason for being, Derry. Maybe in your spare time you can 'fashion' them yourself?" he asked. "Oh, that's right. You have nothing but spare time, Mr. Stay-at-Home Dad."

This proclamation started a fierce row, one that only was ended by my whistling loudly through my fingers. "I don't know about you idiots, but I would like to have an evening. And it's four o'clock, so we have about forty-five minutes of actual daylight before this becomes a two-day job."

"Joyce coming over tonight, Bel?" Feeney asked, his animosity toward my ex- and soon-to-be-current boyfriend still bubbling just beneath the surface.

"What's it to you, Feeney?" I asked, giving him a look that told him shut up or be shut up.

Silence was better and we all agreed tacitly that that was the case, so we continued, the only sound in the foyer the occasional light breaking, accompanied by a curse word that Mom would blanch at. Thank God she and my father were out, something that happened rarely but that brought a certain peace to the Manor.

The lights untangled, we headed outside and into the fading light, the river in the distance, its water level still not what it should have been given the terrible drought we had seen over the past year. I stationed myself at the smallest tree, Cargan and Derry giving me a boost to start the lights at the top and wind through around the thick trunk until I reached the bottom. Derry was in charge of the electricity and went back into the Manor eventually to get thick orange extension cords that would likely give the fire chief fits and starts when he realized that we were lighting the entire tableau from a few outlets inside the Manor. We hadn't burned the place down yet, but there was still time.

We were spread out across the lawn, and one by one the trees were lit to display a gorgeous light show, one that took my breath away. It had been a long time since I had seen the place look so beautiful, my idea of home inextricably linked to this place now and forever. I had resisted it for most of the time I had been here, but now, standing in the twilight with my brothers, one nuttier than the other, I felt a kinship with them that transcended our history. We lived in a beautiful place with parents who loved us, even if they didn't often express it. We had one another and that was a lot more than many people had.

Including Amy. It was there, standing on that lawn and looking at the lights twinkling, that I realized she had every reason to leave, though she always put on a brave face. Our families were different, as many families were, but hers was hard, unyielding in their views, loathe to show affection. The town was sometimes the same, seeming to hold her back. She was supposed to go to college and set the world on fire, but in addition to being beautiful and smart and shrewd, with that wry sense of humor, she was impatient, the electricity of it flowing through her veins.

And now it was possible that she might have been involved in something so serious and deadly that she had no choice but to leave.

"We're going inside for a beer, Bel!" one of my

brothers called, their voices in adulthood all eerily similar in tone and cadence.

"I'm right behind you," I said, but I wasn't. I stood on the lawn for a long time, taking in the spectacle of all of those lights, feeling a peace that I hadn't felt since before I returned home, my own impatience serving to catapult me forward in my career but causing me pain in my personal life. I walked down toward the barren river, the lights helping me find my way even though I could traverse this lawn in my sleep. I crouched down and looked across to the other side of the river where houses dotted the jagged landscape, seemingly suspended in mid-air by strings on the big hill on the opposite side of town. Amy and I used to look across at those houses and wonder what they looked like inside. We knew one person who lived there—Mary Ann D'Amato—but I didn't remember ever going there.

The river was narrow at that point, more narrow than at any other point, maybe an eighth of a mile across, before it took a turn and opened up into a wide expanse where we could fit tens of kayaks across and still not be able to reach out and touch one another as we made our way to Eden Island. My brothers were all inside the house and it was as quiet as it would ever be on this riverbank, so quiet that I could hear the voice calling to me from the other side of the river, the words directed at me.

"Bel. Please leave it alone," were the first words I heard, the sound of that voice one I hadn't heard since I was much younger, less wise. "I'm never coming back, but I'm okay." A voice came through, was clear as a bell, carrying across the bottom of the river, its cracks and scars visible in the moonlight.

"Amy?" I called back.

"Bel, let it go. Please. For everyone's sake. It's just not worth it and I've moved on."

I tried to speak, but couldn't. I started out onto the moonlit ground that used to exist beneath several feet of water, until I hit a patch of water, icy cold and bracing.

"Any further, Bel, and you'll be in danger," the person said—Amy, I was convinced—and I didn't know if she meant from trying to cross the river at night or continuing to find her. "You and everyone else. Cargan. Your mother and father. The boys."

"The boys." That's how I knew it was her for sure. No one called my brothers the boys unless they had grown up with me and had seen the years of shenanigans. They were grown, but they were still "the boys," capable of acting like adolescents at the drop of a hat.

"Amy!" I called out. "Cargan! It's Amy! She's here!" But I knew he couldn't hear me, the boys inside, cracking open the beer that Dad had bought for the Manor and that was supposed to be for the upcoming policeman's ball, as I had come to call it in my head, glamorizing what was sure to be a very boring event.

He did hear me, though, my brother coming up beside me silently, listening, as I did, to the voice being carried by the night air. Even in the dark, I could see his wide eyes, the acknowledgment that he could hear her, too.

"Let it go, Bel," were her final words, the trees on the other side of the river rustling as she disappeared into the night, leaving me with the one admonition by which I couldn't abide.

I could never let it go.

CHAPTER Forty

"How hard did you get hit on the head?" was the first thing I heard when I ran into the Manor, finding my brothers in the dining room, sitting at a denuded table, no tablecloth or place settings on any of the tables.

"It's Amy," I had said breathlessly, the run from the river into the Manor having taken the wind out of me. Part of this new life I wanted to live really needed to include an exercise program that would help me get from totally winded after running to just mildly light-headed.

Derry stood up, his beer still in his hand. "What's that, Bel?"

"It's Amy," I said, pointing out the window and across to the other side of the river. "At the edge. At the bottom. On the other side."

"Someone get this girl a drink," Arney said, and Derry made his way to the bar, where he poured me a healthy shot of tequila and handed it to me.

"Sláinte," he said.

I threw back the drink and sat down at one of the empty tables. I knew it was folly to try to follow her or even look for her in the Landing. She was in the wind again and my one chance to see her and tell her how sad we had all been at her departure was gone.

"Cargan heard it, too," I said. "Heard *her*."

He nodded at my brothers, confirming what I knew: She was back.

The boys knew nothing about the investigation into Amy's disappearance or anything I had found out, so I had to tell them everything. Arney sat with his mouth open. "You called another lawyer besides me when you were detained?" he asked, the one question that didn't need to be asked but that went straight to the heart of his wounded ego. "Bel, really."

"So many words you could have said, Arney, and yet you chose those words," Feeney said, disgusted.

Derry stood by the window, his arms crossed, staring at me. "She's alive?"

"Yes," I said, now more sure than ever. "She's alive."

Derry sat down in a chair and dropped his head into his hands. "And she's been an hour from here ever since? How is that even possible?"

"She was for a time, but now who knows?" I said. "I don't know where she is."

"You're a cop, Cargan. You could find her," Derry said, his knowledge of what went into finding a missing person gleaned from marathon viewings of the various iterations of *Law & Order*.

"And how do I do that, Derry?" Cargan asked, not an insincere or sarcastic bone in his body. He truly wanted to know how Derry thought he could go about finding our missing friend.

"You know cops! And they know cops!" Derry said. "You can all help each other find her."

I wondered if Derry had hit his head, too. Feeney caught my eye, the same thought going through his mind.

"She doesn't want to be found," I said. "Don't you guys get it?" It just dawned on me that that was the case and, now that I had articulated it, it made the most sense of all.

"Then why are we looking for her?" Cargan asked, the one question I hadn't considered. Would never consider.

"We are looking for her because . . ." I started, stopping mid-sentence. We were looking for her because I wanted to find her and for no other reason. And once I gave a voice to that, it would be over for good. "You're right, Car," I said, thinking about what Amy said, that we would all be in danger if I didn't let it go. I stood up. "It's over," I said. "Cargan's right. We shouldn't be looking for her. She doesn't want to be found." I started for the dining-room door and kept going. "It's over," I said as I entered the foyer, feeling foolish for ever having started this whole thing.

Cargan followed me into the foyer. "I heard it, Bel, but I don't know if it's her."

"I've been in this alone, Car, and I'll stay in it alone," I said.

"You're not entirely alone," he said. "I did get you the information on that plate. Dave Southerland is a regular boy scout, apparently. Not even a parking ticket to his name."

"Thanks," I said, my irritation waning somewhat. "It doesn't mean anything in the scheme of things but it's helpful, Cargan."

"You think he's involved?" he asked.

"I don't know anymore," I said before leaving him in the Manor.

I went back to my apartment, leaving my brothers to

polish off the two six-packs they'd taken from the Manor's fridge. I mounted the steps and entered, closing the door behind me and leaning against it, thinking that I would continue looking, if only to find out what she meant when she said to let it go, that we would be in danger if I continued my search.

I lay down on my bed in my clothes and closed my eyes, my phone in my hand. Its vibrating, persistent and annoying, was the only thing that woke me two hours later at a little after eight.

The number was a "private caller," but I recognized the gravelly voice, the inflection. "He's awake, Belfast."

Larry Bernard had some good news for a change.

"And he wants to talk to you."

CHAPTER *Forty-one*

I had to wait until the next day, a trip to Wooded Lake in the evening not a good idea for anyone. Not for me, not for Tweed Blazer, awake and recovering from his stabbing, not for Alison Bergeron, who desperately wanted to accompany me, my phone call to her about this new development putting an urgency in her voice.

"Thank God he recovered," she said, her voice barely a whisper.

"Am I disturbing you?" I asked. "Why are you whispering?"

"I'm in the closet."

"The closet?"

"Yes, the closet in my daughter's room. She is downstairs with Crawford, and if he hears me talking to you about this he might bust a gut."

"Oh, is he as sick of your sleuthing as everyone in my life is of mine?" I asked.

"For sure. I have a long history of butting my nose in where it doesn't belong, so in the interest of marital harmony I'm just going to talk to you from the closet, if that's okay with you."

"Sure. Not a problem."

"Are you going to go see him?" she asked.

"Yes, first thing in the morning," I said.

"I have school. Will you let me know what he tells you?"

"If anything," I said. "Larry said he wanted to talk to me, but who knows about what? Maybe he just wants to thank me for calling the police before he bled out. For being in the right place at the right time."

"Maybe. Or maybe there's something else. Something juicy. Something that will help you solve this."

"I have to tell you something," I said.

"Hurry," she said. "They're coming. I can hear them on the stairs."

As quickly as I could, I recounted what had happened that night.

She gasped and called, "I'm coming!" to her husband and daughter before she hung up.

Now I knew I was completely on my own.

The next morning, a mountain of work awaiting me in the kitchen, I left a little after nine, knowing that I would be pulling all-nighters for the next few nights to make up for the fact that I was no longer focused on my job in the way that I should be, that I had become obsessed with something that might never come to a resolution. My parents trusted me enough to run the kitchen the way I wanted to and didn't seem to worry that I wasn't around as much as I should be. Believe me, I would have heard about it, had they been concerned in the least. They weren't ones to hold back their feelings on any subject, let alone one that concerned the Manor and its success.

Tweed Blazer was still in a prone position in bed, oxygen going into his nose via two small connected tubes. He looked pale and weak but more so than I expected; the burly, hearty guy whom I had met was gone and in his place was a shell of his former self. Archie Peterson sat beside him, his long white hair hitting his shoulders, a copy of *New York* magazine closed and sitting on his lap.

He looked up when I appeared at the door of the room, recognition dawning on his lined face. "You weren't looking for unclaimed barn wood that day, were you?" he asked.

"And you're estranged from you son," I replied, causing Tweed to let out a little cough.

Archie waved a hand dismissively. "That's what he tells all of the lookie-loos. No skin off my nose. How did you like my class?"

"I fell asleep," I said. "You're the guy who started Love Canyon."

"Guilty as charged," he said. "It was a good time while it lasted."

"Can I come in?" I asked.

"If you're this Belfast person he's been asking about, then yes."

Behind me, I heard a familiar voice asking what it took to find a vending machine with a Diet Coke around here. It wasn't a complaint, or even a request, but more of an observation, the musings of a senior-citizen detective who just wanted a shot of caffeine in a can. He came into the room.

"I thought I should be here, Belfast, in case anything important came to light," Larry Bernard said.

"That makes sense, Detective," I said. I moved to the side of the bed and took a seat in a chair that had a blanket tossed over the back of it. I knew it wouldn't be long until at least one of us, if not all of us, was chased from the room; this was a floor for the seriously ill and those who had had surgery in the past few days and I couldn't imagine it was good for three people to be hanging around this guy's bed, two of them looking for answers.

"I've already asked him if he knows who did this," Larry said. "But he doesn't."

"Does this have something to do with you?" I asked, looking at Archie. "Something to do with the old commune?"

"Don't believe everything you read, darling," he said. "Sure, it was free love back then, but ours was a much more conservative communal dwelling."

"Named 'Love Canyon'?" I asked. "That's kind of hard to believe."

"Summer of Love. Peace, love, and understanding. 'Love is all you need,'" Archie said. "Love, baby."

Jeez Louise, this guy was as crazy as a bedbug. If he had been my dad and carried the reputation that Archie Peterson did, I would probably change my name, too.

Larry Bernard was having none of it. "I was in Wooded Lake, Peterson. You might not have been a full-fledged commune, but you were certainly leaning toward being a cult." He leaned back against the wall and crossed his arms. "I'm surprised you've come back to Wooded Lake. Not too many people happy to see you."

"Stop."

We all looked at the bed, where Tweed waved a hand weakly, his voice a throaty rasp.

"Stop." He looked over at me. "She's alive, Bel."

"Amy?"

"Yes. Amy."

"Do you know where she is?" I asked, trying not to get my hopes up and failing.

He tried to smile, but it was more of a grimace. "I do." He attempted to shift position but could barely move. "She talks about you. A lot. Said that you were the one reason she would ever consider going back to Foster's Landing."

"Did you know that it was me when I showed up? That I was Amy's friend?"

"I did," he said. "I'm sorry I lied." He put a hand on his chest, tried to move slightly but couldn't; the pain was too much. "I didn't know if I could trust you. If Amy could trust you. I was protecting her. I was in love with her once. But I haven't told her I know you. It was never the right time."

"Thank you for doing that," I said. "For protecting her."

He gave me an address not far from the center of Wooded Lake. "Go find her and let her tell you everything."

"Everything?" I asked.

"Everything," he said. "It's her story to tell."

CHAPTER *Forty-two*

Larry Bernard followed me out into the parking lot. "Let me go with you. You don't know what you're going to find."

I turned. "This is a one-woman show, Larry."

"I think you're in over your head, Bel." He buttoned his overcoat, pulled the neck in against the stiff wind that blew. "And she's still a suspect in his stabbing."

Not to mention the death of the girl found in her car. I knew that was why Cargan hadn't warmed to the investigation.

"Why?" I asked. "You heard him. They were young when they married. They divorced. They stayed friends. All he wanted to know was if he could trust me and if Amy could trust me. That's all it was." I pushed aside the part in my brain that knew that while I was trying to get close to him, he was trying to get close to me, to find out what I knew and what my intentions were. When it was clear that I was a heartbroken friend and nothing more, he invited me to his home, where he would tell me everything, show me the photo of their special day. It didn't turn out that way, though, someone getting to him first, someone not willing for the truth to come out.

While we spoke, I plugged the address into my GPS, seeing that I was just fifteen minutes away from the place where Tweed said Amy lived.

I opened the door to my car and watched as Larry Bernard, not as young as he used to be by his own admission, scurried to his beat-up Honda, fast but not fast enough. I tore out of the parking lot of the hospital and onto a back road that ran adjacent to the highway, jumping on at the first entrance ramp I came across, playing it cool in the right lane, going just five miles or so above the speed limit so that I wouldn't attract any undue attention. As it was, I had Larry Bernard on my tail; he had heard the address, too. He knew where I was headed. My goal was to get there before he did.

I did, pushing the gas pedal a little more than I thought was safe but wanting to put some distance between me and the detective. It was a very direct route, one that took me off an exit just a few miles up the road and through the center of a charming town; I would come back here again, I was sure, if not to see Amy, then to poke around on a nice spring day, maybe eat at the Turkish place that had a line of would-be diners out the front door. It wasn't long before I turned onto the street that Tweed said Amy lived on—or at least had at some point, this being her last address known to him—looking at a row of well-kept Victorian homes sitting across from a fire station. This place was even smaller than Foster's Landing, which boasted one building for sixth grade through eighth grade and another for the high school itself.

So why hadn't he told me before that he might know where she was? Archie had answered for him. "He didn't know if he could trust you." He had pointed at the bed, at his wounded and weakened son. "Now he knows he can. Because of what you did. How you saved him."

I pulled up alongside the curb and looked at the place that bore the number of Amy's beautiful house, one with a wraparound front porch, little evergreens in window boxes with decorative holly and ivy interspersed. If Amy had done that, we needed her at the Manor to take care of our Christmas decorations; she had done a much better job and was much more creative than I remembered. I got out of the car and walked up the front walk, flat bluestones framed on either side by tiny, manicured bushes, and put a foot on the front steps, the first one creaking slightly. I finally had enough courage to mount the rest of the steps and press the bell, stepping back when I heard its shrill report.

After a few moments, it was clear that no one was home. I went back down the steps and walked around the north side of the house, taking in the meticulous paint job on every corbel, some a beautiful pink, others in a shade of lavender that complemented the other colors perfectly. I looked in a few windows and saw an equally gorgeous interior, spotlessly clean, with complementary architectural details adorning the space: crown moldings, wide baseboards, decorative coffered ceilings.

The person who lived here—Amy?—had crafted a perfect exterior and interior for the life she now lived, and while that didn't seem completely at odds with who I remembered, how could I know? That person had been a teenager, just out of her childhood years, and this person was an adult, with tastes and preferences and a style all her own.

I walked back down the driveway and came face-to-face with Larry Bernard. "She's not here," I said.

Larry's face mirrored mine in terms of disappointment. "I was hoping you'd find your friend," he said.

"I was, too."

"I'd like to talk to her," he said.

"You and everyone else," I said. The thought of the person in Amy's car floated into my head. Although no one had told me outright, someone would want to question her about that.

Bernard and I walked down the path to our cars, parked at the curb. "I'm sorry, Belfast. I thought today might be the day for you. Maybe leave a note," he said. "Maybe she's just at work."

"What about you?" I said. "Won't you be looking for her, too? Isn't she a suspect?"

He rubbed his eyes behind his glasses. "I'm going in a different direction on this one."

"And what direction is that?" I asked.

"Nothing you should concern yourself with," he said, smiling. "Just leave it to me, Ms. McGrath. Belfast." He got in his car and I made a show of getting into mine, too, starting it and even pulling out of the space. But once he was no longer in my sights, the Honda disappearing down a side street, I circled back around and parked across the street from the house, where I could watch anyone come or go.

I stayed there a long time, well into the evening, before realizing that she was never coming home and that if her words to me at the river the night before were any indication, I would never see her again.

CHAPTER Forty-three

I had been wrong about my parents' lack of concern about my disappearance. I had misread the situation to the point that when I arrived in the kitchen the next morning they were both waiting for me, Mom looking less sympathetic than Dad when it came to my explanation of why I had been gone the entire day before.

Dad put his head on the counter, his arms encircling it; he didn't want to hear any more. Mom stood ramrod straight, staring at me. "You know how I feel about therapy, Belfast, but I think that maybe it would help you."

"Yeah, I know how you feel," I said, stripping off my sweater and replacing it with an apron. "You'd rather die than expose your innermost feelings to a stranger." It was a refrain I had heard many times and there was no mistaking her disdain for the wonders of a good therapist. We were supposed to keep our feelings bottled up inside until one day, when we were unable to repress them anymore, they came out in a torrent—usually at a wake or funeral—or they stayed there, killing you with their vice-like grip on your heart and soul. I had vowed that I wouldn't be that person, trying to straddle the line between keeping enough in so that my vulnerability didn't show and letting enough out so that I wouldn't die of a heart attack in my sleep.

It wasn't the easiest way to live, to be honest.

Dad raised his head. "Belfast, that girl is gone and she will probably always be gone. Is this about your breakup with Brendan? A diversion to keep you going so that you're not completely heartbroken?"

I laughed. "No, Dad. It's not that."

Mom crossed her arms over her chest, regarded me for a few minutes. She left the kitchen and went into the adjoining office, where I heard her begin a conversation with someone, her voice a whisper; I couldn't make out any actual words. When she came back to the kitchen, she had a satisfied smile on her face. "Lieutenant D'Amato will take care of it," she said. "I told him to come by so he can get all of the information from you. If she is alive, Belfast, as you say she is, then let the authorities handle it. They will find her and bring her home and give her family some peace."

"This town," Dad said. "Give this town some peace."

"Mom!" I said. "Why did you do that?" Amy's words ringing in my ears, something told me that the last thing she wanted was for the local police to be involved.

Mom looked sterner now than when I had arrived in the kitchen. "We tolerated your investigation into Declan's murder. And in finding Pauline. But this is getting ridiculous," she said, mentioning two situations—two mysteries—that I had insinuated myself into. She tried to soften her tone but was unsuccessful. "You are a banquet chef now, Bel, and we appreciate your help more than you know. But you're distracted and flighty and obsessed—"

"And an adult," I reminded her, this diatribe reminiscent of one that I would have heard in my teens.

"—and you need to settle down and return to what makes you happy."

"Finding Amy would make me happy," I said.

Mom slouched slightly, the conversation weakening her. She looked up. "Well, look at the time. I have Pilates," she said. Before she left the kitchen, she turned to look at me and Dad. "Mal, please pick up where I left off."

Dad stood up. "You really think she's alive?" he asked, a hopefulness creeping into his voice.

"We know she is."

He came over and wrapped me in a hug, his arms strong, his chest soft beneath his paint-splattered shirt. One of its buttons dug deeply into my cheek, but I didn't care. I needed a soft place to land—a safe place—and this was it. He was my champion and my ally, the man from whom I got my emotional side as well as my creativity.

There was a knock at the front door of the Manor and he dropped his arms. "That would be the Lieutenant."

It would be. He was accompanied by Kevin and Jed and none of them looked particularly excited to have this conversation, which to me seemed very strange. We went into the dining room and sat at one of the denuded banquet tables.

The Lieutenant was in charge. "So how were you able to figure out something that the Foster's Landing Police Department and the FBI haven't been able to solve in fifteen years?" he asked.

I shrugged. The tone of this conversation was a bit more hostile than I had anticipated. I didn't expect to be a hero, per se, but I didn't expect to be treated like a perp, either. An annoyance. A pain in the ass. "I don't know. I haven't seen her, though," I said to Jed, his eyes hopeful in the way the other two men's weren't. "I tried to find her, but she never came home."

"Give us the address," Lieutenant D'Amato said.

I don't know what made me do it, but I made up an address, one that didn't remotely resemble the one that Tweed had given me. Based on their body language and the way the Lieutenant was looking at me—angry and somewhat perturbed—it was my first instinct.

She was probably a suspect in that girl's death, and although I didn't know for sure that she didn't do it, in my heart I knew that Amy wasn't a killer.

Unless something had propelled her to be, her own safety at risk.

"That's three hours from here," he said. "You've been going all the way upstate to investigate?" He wrote the address down quickly. "How do you get any work done if you're driving back and forth to Lake Morgan?"

"Didn't we go on a class trip there?" Kevin asked. "To see the caverns?"

"We did," I said. How do you think I came up with this so quickly? I wanted to ask. God, he could be such a dim bulb. It wasn't a coincidence that Lake Morgan was the place I used to throw them off the track. I figured they could be searching that town, and maybe the caverns, for long enough for me to find Amy and let her know that the case was now officially reopened.

Hers was no longer a cold case. Rather, it was getting very, very warm.

"Sounds like you've been busy, Belfast," Lieutenant D'Amato said. "Also sounds like you should get back to the kitchen. Start preparing for our party. You only have a few days."

"It will be lovely and beautiful, Lieutenant," I said. I looked over at Jed, silent the entire time, looking out at the river. "We finished decorating the other night so it will be gorgeous when you arrive."

"Well, talk to my daughter if you need anything else." He stood up, his minions standing up as well. "And Belfast," he said, a warning in his voice, "stick to the kitchen. It's where you belong."

I let them out and stood in the foyer until I heard their car drive off. So in addition to unearthing all sorts of new information about Amy, I had embarrassed the Foster's Landing Police Department. Again.

I went back into the kitchen, where I belonged, apparently. Although I had thought about letting this go and moving on with my life, it was becoming apparent that that was no longer an option. If I was reading the situation correctly—and according to Mom's intimation, I was unable to do that anymore—there were people who didn't want Amy found.

Including Amy herself.

Did that mean I would stop? I thought about that as I started chopping carrots, the rhythmic sound on my cutting board giving me the answer.

Chop, chop, chop. "No, no, no."

CHAPTER *Forty-four*

Fifteen minutes later, I was still chopping carrots in the kitchen, still figuring out how I was going to get out of here and track down Amy's whereabouts once and for all, when a quick knock, followed by the appearance of a person in the kitchen, interrupted my troubled daydreams.

It was Mr. Malloy, my former swim coach, the last person I expected to see in the middle of a school day, his face its usual broad, friendly Irish mug. "Hi, Bel," he said, entering tentatively. "I hope you don't mind me dropping by suddenly, but I had a free period and seeing you the other day reminded me that my wife wanted me to come in."

"You have an event?" I asked, putting down my knife and wiping my hands on a damp rag that sat beside the cutting board on the counter.

"My daughter's Sweet Sixteen," he said. "Can you believe it? I can't."

"Wow, that's hard to believe," I said. "Time really flies doesn't it?" I was still preoccupied from the visit from the police and trying to sound casual, something I wasn't pulling off all that successfully. He hadn't mentioned this when he had been here for Kevin and Mary

Ann's wedding, and as if he had read my mind he addressed that.

"The wedding was so great that we thought that this might be the perfect place." He pointed at his ruddy mug. "And being as we're as Irish as they come, where else should we go but Shamrock Manor?"

"I'm not sure you'd beat the McGraths in an 'Irish-off,' but you'd come in a hard second, I'm sure."

He looked around the kitchen, which after many years of cooking and entertaining carried the phantom odor of many a corned beef simmering in a big pot of flavored water.

"Did I catch you at a bad time?" he asked.

I thought I had recovered from the surprise of seeing him, of being jolted out of my reverie, but apparently that wasn't the case. "Not at all," I said. "Perfect time." I reached up into the cabinet next to the big stainless-steel double sink and pulled out a folder that held menus I had created along with a pricing sheet. I had known Dan Malloy a long time and didn't feel the need to involve my parents in this booking. Besides, right now they were eyeing me to see if I was going to go off the deep end and not doing a very good job of making it seem like everything was normal in that regard. I opened the folder. "How many people are we talking about, Mr. Malloy?"

"'Dan,' please, Belfast," he said. "We've had this conversation, remember? You're an adult now and I'm, well, an older adult," he said, chuckling.

"I guess that's true," I said.

"I would say that Sinead is going to invite the entire sophomore class, so we're talking one hundred students and our family?"

"So, one-twenty-ish?" I said.

"Give or take," he said. "You know how Irish families are. You need a scorecard to keep track of who's speaking to who on any given day. Right now, it's my mother and my youngest sister. Something about someone taking over Christmas dinner or something like that. The claim, as it were, had already been staked."

I was well aware of the Irish grudge.

"We'll see how it goes. Maybe Mom will relent. But I doubt that either one of them would miss Sinead's sixteenth birthday."

We got down to the business of planning for the party, three months in the future, on an evening in early March, when we were notoriously quiet, the rare bride picking a damp and mercurial month in the Northeast to plan her wedding. It could rain. Snow. We could have a hurricane. Or a tornado. Any meteorological event was possible in the third month of the year, but I didn't remind Mr. Malloy of that. Keeping my mouth shut and vaguely suggesting we have a backup date—one that we would gladly give him if the weather proved dodgy—we created a menu that would suit both teens and older family members, as well as a signature "virgin" cocktail that would make the kids feel like they really were celebrating in style, like adults.

"One last thing, Bel," he said.

I put up a hand; I knew exactly what the next question would be. "No," I said, anticipating the question. "You do not have to have the McGrath Brothers band play at your daughter's Sweet Sixteen."

He let out a relieved sigh. "Okay, thanks. Sinead really wants a DJ and I wasn't sure if having your brothers play was part of the deal."

I led him into the foyer, the heavy lifting done, in terms of planning. "Making you and your guests happy is our only deal," I said, sounding more like Dad with every passing day.

Speak of the devil, and he shall appear. As if right on cue, smelling a client, Dad emerged from the office, talking before he focused on Dan Malloy, his eyes trained on a sheaf of papers in his hand. "So, Belfast. Did you tell the police everything you know?"

I shot him a look that asked him, telepathically at least, to shut it, but he mistook that for confusion, the need for more information.

"About Amy," he said. "How you found Amy?" He finally looked up and, seeing I was with another person, put his lips together.

"Dad, we'll talk about it another time," I said.

Dan Malloy's face went white. "Amy? Amy Mitchell?"

I looked from Dad, stricken that he had blurted this out in front of a client, back to Dan Malloy, stricken, it would seem, for another mysterious reason.

The jig was up. The cat was out of the bag. "Yes," I said. "Amy Mitchell. She may be alive."

He recovered quickly. "That's wonderful news. So, she's okay?"

"We don't know. We hope so," I said. I changed the subject. "Dad, Mr. Malloy here has booked the Manor for a Sweet Sixteen in March."

"That is wonderful news!" Dad said, clapping the guy on the back and leading him to the door, one hand on Malloy's meaty biceps. "You'll have a grand time here at the Manor. . . ."

I wasn't listening anymore to Dad's exhortations

about the Manor, my cooking, how Sinead Malloy's Sweet Sixteen party would be the event of the century, at least where the teens were concerned, or how the place would be dolled up for St. Patrick's Day, complete with a green disco ball.

No, I was thinking about the utterance of Amy's name, and at the sound of it, Dan Malloy's ashen face.

CHAPTER *Forty-five*

It wouldn't be long before the police were back, having figured out that the address I had given them was a phony. I had a friend who had moved to the town that I had referenced and I had remembered her street name but nothing else. I didn't even know if the house number I gave them existed. Maybe they had put the address in their GPS and come up empty, aborting their three-hour drive north, or maybe they had gone anyway, a wild-goose chase that would end with my being put in the slammer. My money was on the latter. The last few months had seen an uptick in crime in the Landing—two murders at the Manor alone contributed to that—and our police department really wasn't up to the challenge, having spent years investigating vandalism, the overdue library book, and, in one example of a deep dive into something that really didn't matter, the case of a missing mint-condition Mickey Mantle baseball card, something that had kept them occupied for months. (It was in a sugar bowl in the owner's grandmother's basement apartment. Case closed!) That left me six hours to finish prepping for the policeman's gala that would take place the next night, "gala" the word I had assigned it to make it seem more festive in my mind, and then get back to the business of answering the myriad unanswered questions that still remained.

On this last day of school before vacation, snow was on the way. I could see it in the rapidly forming clouds, gray and dark, on the horizon. I could feel it in my bones, a chill beneath the cold that signaled we were due for more than a dusting. I spent the day in the kitchen, formulating my responses to Lieutenant D'Amato's questions about the address I had given them, how it was probably a strip mall now, or even nonexistent. I had to have a plan, my answers at the ready, and as I diced some onions and cut up some cucumber for a crudité I thought about what those might be.

I decided, finally, that ignorance was both bliss and my best course of action. After a few hours, my prep done, I still had heard nothing from them and decided I would take a ride past the police station just to check out whether they were still there, knowing that if they were going to go out in an official capacity they would take the Lieutenant's "company car," as it were, an oatmeal-colored sedan that I wasn't sure they even made anymore. It was solid, an American car, one befitting an older guy who probably had lower-back pain (just a guess; he was constantly grabbing his hips and wincing) and who had no idea what his carbon footprint was or how this car was making it larger.

I drove down the hill away from the Manor, circling through the residential neighborhood at its foot and through the village toward the train station. School was letting out and with it a throng of noisy students, oblivious to cars on the narrow streets, crossing against the light, running for their lives, or so it seemed. I caught sight of Brendan, a full foot taller it seemed than the group in which he was walking, stuck in the midst of what seemed like an army of tiny girls, all wearing backpacks and all jockeying for Mr. Joyce's attention. I pulled over at the curb.

"Hey, Mr. Joyce!" I called. "I really didn't appreciate that C on my latest painting."

The girls stopped, looking from me to Brendan and then back at me, not in on the joke, or any joke for that matter. I had forgotten what it was to be in my teens, the world a very serious and dramatic place, especially for me. Everything that my parents said to me was stupid and everything my brothers uttered in my presence a gauntlet thrown down for an oral argument or worse. Looking at Brendan and thinking back to the events of earlier that day, I thought back to the one teacher to whom I would complain during those early mornings at the pool, my Speedo wet and my skin pricked with goose bumps, a guy who was committed to our team and its success, who would listen to our problems and offer some kind of platitude or useless advice, sometimes on our side, but more often on the side of authority. Our parents. Our teachers. Our priests.

Brendan ran over to the car and jumped in, grateful for the diversion. "Where's your car?" I asked.

He turned and looked at me. "Are you daft or are you just playing with me, Bel? Because that's not a funny joke. Not at all."

"Oh, right," I said, putting my hand to my forehead. "I got hit in the head, remember? Maybe it did some damage to my hippocampus."

"Your 'hippocampus'?" he asked.

"Yes, part of the limbic system. Where memory is stored."

"I was an art major, Bel. I have no idea how the brain works." He leaned over and put his arms around me, his mouth soft and warm despite the chill coming off his cheeks. We hadn't kissed like this in a long time and I had almost forgotten what it was like, how he tasted.

"You had a ham sandwich for lunch today, didn't you?" I asked, pulling away.

"Pea soup," he said.

"Cafeteria pea soup?" I asked. "That doesn't seem like a good idea."

"No. My mother's. I rarely eat in the cafeteria," he said. "And you were close on the ham sandwich. Mom puts a ham hock in there for flavor."

I pulled away from the curb. "Of course she does. There's no other way to do it."

"What brings you to this part of town?" he asked, throwing his backpack over the seat and into the back of the car.

I got to the stop sign at the corner and looked both ways before proceeding. "I told a little white lie today and it may come back to bite me in the ass." I pulled onto the street on which the station house resided, driving slowly. "Tweed gave me an address for Amy. I gave the cops a different one."

"Come again?" he asked. "You have an address for Amy?"

"I do," I said, slowing to a stop at the curb across from the police station. "I went there. She either doesn't live there or wasn't home."

"Where is it?" he asked, not focusing on the part of the story where I had lied to the police.

"Up north a bit," I said. "Aren't you going to ask me where I sent the cops?"

"She's alive?" he said. "You know for sure now that she's alive?"

"I thought we had established that, Brendan." I turned to him. "You know that."

He looked out his window, away from me. "It's just very real now." As he faced me, I could see that he had tears in his eyes. "You must be so happy. To know for sure."

The last man I had seen cry was my father, someone for whom tears flowed freely, an old softie if there ever was one. He was the exception, though. Most of the men I knew were hard and tough, my brothers leading the pack in that regard. Hardened by Mom and her protestations to "be a man" and toughened by her in the same way. She meted out harsh punishments for the slightest of transgressions, nary a tear shed lest the punishment, which never fit the crime, get worse. Dad was allowed to cry, but no one else was, so seeing this big guy, softer than I knew apparently, shedding a tear over my lost friend was disconcerting. A little upsetting.

I didn't think about that longer than a few seconds because the air in the car had changed and not for the better. I scanned the parking lot for Lieutenant D'Amato's big sedan and, not seeing it, drove around the block again, wondering if I should go inside and check on the status of Kevin and Jed and D'Amato or if I would arouse suspicion. I decided I had nothing to lose, and circling the block, Brendan having regained his composure, I pulled up to the curb again.

"Wait here," I said to Brendan, jumping out of the car and walking across the street to the parking lot.

I walked up the long flight of steps and entered the

station, my first encounter with the lovely Francie McGee, town gossip and all-around harridan. She also held the position of FLPD receptionist. "What can I do for you, Bel?" she asked, her eyebrows in a permanently raised position, her disdain for me evident. I don't know what I had done to Francie McGee to make her loathe me so, but ours was a troubled relationship, one that had recommenced when I had returned, my trips to the police station happening with alarming regularity.

Over her head, the station was abuzz with people. I could see the parking patrol lady moving about the room. She was someone from whom everyone ran when she announced her presence. There were some uniformed cops, two of them huddled by the water cooler, deep in discussion, their body language suggesting their conversation had something to do with football, one cop mimicking a quarterback throwing a ball. There was Jed, sitting at his desk, his head bent over a stack of papers.

And here came Kevin, a look of confused surprise on his face, like I was the last person he was expecting to see.

Kevin put his hands on the low wall that separated Francie from the squad. "Bel, what's up? What are you doing here?"

I moved around Francie so she couldn't see my lips moving or, I hoped, hear our conversation. I leaned in close to Kevin. "I would have thought you'd be on your way to Lake Morgan."

He cocked his head, a golden retriever trying to understand a multi-syllabic question. "What?"

"Lake Morgan." I leaned in closer. "Amy's address?"

"Oh," he said. "Loo told me and Jed to stay behind."

"Why?" I asked, Jed and Kevin being two major pieces in this puzzle, two cops who were in on every aspect of this investigation, not to mention story.

"He said he wanted to go by himself."

CHAPTER Forty-six

I couldn't drop Brendan off at his house soon enough. With a promise that we would see each other again soon, I sped back to the Manor, my thoughts not on my erstwhile boyfriend but on the Lieutenant and his striking out alone. I parked the car and went through the big double doors; I found Cargan in the office, thankfully alone.

"Where are Mom and Dad?" I asked, out of breath from the exertion of running a full five hundred feet.

"You have got to get into an exercise program, Bel," Cargan said, looking up from the computer screen. "You're going to have a heart attack." He clicked on the keyboard for a few seconds. "And good news. The Crawford wedding is booked. Signed, sealed, and delivered."

I waved that off, putting my hands on my knees. "That's great." I took in a few deep breaths. "Now I'm going to tell you something and you have to reserve judgment. I just want an answer to a question."

He closed the laptop and gave me his full attention. "Why do I feel like you're going to tell me something that's going to make *me* have a heart attack?"

"I have an address for Amy, Car," I said. He sat up

straighter in his chair, half getting out of it, his hands on the desk. "Dad didn't tell you?"

"No. Dad knows?"

"Dad knows," I said. "He made me tell the police what I had found out." I pulled at a stray thread on my sweater, unraveling an entire row of stitches, just like what was going on here, the disparate threads pulling apart a story that had a beginning and no end. I had to let Cargan know about my deception, even though I knew he would not be happy. His brothers in blue were important to him and their bond may have been more than ours. I blurted it out. "But that's not the address I gave to the FLPD. I gave them a fake address."

He sat back down, defeated. "Oh, Jesus, Bel."

"I know," I said. "I told the Lieutenant, Jed, and Kevin. But here's the weird thing."

The fax machine sputtered to life, scaring both of us. Cargan turned and looked at it, pulling out a sheet of paper and tossing it on a pile on top of the desk.

"Only the Lieutenant went." I had that same feeling that I used to have before I entered the confessional at church: a tingly, every-nerve-on-fire sensation that spoke to my guilt and my inability to embrace any kind of contrition related to it. Back then, I was a sturdy little ten-year-old and my sins ran to coveting Amy's pink bike and calling one of my brothers an idiot. Now they were more corrupt. Lying to the police? That was probably the worst one yet.

Cargan's response was defeated laughter, his body shaking, his eyes tearing at the thought of what I did, the deed so overwhelmingly bad, a terrible decision, that his only option was to find the humor in it. "Oh my

God," he finally said. "You know you're going to have to keep lying about this? Tell them that that's what Tweed told you and never admit that you lied, right? Blame it on his addled state?"

"That's one way to handle it," I said, my fingers on their own, worrying that thread again. If I kept it up, I'd be topless in no time. I shoved my hands in my pockets. "I guess."

He wiped his eyes. "Where is she?"

I gave him the real address.

"That's not terribly far," he said, checking his watch. "But too far and too late to go up and back now."

"You're willing to wait?" I asked, hoping that this revelation, my deception, wouldn't completely upend our relationship, one that I had come to count on and cherish. I never thought I would say that about one of my brothers, but without a real friend in town, besides Brendan of course, Cargan was my rock. My go-to. My older brother who looked out for me and me for him.

"I've been waiting for over fifteen years," he said. "Another day won't matter."

When I woke up the next morning, refreshed after a dreamless sleep, I wrote a letter, the longest letter I had ever written. I didn't use my computer, preferring to put everything down in my own handwriting, a letter to Amy asking her all of the questions I needed answers to when I got there. If she wasn't home or wouldn't let me in, I would leave this missive, one that would let her know that whatever had happened all those years ago was forgotten, that it was safe to come home.

I knew I was being naïve. There was still the issue of

that dead girl, someone for whom there had been a memorial this week, her parents' grief having been awakened like a sleeping giant, angry and raw, their faces belying the fact that their daughter had been dead for a long time. No, she had just died and it would always be like that, waking up and finding out—remembering— that she was gone. The thought of that kept me in my chair for a long time, holding the letter between my fingers, wondering if anything I said would make a difference, bring her home.

Our friendship hadn't died that night, something I reiterated over and over again in the letter. I gave her all of the pieces of the puzzle I had, from that first drive to Wooded Lake to the day before when I gave the Lieutenant that fake address, anything to keep the police off her trail until I found her. I wrote the last line before signing my name.

"And if you were here, we'd laugh out loud at the thought that tonight, if I am not in jail, I will make dinner for the entire police department of Foster's Landing. Remember when we ran from the police? When we used to kayak away as fast as possible that year they got the new police boat and used to troll the river, looking for us? Those days are gone, Amy, and now I'm a responsible citizen and master chef, but working for my parents. The more things change, right?"

It was early, early enough to get up and back before I needed to be in the kitchen, early enough so that I wouldn't see Cargan, whose last words to me the night before led me to believe that there was no way I was going up to Amy's by myself; he, the responsible one, the one who knew how to do a proper investigation, find a missing person, was coming, too. Except that he wasn't, and as I drove down the hill toward the highway out of town I didn't feel one morsel of regret.

When I arrived, she either still wasn't there or wasn't answering. On the porch of Amy's house, my heart racing just a bit, I pushed the letter, in a sealed envelope, through the slot in the big ornate front door. As I walked to my car, I passed a woman walking a small white dog; she stopped and gave me a smile. "Can I help you?" she asked. "I saw you go up the walk there. I live on the second floor."

I had assumed the house was a one-family, not a place with an apartment. I felt as if I had struck pay dirt. "My name is Belfast McGrath. I'm looking for someone. Her name is Amy," I said. "She lives there." I pointed to the house behind me.

The woman, her face kind and lined in the way that a happy person's was, someone who had smiled a lot in her life, grew sad. "Oh, I'm sorry, honey. There's no one named Amy downstairs."

"Bess?" I asked. "Bess Marvin?"

"No," she said, giving the dog a little tug before it went into the road. "Just a young man. An artist, I think. Beautiful watercolors. I have one in my sitting room."

"Did a woman named Amy or Bess ever live there?"

She shook her head. "No. I own the house, honey. I do the rentals. There's never been an Amy or a Bess. A Kathleen and a David and a Priscilla. But not your friend."

"I never said we were friends." I looked closely at the woman. I didn't know her and would never be able to tell if she was lying and it was in that moment that I rued not having waited to take Cargan with me. He would know.

"I just assumed," she said. "I'm sorry I can't help you." She scurried off, less interested in talking to me now that she knew my real purpose for being there.

I stood there for a moment, staring at the house, listening as the woman went inside and the front door slammed.

The woman was lying; I could feel it in my bones and wondered if I had picked up some of Cargan's special powers along the way. I made my peace with all of it in that moment; if Amy never came back, never contacted me, I would have to move on, something that would take some time. But I had to let it go. I had to think that she knew that I was around, but then again, maybe she didn't. I wondered if Larry Bernard had found her and had questioned her in relation to Tweed's stabbing. Surely he would have told me, just to assuage my fears of what had happened to her. Or maybe he wouldn't. I was ascribing more logic—more closeness—to our relationship than what actually existed.

Although I tried not to go there, I wondered if she was on the run again, if something strange and inexplicable and violent had happened that night, something that I didn't know about that had made her run and never return to Foster's Landing.

Cargan was in the foyer when I returned a few hours later, his demeanor the same as always, his face inscrutable. "Nice drive?" he asked.

I walked past him toward the kitchen. "Nice drive."

In the kitchen, I butchered six tenderloins and set about putting together the cheese course that Mary Ann had requested. Thankfully, she hadn't contacted me much over the past several days, her last text admitting that she knew I "had this" and that I wouldn't let them down. I had cooked for their wedding, so they already knew what I was capable of; they had experienced it with their own eyes and taste buds. I was grateful for her lack of interference. She was letting me do it my way, to have free rein over the preparation of what I assured her would be one of the best meals anyone in Foster's Landing had ever had. Because while I was insecure about a lot of things, I was sure of one thing and that was my skill in the kitchen.

The dining room was abuzz with the other staff putting together the tables and assembling chairs. I kept my head down, my heart skipping a beat every time the door to the kitchen swung open, waiting for the moment when Lieutenant D'Amato would show up, point at me, and scream, You lied! in front of my parents, my brothers, and the entire Manor staff, my humiliation and guilt on display for all to see. In a spare minute, I googled "lying to police" and hastily put my phone back in my pocket when the results came up. Apparently, that wasn't a good thing to do, to not tell the police the absolute truth and have them find out.

The day progressed and nothing happened, but I still didn't rest, knowing that at six o'clock he would show up, as would Kevin and Jed and a host of other local law enforcement, and it would be a matter of time before I was hauled away in handcuffs, my mother clucking disapprovingly as she worried her pearl necklace, Dad going into a full-blown meltdown, loud, heart-wrenching sobs filling the vastness of the foyer.

As I made the final preparations on the meat, I noticed my hands shaking. Get a story and stick to it, I thought, making up a tale that no one would believe but that would maybe buy me some time until I figured out exactly what to tell the Lieutenant about this whole crazy story—this journey, really. In between chastising myself for not telling the truth, I justified it at the same time. I went into the walk-in and stood there, forgetting why I was there and finally saying to no one, "She doesn't want to be found."

She told me herself just a few nights earlier. Or had she? Had I imagined it or had it been someone else? My obsession was slowly turning into insanity and I had to get back to normal, to an emotional equilibrium. I had carried this around long enough, the guilt, the shame, the idea that I—as many in this town thought—had something to do with her disappearance or maybe had facilitated it even.

I needed to change the narrative, both in my head and in this town.

Standing in the walk-in refrigerator, my letter probably still sitting between the screen door and the front door of Amy's beautiful Victorian, I decided that once and for all, I would let it go. It was over. She was gone for good. I needed to make sense of my place in this world and what it meant that the last words I had ever said to my best friend, my sister from another mother, and that she carried in her heart, too, were, *You'll be sorry.*

We were young and we had certainly been foolish, but I would never forget her kissing Kevin, my boyfriend at the time, in front of me, the look of hard contentment and victory on her beautiful face, her betrayal and my words leading us to this place.

She had betrayed me, but she wasn't a killer. I had known her almost as well as I had known myself. That girl's death, though, was beyond what I could look into or investigate; I would leave that to the police. I had to walk away. It had been Cargan's approach all along, one I finally understood.

The cold of the walk-in seeped into my bones and I shivered, finally remembering why I had come in. Eggs, I thought. I need eggs. I took a deep breath, letting all of the tension go, trying to erase the past, and walked from the refrigerator and back into the kitchen, the eggs in my hand, a small measure of peace in my heart.

CHAPTER Forty-seven

Cargan peeked through the small window that looked into the dining room, giving me a blow-by-blow of the attendees, their dates, and the mood of the room. "Francie McGee is wearing her best, formfitting, knit-jersey dress," he said.

"What do you know from a knit-jersey?" I asked.

"I read *Vashti*," he said, referring to that online magazine for women that Margaret Dunleavy had told me about. "I know knit-jersey, and how to pluck one's eyebrows for maximum drama and effect, and what contouring looks like," he said, without turning around.

"And that should dispel any doubt as to why Feeney sometimes calls you 'Nancy,'" I said.

"I'm always trying to figure out how the other half thinks." He continued his sartorial observations. "It's a little snug for my liking, Francie's dress, but I gotta say, she cleans up nice."

"Don't go getting any ideas, Car," I said. "She hates me for some reason and I can't have you going with a woman with those kinds of feelings. Knit-jersey or not."

"I'll keep that in mind," he said. "Hey, have you heard from that cop? The one in Wooded Lake?"

"Larry Bernard?"

"If that's his name, then yes."

"No. I haven't heard from him," I said. And I wondered if I wanted to. As kindly as the old guy was, I was afraid of what he might tell me with regard to Tweed's stabbing and the identity of the person who had hit me over the head, if what had happened was a result of my digging too deep and exposing an innocent guy to deadly violence. A few days. That's all I needed to get my head straight. Just a few days before I delved into that unresolved question again.

"It would be nice to know who did that to you," he said, his voice as calm as if he had stated the menu that I had prepared. "How can you move on so easily from that?" he asked, turning around.

"I'm tired, Cargan," I said, and that was the truth. Since I had come home several months earlier, I had seen one guy tossed from the balcony to the foyer floor below, found a groom taking his last breaths in the Manor restroom, and now this. I had come home to regroup and to rest, to ply my trade at the place I once called home and now did again. I hadn't come home to be more stressed than I had been in my previous life. My head still hurt and my heart definitely ached, but was I okay with not hearing from Larry Bernard for a few days? You bet.

Colleen came into the kitchen. "Cheese course is going over well, Bel. Lovely job you did this time."

"This time?" I asked. The girls were nothing if not passive-aggressive when it came to my food. They preferred the food of the old Manor: starchy, meaty, and soggy, at least where vegetables were concerned. The new Manor was a place to which they weren't accustomed. It was a cut above, something they were still getting used to.

"Let me know the timing on the entrée," I said, going over to the window to take a gander at what was happening. Cargan had returned to the stage and was tuning his violin. Mary Ann and Kevin were at the bar, Kevin in the midst of a story that required a lot of gesticulation, his beer slopping over the sides of his pint glass, Mary Ann gazing at him adoringly. Tonight she was in a show-stopping black dress and strappy high heels, revealing a slim figure that was usually hidden beneath baggy nursing scrubs. She laughed at something her husband said, tossing her hair over her shoulder. He was funny, but he wasn't *that* funny.

The servers were still passing canapés; Lieutenant D'Amato reached out and plucked a pig in a blanket from Eileen's tray, smiling at her and taking the napkin she offered him. Over her head, he spied me in the kitchen and his demeanor changed, a mask of consternation covering his usual jovial expression.

So there it was: He had gone to Lake Morgan and he had discovered my deception. I backed away from the window and made myself as small as possible between the doorjamb and the wall, knowing the whole time that he knew I was here and eventually, no matter how hard I tried to hide, he was going to want to talk to me. It was just a matter of time. Maybe it would be tonight after his officers and staff enjoyed the dinner and dancing or maybe it would be tomorrow after I spent a night tossing and turning, hoping against hope that I wouldn't be arrested for obstructing justice or whatever else I was guilty of.

I had a few questions for the lawman myself, namely, How was it that I could find Amy after a few intense weeks of looking? and Why did you go to Lake Morgan alone? By myself in the kitchen, my head bent over individual plates of cookies and petit fours, I pondered that, my mind eventually returning to the task at hand, the questions still there but lying dormant. In the dining room, the din got louder as the open bar was frequented and the hour grew late. The boys were into the disco portion of the evening, Cargan's violin prowess on display during a particularly raucous rendering of "Disco Inferno" by The Trammps, a song that Feeney loved to sing but rarely had the chance. I continued plating the dessert, listening to the fun being had in the room next to the kitchen, enjoying the temporary quiet, not looking up when I heard the door, the one that led from the foyer, open, a few small footsteps approaching the counter.

"Not quite done yet," I said, my eyes still focused on the plates. "Give me a few minutes, Colleen," I said, Eileen not being known for her anticipation of service.

When she didn't respond after a few seconds, I lifted my head and took in the sight of the person in front of me. She was tall, slim, and now a brunette, but her face hadn't changed all that much. There was a wrinkling around her eyes, wrinkles that all of us had now, and the beginning of laugh lines around her mouth suggesting that her years away from the Landing had been full of frivolity and a life well lived. Or maybe it was hardship, the lines suggesting struggle. I decided I couldn't tell. Her hair was short, not the straight plane that had hung down her back when we were kids.

"Hi, Bel," she said casually, as if no time had passed. I dropped the piece of flourless chocolate cake I was holding, the breath going out of me like a hot-air balloon, rising and rising until I couldn't breathe. I got out only one word before I felt the world spinning around me, my feet losing traction on the cake-covered floor.

"Amy."

CHAPTER *Forty-eight*

She was still there when I came to, Cargan standing beside her. I hadn't gone very far, just a minor slump, my hands still gripping the counter, my pants and chef's coat still pristine and not covered in the goo at my feet. There was a dish towel covering the window that looked into the dining room and a large wooden spoon through the door handles, preventing anyone from coming inside. The door that led to the foyer was bolted shut as well.

"Why now?" Cargan was saying. "Why this time?" He helped me to my feet, careful to avoid the chocolate cake. In the next room, the band was playing without him, as they often did when he took an unplanned-for break.

Amy looked around the kitchen. "This is the last place I thought I'd ever see you, Bel. And that's saying a lot, being as you spent most of your life here."

"I've been looking for you," I said, my voice sounding unlike my own, thin and reedy. "I went to your house. I left you a letter."

She pulled the letter from the pocket of her leather coat. "I got it. And that's why I am here."

"That *is* your house?" I asked. "I met a lady who said it wasn't. That you had never lived there."

She smiled. "That's Roberta. I have lived below her for the last five years, but I told her to never answer any questions about me. She's got a secret of her own that I keep, though it's not on a level with my secret."

I assumed that meant that Roberta's secret was on a par with not recycling, or putting her garbage out before pickup day. No one's secrets could rival Amy's.

She continued. "I knew you'd try to find me. I knew you'd probably actually do it one day." She paused. "And I didn't want to be found."

"So why now?" I asked, repeating my brother's question. "You were here the other night. Across the river. You could have talked to me then, but all you did was warn me."

Confusion passed across her face. I still couldn't believe that I was looking at her, that she was standing in front of me, but Cargan was there and he saw her, too. She wasn't an apparition; she was real.

And for that, I wanted to kill her.

"That wasn't me, Bel." She frowned. "That might not have been anyone," she said, my obsession with finding her something I couldn't hide. After all these years, she could see what I couldn't.

"Do you know what this has been like? How your family has felt? Your friends?" I asked, my throat choked with unshed tears. "Me?"

"I'll tell you everything, Bel," she said, "but that wasn't me across the river." She was more self-possessed now than as a teen and that was a pretty hard feat to pull off because she had been the most confident teen I had ever seen. An old soul, as Mom would say.

"Did you murder that girl, Amy? Or is it Bess?" I asked. "The girl they found in your car?"

The weight of so many years flashed in her eyes, the time on the run. "I didn't hurt that girl, Bel. You know me better than that."

"But things happen!" I said. "And you left. What am I supposed to believe?"

We ignored the banging on the door from the dining room, someone pulling at the handles on the other side, only to find that they were locked out. The only door whose entry Cargan had failed to bar was the one that led from the office into the kitchen, and after the banging on the other door had died down someone came through the office and into the kitchen, Mary Ann D'Amato-Hanson looking as serene as she always did, standing at the far end of the counter. "Bel, it's getting a little crazy in there. Close the bar maybe? At least for a little while?" She either was oblivious to Amy's presence or didn't recognize the other woman in the room. It took her a minute, looking back and forth between the two of us, before the realization of Amy's identity dawned on her. "Oh my God," she said, her hand going to her mouth to cover a gasp. "Is it you? You're back?"

"It's me," Amy said, a trace of fear crossing her face. "I came back, Mary Ann."

"Why? When?" Mary Ann asked, the questions that were in my mind but that I was too addled to ask.

"Because I don't want to run anymore. I want to tell the truth."

The party was really getting going in the dining room, whooping laughter and a cacophony of inebriated male voices blending together into one raucous racket. Mary Ann didn't seem to feel the same joy that I did over Amy's appearance. "But nobody wants to know the truth, Amy. I thought we agreed on that." Mary Ann's face turned hard and a little menacing. "You weren't supposed to come back," she said, her hands hidden beneath the counter. "We made a deal."

"I'm done running, Mary Ann," Amy said, the calm in her voice belying the tenseness of the situation. "You can kill me now if that's what you want, but I'm done running. It's over, one way or another."

Without my even noticing, Cargan had cut the distance between himself and Mary Ann in half.

"Kill you?" I said. "Why would she want to kill you?" That's Mary Ann D'Amato, I wanted to add, not some killer. That's the girl who fostered more animals than I could recall, the girl who had taken the science teacher's boa constrictor for an entire summer, feeding it rodents and keeping it healthy when none of us wanted anything to do with it, even Feeney, who everyone thought was the best suited to the task, an oddball with strange tendencies. The girl who had befriended me after I returned to Foster's Landing, making sure I went to at least one girls night out.

"Kill me, Mary Ann," Amy said. "It's been a long time coming." Her shoulders slumped slightly, but her tone was resolute.

I looked from Amy to Mary Ann. "It was *you*," I said. "The other night. At the river, warning me away from trying to find her."

"Bel, you are such a sweet soul," Mary Ann said, the saccharine in her voice something I had missed all these years, the patronizing lilt that suggested I was less than her and always had been. "Bless your heart. Such a doll." She looked at Cargan. "And we always thought you were the one who needed protecting. You were the one that surprised us all."

"What is she talking about, Cargan?" Amy asked.

"It's a long story," my brother said, as enigmatic as usual. It was a long story, and if I hadn't heard it myself I would have found it totally unbelievable. Finally, he looked at Amy, a girl he once loved. "I'm a cop."

"And knowing what we know," Mary Ann said, keeping an eye on him, knowing he was capable of leaping into action at a moment's notice, "let's just pretend that we're four old friends, that one of us isn't a cop, and one of us didn't kill someone by accident a long time ago. And that one of us," she said, looking directly at me, "couldn't leave well enough alone, so filled with guilt and angst that she had to go further than anyone else had up until this point to find a girl that, really, no one ever cared about." She raised her hands, a gun hanging limply in one of them. She waved it in the air. "I guess you're wondering why I have this." She placed her purse on top of the counter.

"The thought crossed my mind," Cargan said.

"You're a leftie," I said. Larry Bernard had made a strange proclamation about how the person who had hit me had been a leftie.

"How's your head, honey?" she asked, the nurse in her making its presence known. "That wasn't part of the plan."

"And stabbing Tweed?" I asked. "That was?" I was confused and it had nothing to do with the bump on the back of my head, now a distant memory. "How did you know about Tweed?" I asked.

"Remember when Hallie said that people always thought you knew more than you did?" She didn't wait for my answer. "I was one of those people. I know what you told Kevin and did some digging myself. You made a mess of things, Bel."

I didn't know how that was true, but I let her continue.

"I was going to get in and get out," she said. "I really had no choice. He could have seen me. Could have identified me if that old detective had started digging around."

"And how would they have linked this to you?" Cargan asked. "That's a bit of a long shot, even for the best detective."

"Is that the old guy who has been following me around?" Amy asked. "The one who looks like a Jewish Columbo?"

"That would be the one," I said.

"I wish you had just left the past behind, Bel," Mary Ann said, her disappointment in me on display. "I don't know why it was so important to you to find . . ." Her words left her. "Her," she finally said, pointing the gun at Amy.

"Put the gun down, Mary Ann," Cargan said, his arms straight out in front of him, his hands still a good ten feet from her, too far to do any good or avoid the inevitable.

"Or what, Cargan?" she asked. "You'll ask me again? I have a gun. You have nothing."

A room full of cops right outside while this happened in the kitchen, the sound of my brothers playing on, this time a jazzy samba, everyone oblivious to what was happening in the kitchen.

Kevin appeared behind his wife, his body language suggesting he had spent time at the bar, his face displaying confusion at the scene before him. "Honey?" he asked. "What's happening?"

"Not now, Kevin," she said without turning around. "Go back to the party."

"Amy?" Kevin said, the presence of our friend finally registering in his alcohol-soaked brain.

"Get Daddy," Mary Ann said to Kevin. "Tell him that Amy is back and she is going to confess to murdering that girl."

I looked from Mary Ann to Amy. "Is that true, Amy? Did you kill that girl?"

"No," she said. "But someone in this room did."

CHAPTER *Forty-nine*

A lifetime ago on a muggy summer night, our kayaks cruised along, the water getting deeper as the tide came in, the excitement palpable as we raced out to Eden Island, our days here numbered, all of us leaving for school in a few months, our carefree summer days soon to be replaced with summer jobs that would help with tuition and keep us in beer for another semester or two. Amy floated next to me, her mind on something.

"What gives?" I asked.

"Just taking it in," she said, the Manor on our left as we skimmed the surface of the placid river, the current pushing us along, our paddles almost unnecessary. It would be hell getting out if we didn't leave before the tide went out, a natural, regular event that would require us to carry our kayaks to higher ground. Unless we wanted to carry them the whole way, we knew we had to time our partying carefully.

"I can't believe we're leaving soon." I had mixed emotions. On the one hand, I couldn't wait to get out of Foster's Landing and away from my family. Strike out on my own. Live my own life. On the other hand, and according to the voice in my head, I wasn't sure I was ready, if I could really do it. I would be leaving Amy

and Kevin behind, too, and the thought of that was almost more than I could bear, Amy being my steady rock
in every storm, academic, personal, and emotional, and
Kevin being the love of my life, someone who would be
mine, always. We had promised each other, vowed to
stick together even when separated, him heading one
way and me another before, I hoped, transferring to a
culinary school. We would be true blue, and when it
was all over we would come back together and live the
life we were meant to, one couple who had loved each
other for a long time.

We reached the island and saw that our usual party
planners were already there: Mickey McGee, Francie's
cousin—of legal age with slippery morals—the guy
who bought all of our booze, holding his hand out for
our monetary contribution upon arrival; Kevin; a group
of kids from the high school five miles north of us, some
football players and their cheerleader girlfriends; a few
unfamiliar faces; and a host of other kids from our high
school, all ages, all classes. We had all come together for
an epic evening of partying, our kayaks, numbering
about fifty, strewn about on the narrow shoreline, the
water creeping up, settling under them, lifting them with
each little wave that crested.

I grabbed a beer and mingled with the kids who had
assembled, avoiding Francie's cousin, a guy who got a
little handsy as the night wore on and who Amy had
warned me was a "perv." There was no warning necessary where Mickey McGee was concerned; I had wit-
nessed and experienced his perviness myself, so after
slapping a twenty into his hand, certainly more than the
cost of a six-pack, I gave him wide berth.

A storm was coming; how soon it would arrive was

anyone's guess. It was brewing outside around us and inside all of us, tumult of the exterior, natural variety and also of the interior, a tuning of nerve endings, nervous and anxious and excited all at once for what was to come, what we would leave behind, what would happen to us after we were washed clean of this place and the history and memories we carried.

Many years later, I remembered Brendan Joyce. He arrived in his bright green kayak, a kid from across the pond, someone whom I never really got to know. He wasn't exactly an outsider, but he definitely wasn't an insider, either, a guy who hung around the periphery of the group that I helmed, an amiable sort whose presence didn't register on anyone's radar. He was like that giant, lumbering dog in the pack, the Saint Bernard or the big retriever, the one that the little dogs dominated, his size not lending him any presence in a large group. He was quiet and a bit shy, never saying much, drinking his beer in silence, laughing at everyone's jokes. When he was there I saw him, but when he was out of my sight it was like he had never existed at all. He blended in and was completely forgettable, all at once.

In the distance, I saw Cargan gazing out at the water, testing the tide with his hands. At some point, he would try to get me to leave but wouldn't be successful, doing something for which Mom would never forgive him, or for which he would not forgive himself: He would leave me there, sick of arguing with a sister with whom he had a special bond but who could be immature and intractable and just generally annoying in her stubbornness.

Mickey McGee had bought a lot of beer and I, not one to temper my imbibing on a night like this, partook of the stash, determined on this night that I would drink my twenty dollars' worth. The night grew hazy, and I started to find the people around me either hilarious in their recounting of some ridiculous story or tiresome; the mood changed with the level of my intoxication. I was getting drunk and I knew it but was powerless to stop it. We only had two more months, a few more weeks. This would all come to an end and, with it, everything I knew, the familiar being erased by every new experience and every new acquaintance. I knew I would never make friends like these; there couldn't be people out there who were as special as Amy and Kevin, and even Cargan, my silent brother who didn't say a lot but when he did made it count. There was no one else in the world like these people; that I knew for sure.

Amy and Kevin were parked by a tree, Kevin leaning up against it casually, Amy close to him, her hand placed beside his head, a stance that suggested more than friendship. They were oblivious to my presence, Kevin smiling broadly at something Amy said, clearly drinking in her attention, hanging on her every word.

It was hard to tell whose head went in first, whose lips touched the other's in a gesture sensual and romantic, but it happened, right in front of me, my mind going from fuzzy and jumbled to crystal clear and sharp in a matter of seconds. It was only a brief kiss, nothing more, but to me, at that precise moment, it represented the worst thing that could happen. And now, on this night, the one that we had all looked forward to with such excitement. It was ruined.

Amy turned and before her face turned contrite it wasn't lost on me that there was a small smile there, a look of victory. She had something that I had once called my own.

Before I walked away, deeper into the copse of dense trees in the center of the island, I turned back and with a venom I had never heard in my voice before uttered the last words I would ever say to her.

"You'll be sorry."

CHAPTER Fifty

In the kitchen at the Manor, the memories flooding my brain like the rain did the island that night so long ago, I stared at her while she finished the story. Mary Ann D'Amato implored her to stop talking but was not at the point where she was ready to shoot. The gun was still pointed at Amy, shaking in her small hand, the weight of it weakening her. I could see it and so could Cargan; she propped her left hand up with her right to steady it. Kevin was the only one still unsure of the proceedings, wondering what he had drunkenly wandered into. His wife was unpredictable, though, having turned into someone none of us recognized, and that was a concern. She could turn again.

"I left and went to the center of town after that," Amy said. "I left my kayak at home and walked for hours, not sure why I had done what I had done." She couldn't look at me and I didn't want her to. "Why I kissed him."

"It was my fault," Kevin said, his words sure but slurred. "It was me. I did it."

"You did it to hurt me," I said.

"I did it to hurt you," Kevin said, nodding, accepting the blame. "It was all too much. We were way too serious. I wanted it to end but couldn't tell you."

Cargan stared at the ceiling, embarrassed for me. Even after all this time, it was hard to hear that I had misread the situation, that what I thought wasn't even close to the truth. I thought that Kevin was in it for the long haul until he wasn't. It was still a blow, me thinking that the relationship had died a natural death.

"I finally walked home and got my car, driving it to the edge of town where I knew there was another party." She pointed at Mary Ann. "You were there."

The story was taking a turn; we could all feel it, but behind Mary Ann's eyes was the thought of whether she would stop Amy or not, whether she had the guts to actually shoot her in front of all of these people, a group that now included her father, looming in the doorway of the office, knowing what was happening without saying a word.

"That girl . . . Kelly . . . she was drunk. And high. As was everyone else." Amy put her hands together, as if in prayer. "Even you, Mary Ann. The most perfect girl in Foster's Landing." Her voice was barely a whisper, but it held the accusation. The truth. "Even you."

There was a strange sound building in Mary Ann's gut, rising from deep within her, something feral and not human.

"I decided to leave the party at the same time you did, and that's when I saw what happened."

We waited, knowing that although this would be the truth, the final missing piece of the puzzle, we also knew that it would be the worst part.

"I saw you hit her with your car and I saw you drive over her." Amy started crying. "And then I saw you back up over her until she was really gone, really dead, and you didn't even know until I stopped the car and ran into the road screaming for help." Tears were running down Amy's face at the memory. "I was hysterical. You slapped me so hard that I still can't hear completely out of my right ear." Mary Ann's hand trembled even more as the retelling got darker and more sinister. "You put her in my car, but she was already gone."

"I told you then and I'll tell you again: No one would ever believe this, Amy," Mary Ann said. "Because you were you and I was me." Her voice dripped disdain like an oily slick of something rotten. She had become someone I didn't know in that moment and the ones that followed.

"Meaning what?" I asked. "Everyone loved Amy. They still do."

"How could they?" she asked. "She was a bar owner's daughter, a girl from the wrong side of the tracks." Mary Ann laughed. "Who would believe that lush's daughter about anything? Especially now after what he did to Bel and Cargan? After he stalked her and shot Cargan? Your family is trash, Amy. They always have been."

Amy ignored her. "She made me drive to the edge of the river, to that big hill over the rapids." "Rapids" was an exaggeration, but the water was deep and it did gush through the rocks with a force we hadn't seen since the drought hit. "She put the car in neutral and pushed it into the river and it sank," she said, sobbing now. "I helped her. And every day I live with that."

The boys started playing one of Feeney's favorites, a Bee Gees/Barbra Streisand duet called "Guilty." He had crafted the set for tonight with great precision, focusing on songs that were related to our law-enforcement clientele.

Amy ran a shaky hand over her eyes. "And when I started to leave, when I started to go back to the village, she told me that no one would ever believe me and that, if I told, it would be me who would go to jail. It would be me who she blamed. That it was me who had hit and killed that girl." The story finished, Amy slumped a bit, out of details and seemingly out of air. I put my arm around her, held her up, feeling the familiar boniness of her shoulders and seeing the lines of her face up close, marring what was still a nearly flawless complexion. "It was my word against hers." She spat the last part out, glad to have it over.

The Lieutenant finally spoke and I was grateful for that as well as his presence. If anyone was going to get through to her, it was him. "Sounds to me as if your guilt has gotten the best of you, Amy. And that's why you're back. Case closed. Now we know who killed that girl," Lieutenant D'Amato said. "Give me the gun, Mary Ann."

"Oh, thank God," I said, listening with one ear to Feeney's rendition of a song from around long ago, its peppy tune at odds with what was happening here, or even what it was about. A love gone wrong.

We have nothing to be guilty of.

His daughter dutifully handed the gun over to her father, who emptied of its bullets, wiped it clean with one of my dishrags. My breath came out in one jagged exhale. It was over and he had seen it all. He knew the truth.

We had nothing to be guilty of.

It was only when he started toward Amy, his face taking on an angry redness, that I knew that what I thought was going to happen was in direct opposition to what would really happen.

It hit me like a punch to the gut, just like one from one of my brothers back in the day when fighting was all we could think to do, peace not in our repertoire. He was never our ally, never on our side. He knew all about this for all these years, and while he paid lip service to finding Amy and bringing her back, it was all a charade for us, her brother, her father.

He handed the gun to Amy, who, as surprised as we all were, took it. "And now, I'd like everyone to leave the kitchen," he said. "Except for you, Amy," he added, pointing his own gun at her, more sure-handed and confident than his daughter had been, his posture suggesting that with the slightest provocation he would use it and not have a second thought about it.

"Death by cop. It's a convenient way to go," Cargan said, exposing the Lieutenant's hand. "If you're a murderous small-town cop with a crazy daughter and a vendetta." He linked his arms across his chest, considered that. "And what are you going to do with us? You've already tried to get rid of one witness."

I looked at Cargan. "What are you talking about?"

"Tweed," Cargan said. "There's no way that Mary Ann could have done what was done to him. It was you, Chief, wasn't it?" Cargan asked. "But now there's more of us who know. What do you do now?"

The chief hadn't thought about that, a flicker of doubt crossing his face.

"She killed someone and covered the evidence," I said. "She's a murderer." After all these years and hearing about the wonderful Mary Ann D'Amato, I still couldn't reconcile our shared history with this craven act.

"Get out," the Lieutenant growled.

"You'll have to shoot us all," I said. I pointed at the desserts on the counter. "And then no one gets cake. That would be a shame, wouldn't it?" I asked, the babbling sounding reasonable to me even though my plea was completely at odds with what was going on in the room.

Cargan gave me a sly look and with one graceful movement jumped atop the stainless-steel countertop, dislodging a few plates. Everyone was stunned by the grace with which he ended up where he did, high above us, including the Lieutenant, who stared at my brother as if he were witnessing the moon landing at Shamrock Manor. Once there, Cargan began to dance a spirited jig on the slippery metal, one that ended with him flying through the kitchen and onto the much larger man, pointing the gun at the ceiling and letting off several rounds, ceiling tiles raining down on everyone. I pulled Amy onto the shelf beneath the counter, knocking aside giant pots and pans, hearing the music in the dining room stop abruptly and the kitchen door being broken down with a splintering crack. A myriad of voices came together in a panicked command, variations on a theme.

"Stop or I'll shoot."

And shoot they did, our kitchen filling with the smell of cordite, the sound of shell casings hitting the floor like candy falling out of a piñata.

When it was done and it was silent for more than a few sustained moments, I slid out from under the counter, dragging Amy with me, the two of us sitting on the floor, our backs pressed up against the wall that the foyer shared, my hand still gripping hers. Her brother was the first to come to her, hoisting her into a standing position, wrapping his arms around her, his sobs filling the small, noiseless, empty spaces that filled my kitchen. She held on to him like he was a life preserver in an angry sea, the two of them weaving back and forth, two siblings separated for over a decade and a half.

As she was led out of the kitchen, her wrists encircled with handcuffs, Mary Ann D'Amato offered me one parting shot. "I tried to warn you, Bel."

I didn't know what that meant.

"That night at the river?"

I stared back at her, the woman I once admired and even felt a pang of jealousy toward.

"I warned you that if you kept at this, it wouldn't end well. For anyone."

She had been right.

CHAPTER *Fifty-one*

I went back to the start. Back to the beginning. The next day, I walked out to Eden Island, my kayak useless in the barren river, still patchy after the drought, rocks jutting out. I bundled up, pulling a scarf around my neck and putting a hat over my red curls. It wasn't very far, but it took me about an hour, picking over the stones and in between unexpected pools of water, and by the time I reached the edge of the island the sun, high in the sky when I left, was dipping now, clouds covering what light there was.

I walked up onto the bank and stood, my hands in my pockets, my reason for being there less known to me now than when I left. The policeman's gala wasn't exactly what we had hoped it would be, a thought that was a massive understatement, and after it was over everyone was exhausted, hungover, and not wanting to see one another ever again. What had happened was ugly and torrid and now cast doubt on everything the Lieutenant had ever done in what was once a storied career in our little village. It was two days later and everyone knew about Amy Mitchell's miraculous reappearance, some overjoyed, others tentative and shaky at the thought of why she had left and now, why she had returned.

It was after a few minutes of staring up at the clouds, of trying to make sense of a world that made absolutely no sense anymore, that I realized I wasn't alone. Kevin came out from behind a tall copse of trees, his face ashen, his body suggesting that he was broken, officially and forever. "Hey, Bel."

"Hey, Kevin," I said. "What are you doing out here?"

"I guess I could ask you the same thing."

"Just wanted to visit where it all began."

"We call that the 'scene of the crime,'" he said.

"In this case, almost literally," I said, finding a big, broad rock with a flat surface and sitting down. "Where's Mary Ann?" I asked, Kevin off to my right looking into the distance at the Manor.

"Jail, Bel. She's in jail. Where do you think she'd be?" he asked.

"No bail?"

"No bail," he said. "Amy could be charged as an accessory."

"I guess she could," I said. "But she won't. She's cooperating with the police and that has to count for something. It's not like we don't have a full confession from . . ."—here I stumbled over what to call the woman none of us had ever really known—". . . your wife. Or her father." Amy was staying with Jed, the whole thing still a mess. "One thing I don't understand, Kevin."

"What's that?"

"Stabbing Tweed. What purpose did that serve?"

"She didn't do that," he said. "My father-in-law did. Cargan was right."

"The Lieutenant?"

"Yes," he said. "This whole thing stinks to high heaven, as your dad would say. Once they found out that you were close to finding Amy, that Tweed was part of this, they went up there together."

"My God," I said.

"Loo would have done anything to protect her," he said. Silence was the only response I had.

"She's awful," Kevin said, shaking his head. "You know what she told me? That she put that photo in Brendan's wallet to throw you off the scent. That you were getting close to figuring it out. That she wanted to implicate him in all of this."

She had been right. I had been close. And my brother had been right to believe Brendan when I couldn't.

Kevin was pacing the little patch of ground at the base of the island, his feet taking him in circles, his mind a jumble. "You had no idea," I said.

"Do you think I would have married her, Bel? I'm a cop," he said, as if that needed repeating. I knew that. I also knew that it might be hard to continue in that capacity for the foreseeable future. Things had unraveled quickly and didn't seem to be reparable.

"You suspected. I saw you at the river one night when you thought you were alone. I saw the look on your face when you told me you were engaged. I saw you at your own wedding. If you didn't know, you suspected."

"Or I realized I didn't really know her," he said. "There was always an element of that."

The clouds had completely covered the sun and it was now a typical gloomy Northeast kind of day, the kind that my parents felt completely comfortable in, the dank murk reminding them of Ireland. I pulled my scarf tighter around my neck and thought it might be a good time to start going back home, even though it was only early afternoon and it would be hours before the sun really set.

I had to ask. "What's next for you, Kevin?"

"What's next for you, Bel?" he asked in response.

"Oh, you know," I said. "A wedding here, a communion party there. The kitchen at the Manor. I probably won't venture out much because, as we've seen, that's never a good idea."

He noticed the approaching clouds, too, and started for the edge of the island. "I'll probably take a leave of absence. I'll sell the house. I may leave for good." He looked at me. "Can you think of a reason for me to stay?"

He searched my face for an answer, but this new-found interest in me and my whereabouts was misplaced, about fifteen years too late. A Band-Aid. A balm to a very open wound. No thank you. "I can't," I said, his face falling. "I can't think of one."

A third person joined us, settling in beside us, just like old times. We were silent for a long time, listening to sounds, in the distance, of cars rumbling over the bridge.

"Why now?" I finally asked my best friend from a long time ago.

I had never really seen Amy cry real tears like the ones running down her face. "I got really tired," she said, her voice choked behind the sobs, her shoulders shaking. She leaned in and put her head on my shoulder. Kevin reached around and, finding his arms not long enough, scooted around until we were in a circle, our heads bent together in silent prayer for what had been done and what had been lost.

"I don't know who you are anymore," I finally said, lifting my head to capture some of the waning light, hoping that would reveal something.

"I'm exactly the same," Amy said.

"There's no way you could be," I said. "I'm different. Kevin's different. We all changed."

She thought about that for a few minutes. "You're right," she said. "I'm hoping I'm better."

It was Kevin who finally gave voice to what I was thinking, the one thing I didn't want to say out loud. "What you did hurt all of us but especially Bel, Amy. People in this town have never treated her the same. They think she had something to do with your leaving or that she knew where you were." He was a simple guy and used simple words, his last words of the day to both of us the ones I wanted to say but couldn't. "You owe her an apology. You need to make this right."

"That's going to take some time," Amy said.

Kevin got up, the conversation, the events, the whole heft of the memories, turning him into a new person, someone with something to say, commanding us to listen. "Make it fast. Everything's been ruined, but you can still make it right." He leaned over and kissed the top of my head, walking past Amy and out onto the dry riverbed, the two of us watching as he got smaller and smaller until he finally disappeared.

"So Tweed," I said.

"He's a great guy," Amy replied.

"Seems like it. So why did you split up?"

She thought about how she would answer that. "Well, we were too young. And I was too damaged. Maybe there will be some day when we can figure it out."

"And Dave Southerland?"

"Rebound man."

I shook my head. "This is all completely unbelievable."

"I guess it is," she said. "I was young. That's all I can say."

I wish she had a better answer. "I have more questions," I said.

"Shoot."

"What do you do now?" I asked. "For a living?"

"I'm an editor of an online magazine for women. *Vashti*? Have you ever heard of it?" she asked.

I thought back to Margaret Dunleavy and that unpleasant night in the craft-beer bar as well as Cargan's assertion that he read it and that's how he stayed current on women's issues. "I do."

"We consider Vashti to be one of the original feminists," she said. "She went against her husband in a time no one would think of doing that."

She was still in there, the girl I had known hidden behind an older face, a shorter haircut. She was still the girl with a strong core. I could see the spark in her.

"We don't have to cover everything at once, Bel. We have a lot of time."

"And how do I know you won't disappear again?" I asked.

"Because the truth is out there now. I don't have to run."

Overhead, the sky darkened some more so that soon it would be pitch black out.

She put a hand on my arm. "You had a good family. All those protective brothers."

I let out a snort, derisive and pointed. "Not so protective."

"But they were," she said. "They looked out for you and made sure you were part of the fold." She wrapped her arms around herself to ward off the chill. "My family wasn't like that, Bel. Sure, you grew up there and you think you know what I'm talking about, but my father was a hard man and my mother grew hard as a result of that. Jed was so busy protecting himself that he didn't have time to look out for me or my sister, so we were all on our own, three kids trying to stay clear of Oogie's rage. If I hadn't had to leave, I probably would have anyway."

"I never saw your father like that." But that wasn't true. "Until he almost killed my brother and me, thinking that I knew something I didn't."

"I never let you see that part of it," she said. "Think about it. We played at the Manor mostly."

"That's because there was no better place to play than the Manor. All those rooms, all that land, direct access to the river. It was paradise."

"And my family wasn't there. They wouldn't have protected me like yours did for you," she said. "I couldn't go to them when this happened. I was the party girl and Mary Ann D'Amato was the perfect girl. No one would ever have believed me, believed that what I had seen was not a direct result of my carelessness. We were the Mitchells, from the wrong side of the tracks, and she was Mary Ann, the daughter of the chief. She said it herself." She bit her lip, considering all of that. "That's what she told me and that's what I thought. That's what I believed and what she still believes now. So I ran."

"To a commune?" I asked.

"It was hardly a commune by that point," she said. "More like a summer camp for the lost."

She wasn't the only one to characterize it like that. "And how did you hear about it?" I asked.

"I got off the train in Wooded Lake and went into town. That's where I met Tweed," she said.

"Your ex-husband."

"Sort of," she said. "That wasn't really legal. That was more of a Love Canyon ceremony. Archie wasn't one for legalities." She smiled. "He's a nice guy. Tweed."

"He really is," I said, thinking that the minute I got my answers from her I needed to see him. To apologize for not being honest, for dragging him into this mess. He had lied, too, but would understand that what we did we did to protect each other, and Amy, from the truth and what would happen if it got out.

"And what about Archie?" I asked.

"Ah, a lech, for sure," she said. "He never laid a hand on me. Tweed saw to that."

"So why did you leave him? Tweed?" I asked.

"We were kids. I was broken. It never would have lasted." She looked down. "And there was the next guy," she said, looking up, her mouth caught between a smile and a grimace at the memory.

"Dave Southerland?"

"Like I said, a rebound guy."

"He's pretty pissed off."

"Yeah, I wasn't a great wife to him, either." Her shoulders slumped, sadness coming out of her every pore. "I wasn't a good friend to you, Bel. I kept secrets the whole time we were friends. I kissed Kevin that night and I still don't know why."

"Yeah, that was pretty shitty," I said.

"And there was what I did to Dan Malloy. My relationship with him . . ."

"The coach?" I asked, aghast. "Relationship?"

"How do you think I got the money to leave?" she asked. "I went to him and asked him to get me out of town." She laid it out for me. "He gave me five hundred dollars and a train ticket. That was enough to start over."

"But why would he do that? Why would he help a teenager leave town? Why didn't he tell the police?"

"He probably did." She paused. "Think about it. Think about what you know now." She looked at me and it was all there. She didn't go any further about her "relationship" with Malloy but it was clear that something had happened. I didn't want to know what. I had heard enough already.

It all made a strange, perfect sense. That was just the sort of thing that Mary Ann's father would have kept a secret so that his precious daughter remained blameless. And Malloy wouldn't have raised it again for fear of being caught. It was a cover up inside of a ball of lies that seemingly had no end.

"Was it, Bel?" Amy asked after a good five minutes of silence.

I looked over at her.

"Ruined?" she asked.

"Pretty much," I said.

"So why did you come back?" she asked.

"Because there was nowhere else to go," I said. "There was nowhere else to hide from this."

On our way home, Amy, Kevin, and I having gone in different directions, something we had done a long time ago, I had one thought.

We were too young to feel this old.

CHAPTER *Fifty-two*

So many secrets.

Secrets in my family.

Now secrets in our town.

Amy carried the most secrets, keeping them close.

I finally asked Amy where we went from here, but she didn't answer because she didn't know. Only time would tell if we could be friends again or even if we wanted to.

When I got home, drained from our meeting, I e-mailed Dan Malloy and said that I was sorry, but we had double-booked the date of his daughter's Sweet Sixteen and that he'd have to find another place. He never responded. To think that he had helped her escape and whatever else he had done, had been dumb enough to believe whatever story she had told him, was more than I could bear. I didn't want to see him or his happy family. This was the Landing, though; it wasn't big and there weren't a lot of us. I was sure to see him again and I was still figuring what I would say to him to "encourage" him to retire, despite that event being a decade or more off for him. Blackmail really wasn't my thing but neither was guys in their twenties having relationships with teens so when all was said and done, I sent another email a few weeks later that contained one line:

I know everything.

Duffy Dreyer, the reporter who had tried to unearth new evidence about Amy's disappearance and was unsuccessful in doing so, e-mailed me no fewer than eight times, but I wasn't talking. I instructed my family to keep her out if she came to the Manor. If she found me somewhere else, I would remain silent. I had done what she couldn't do and I didn't need to talk to her about it.

I hadn't spoken to Tweed Blazer since all had been revealed but knew that there would come a time when I would want to, would want to thank him for protecting her and keeping her safe. To maybe get back her dolphin charm. Eventually, days passed and everything started to return to normal, whatever that meant in the land of Shamrock Manor. I don't think Mom was ever going to get over her girl crush on the woman she thought Mary Ann had been. And as we celebrated New Year's dinner in the residence, all of us around the big hatch-cover table that Dad had built many years ago to accommodate his growing brood, the mood was less than joyous, even with the happy sounds of my nieces and nephews running around the place.

There was a knock at the door and two of my brothers jumped up, Cargan and Derry both racing to let in whatever visitor was outside. I peeked around the corner from the kitchen, where I had stood over the stove trying desperately to fashion a gravy that just wasn't coming together, my culinary skills also in a depression, it seemed. My brothers looked surprised to find both Brendan and Kevin standing there, the former holding a huge spray of flowers, the latter a giant bottle of bourbon.

By the looks of things, Derry had invited Brendan and Cargan had invited Kevin; to what end I had no idea. I wiped my hands on my apron and went into the hallway.

"Is this the ghosts of Christmases past, compliments of my ex-boyfriends?" I asked. "If my old fiancé walks in, I'm leaving."

Brendan thrust the flowers at me. "You've been through a lot. I just want you to know that I've been thinking of you."

I had been distant from him since that night of Amy and Mary Ann's confrontation. I was holding back and I wasn't sure why. Maybe the thought that he, too, had been there that night, a memory I had long repressed, had sullied the idea of him for me.

Kevin handed me the bourbon. "My family's not really talking to me right now. They're 'embarrassed,'" he said, air quoting the words and sounding like a teenager who'd been grounded.

I don't know if "embarrassed" really summed up how his family felt, but I let the word hang. The revelation about Mary Ann had probably ruined their Christmas and maybe more to come. I took in Kevin's disheveled appearance, his slack jaw, and realized that he had partaken of some other kind of alcoholic beverage—or six—before arriving and I looked at Brendan. "Please tell me he didn't drive."

"Found him wandering toward the Manor and picked him up," Brendan said.

Derry patted Kevin on the back. "Come on, friend. Let's get you some coffee."

I didn't want to disabuse Derry of the notion that coffee would help sober up a drunk person, but if it got

Kevin out the room and away from the rest of my family's prying eyes so be it. Let them have coffee. I put Brendan's flowers on the counter, grabbed my sweater, and took him by the hand. "Let's go outside." I heard Mom call out a halfhearted, "But we're eating soon!" as the door slammed behind me, Brendan and I going to the patio behind the Manor and taking a seat on the cold, stone steps that faced the barren Foster's Landing River.

He was visibly upset. "I haven't heard one single, solitary word from you since . . ."

"Since Amy came back?" I said. "You're right. I am still processing everything that happened. I kind of needed to be alone with that." Why did I do this? Why did I push him away with regularity? Was it because I had been so wounded by Kevin, by my ex-fiancé, Ben? Sitting here at the back of the Manor, the sun already set, the air frigid, I wondered what it was that made me sabotage this relationship at every turn. Would I continue to do that?

"You are?" he said. "Well, so am I." He shook his head. "You are one selfish person, Belfast McGrath."

"I'm not selfish, Brendan, but I am self-preserving."

"Whatever that means." He turned and put his big hands on both sides of my face. "Don't let yourself harden to this. To me."

He was right. I had hardened and I wasn't sure why. Amy was wrong about me; I wasn't as soft as she thought. "I don't know if you have time to wait for me to thaw out. To soften up."

He dropped his hands. "I just have to know if you love me. Like I love you."

CHAPTER Fifty-three

Before I knew it, it was spring and then the month of May, which started a busy time at Shamrock Manor. And the end of the month arrived at top speed. I opened the local paper and scanned it for the latest news. The front page held a story about a beloved coach and teacher, one Dan Malloy, who had put in his papers and was retiring at the end of the month, a move to North Carolina in his future. He was "changing careers," and heading South to start a new life. You can run, Dan, I thought, but you'll never hide.

Erin Crawford and Fez—surname unknown—got a beautiful day for their wedding and everyone was at the battle stations, awaiting their arrival. May was in the kitchen putting the final touches on the cheese tray and the boys were on the stage, tuning their instruments, looking as happy as they could given their "creative differences."

The Crawford/Bergerons, one of the happiest blended families I had ever seen, arrived at four o'clock sharp. On second thought, they were the happiest family I had ever seen, mother and stepmother, father and stepfather, all happily talking to one another and their guests, Bobby

Crawford finally looking relaxed and content, the wedding of his daughter now a done deal, no turning back. Over the last several months, Alison and I had become true friends and I had even met her in the city a few times for drinks and dinner, though never at The Monkey's Paw. That part of my life was over and I was embracing my new one with gusto. It seemed that having a friend made all the difference and with the reappearance of Amy, whose adult self was still unknown to me, maybe someday I would have two.

As for my love life, I had softened. And he had waited.

Alison knocked at the kitchen door before entering. "I don't want to interrupt, but I did want to say hi," she said, not entering the kitchen, which was its usual wedding-day beehive of activity.

"You can come in," I said, "but be careful not to get too close to anything. You look like a babe, Alison!" And she did, clad in a champagne-colored raw-silk pantsuit, her hair straightened and a blush-colored wrap around her shoulders.

"Thanks," she said. "You'd be shocked to learn, I'm sure, that most mother-of-the-bride dresses made me look like Bea Arthur. Big gals shouldn't wear sequins. Or a gown. So, I got special dispensation from the bride to wear a pantsuit."

"So glad you did," I said. "I would give you a hug but . . ." I waved my hand around the kitchen, food and all things that could stain her outfit everywhere around us. "Well, food."

"Gotcha," she said. "Will you come out and join us for a glass of wine at some point?" She grimaced a little. "I still feel kind of weird that you're cooking in here and we'll be out there partying. We're friends now and it just doesn't seem right."

"There's no place I'd rather be," I said. "But I will come out when things wind down."

Alison turned and started for the foyer but poked her head in one more time. "You've got a visitor," she said, smiling.

I wiped my hands on a dish towel and smoothed down my apron. Life had changed a lot in the last several months and for the better and I had found a way to let myself soften. To love. I walked toward the foyer, but the visitor, as Alison had called him, was already on the way in, his hard shoes in his hand, ready for a spin on the dance floor, his favorite place to be.

I looked at Brendan and my heart felt a little fuller, fully thawed. "Hi there, handsome."